MAX DUNCAN
THE
DEVIL'S BACKBONE

DALE BRONSTEIN

outskirts
press

Max Duncan
The Devil's Backbone
All Rights Reserved.
Copyright © 2018 Dale Bronstein
V4.0 R1.0

This is a work of fiction. The events and characters described herein are imaginary and are not intended to refer to specific places or living persons. The opinions expressed in this manuscript are solely the opinions of the author and do not represent the opinions or thoughts of the publisher. The author has represented and warranted full ownership and/or legal right to publish all the materials in this book.

This book may not be reproduced, transmitted, or stored in whole or in part by any means, including graphic, electronic, or mechanical without the express written consent of the publisher except in the case of brief quotations embodied in critical articles and reviews.

Outskirts Press, Inc.
http://www.outskirtspress.com

Paperback ISBN: 978-1-4787-5749-8
Hardback ISBN: 978-1-4787-9482-0

Library of Congress Control Number: 2017917221

Cover Photo © 2018 thinkstockphotos.com. All rights reserved - used with permission.

Outskirts Press and the "OP" logo are trademarks belonging to Outskirts Press, Inc.

PRINTED IN THE UNITED STATES OF AMERICA

*Exposing oneself to total and complete embarrassment,
is the first step to building true character.*

For Centuries the Bahamas has offered safe haven to criminals, dating to the time when ship wreckers worked their craft as far back as the 1600s. In 1648, William Sayles and his Eleutheran adventurers landed in Nassau's harbor while searching for a place to establish a Puritan colony. They continued their search south to an island, which is now known as Eleuthera, and it is where a reef called the Devil's Backbone wrecked their ship. And so the surviving crew became the first English settlers in the Bahamas and in Nassau, wrecked ships became a livelihood for the city's less moral-minded settlers.

When bad weather and inaccurate maps didn't bring enough ships ashore, the settlers would put lights out on the reefs to lure ships onto the rocks. It spelled ultimate doom for the ships and crew, but was a very lucrative business for the pirates. The English government never openly approved of these practices, but like it or not, they inadvertently put their seal of approval on the beginnings of piracy.

But now fast-forward to the future where the practices are still alive and well, but just in different form. Now, the fortunes of world economies are being manipulated while communist countries are stripped of their wealth. Millions of people are losing billions to con men, corporate raiders, stock manipulators and tax dodgers who safely sail off into the sunset on their mega-yachts. And just like an old fashioned cream separator, billions flow from the bottom up, and are then skimmed off to a select few.

But where does all this money and wealth go? It's like a giant vacuum sitting there sucking in the billions as they flow to the top, and then stashing it away in any one of the not-so-selective places ready to take it in. There are dozens of offshore tax jurisdictions, each facilitating a very different need when it comes to sheltering or hiding money. And the Bahamas has been a safe bet ever since the days of William Sayles.

Nowadays, the hustlers, scam artists and Oligarchs, along with some of the world's biggest corporations, use offshore structures to shelter billions in tax dollars, or to stash away their illicit fortunes. But recently, and mainly driven by the need to keep tax dollars at home, countries and governments have banded together to close the tax loopholes that have made offshore jurisdictions attractive and viable.

So how does it all work? For the smaller scale client, a petty stock manipulator or tax dodger will simply set up offshore accounts with private banking facilities in any one of the numerous jurisdictions and transfer the money into these accounts. With the bigger clients they will purchase homes and become permanent residents, which allows them to leave the tax jurisdiction they then live under and no longer be liable for taxation.

They can live without fear of prosecution, while freely travelling back to their home countries and living off the vast sums of money they have stashed away. It is not uncommon for 'investors" to arrive in the Bahamas in their private jets and drop tens of millions of dollars on homes or private Islands and then spend the winters aboard private yachts the size of small cruise ships.

However, all that glitters is not gold. Many of these offshore jurisdictions have their own resident modern day pirates who are well equipped to relieve these unsuspecting "investors" of some of their ill-gotten gains. They lay in wait, like the calming surface waters that wash over the Devil's Backbone as they lure them away from the safety of the open ocean. And then once inside the reef, there is little chance for escape.

And therein lies the rub.

PROLOGUE

Paradise Island, The Bahamas
1:42am:

The temperature was still a stifling ninety-two degrees, and the air hung thick with humidity as Howell made his way down the tree-lined path to the parking lot. He had only been outside a few short minutes but could already feel his shirt sticking to his back, the faint breeze drifting in from the harbor giving little relief as it rustled through the fronds above him.

It was late, and with the exception of the cicadas echoing their lonely song in the distance, the area was totally deserted. The tourists and maintenance workers had long since retired to their homes or the comfort of their air-conditioned rooms. But as he passed through the shadows of the giant palm, he felt a prickle in the back of his neck.

He stopped, and felt the gravel crunch under his feet as he turned and stared out into the darkness. The seconds passed, but there was nothing. But then he took one step forward and it was as though his head exploded as a thousand shards of light ripped through his left eye. The blow landed with vicious force, snapping his head to the side sending him sprawling face first to the ground.

The cicadas went quiet, and a deadly silence fell over him. He did not know how long he'd been unconscious, but when he came to he heard a faint gurgle as he struggled to breathe through the thick paste of blood and sand that pooled beneath him. Choking, and barely breathing he somehow managed to roll himself over, and as he sucked jagged breaths of air deep into his lungs he felt the panic set in.

"Nice watch, Howell, it's good to see you've been moving up in the world," echoed the cold and lifeless voice.

It was a voice from the past, a voice he had heard only once before. But the memory shook him to the core as he felt his prized Cartier watch being ripped from his wrist.

Five hours earlier Howell had been inside the Shores Hotel and Casino:

"This place is something else," he said as they strolled down the corridor of high-end shops and checked out the endless parade of beautiful women that passed them by. He was on his way to dinner with Rafael, his good friend and client from Venezuela, who had just flown in on his private jet and was spending the night in one of the pricey waterfront suites.

"It certainly is, my friend," replied Rafael as they stopped in front of Armand's, with an incredible array of expensive jewelry and watches on display. Obviously having spotted something he liked, Rafael bolted inside and was standing in front of the showcase filled with watches when Howell caught up to him.

"I'll take two of those," he said to the saleswoman. He pointed to a pair of matching Cartier Pasha Seatimer watches as he pulled out a stack of one hundred dollar bills.

One for him, and one for his latest, much younger girlfriend who was waiting for him back on Miami Beach. Not wanting to be outdone, Howell put a Calibre De Cartier on his platinum American Express.

The store clerk hand delivered the watches to their table at Zen, the ultra chic Sushi restaurant located down the corridor from the shop. It was just one of his many over the top acquisitions that not only symbolized his success, but accentuated his flamboyant lifestyle.

"There is no time like the present to start enjoying," he boasted as he tossed back a forty-dollar shot of Saki.

Until recently Howell had been slogging it out in the private banking system, hating every minute of every day as he pandered to the pathetic whims of his rich and demanding clients. But his relentless determination had finally paid off, the tide had turned, and it would soon be himself who was seated on the other side of the table.

Things were finally going his way, and he had been on a roll since orchestrating the buyout of his small bank and trust just a few months earlier. The eight-figure payout had put him squarely on the inside, and he was no longer just a two-bit player competing for clients in the seedy underworld of offshore banking. He was living in the moment.

It was intoxicating, and he couldn't get enough of the fast-paced life he had been craving for so many years. And The Shores was the perfect place for him; a playground for the ultra rich where mega-yachts lined the docks of the private marina and the high rolling owners filled the casino and bars.

The most exclusive was the Private "Members Only" club right above the casino, where they indulged in expensive liquors and locally hand-rolled Cuban cigars. Many would covet the young women who came in search of the action, in hope of being invited back to one of the floating palaces where the real parties took place.

It was nearly 1:00am., and although his friend had long since retired to his suite, Howell had continued to party. It was the fourth night in a row that he had hit the club and it was finally catching up to him. He was tired, or more specifically, he was physically exhausted and losing the battle to stay awake as he fought to find his second wind.

The two young girls at his side however, were singing at the top of their lungs and gyrating to the music as an exotic blend of cocaine and Crystal flowed through their veins. He didn't partake in the drugs but he did have a weakness for the champagne and wasn't ready to leave just yet as he searched the crowd for a waitress to bring another bottle.

The blond on his right had her legs draped high across his, her skintight mini riding dangerously high, leaving little to the imagination. He knew what lay ahead if he managed to last out the evening. She had her arms wrapped around his neck and he could feel her lips as they brushed softly across his ear, but he couldn't hear a word she was saying as the music drowned out her faint and raspy voice. She was young and stunningly beautiful, and he could feel himself getting aroused as her firm and recently enhanced breasts pressed hard up against him.

The three were laid back on the sofa in the bottle-service-only area reserved exclusively for invited guests and high rollers, well away from the mob scene that usually surrounded the overcrowded dance floor and bar area. But the service was slow tonight and he made a note to have a word with Tyrone, the floor manager, when he saw him next as he scanned the crowd in the nearly 9000 square foot club.

"Finally," he said aloud as he spotted a waitress heading in their direction. She had a tray held high with a bottle of Grey Goose Vodka set in a sterling silver canister with three sparklers splattering molten metal onto the crowd as she sashayed past. The sparklers signified bragging rights for the table; every time a bottle was ordered a sparkler was added. And at $500 a pop he estimated the table's tab to be around $2000, nothing compared to what others were spending.

He had been at this very table just a few weeks earlier, when the local real estate developer he was with dropped over $20,000 without blinking an eye. But this was Tuesday, and although there was no question the girls were hot and ready to party he decided it was time to leave. The bar had his information and he undoubtedly would see the bill online in the morning, duly inflated as usual.

He thought about getting their numbers, but decided not to bother as he pushed himself up from the table. The girls just smiled at him as they curled up beside each other and watched him leave. He had been more than generous, and they were more than happy to go home together.

The music was near deafening as he passed by one of the giant speakers, and he could still feel the bass reverberating off of his ribs as he took the escalator down to the main entrance below and into the exterior lobby. Once outside he looked up at the suites above and wondered how in the hell anyone could possibly sleep with all the noise.

"But then again, who comes here to sleep," he said aloud as he walked to the valet desk with the hopes of getting his car brought up. But as was the norm for this time of night, the girl advised there were no attendants on duty as she handed him his key with a smile. And then requested the customary $15 fee.

"Fucking rip-off," he mumbled, tossing her a twenty dollar bill and snatching his key from her hand. But then he stopped and apologized as he gently handed her another five.

The parking lot was well off to the side the hotel, and it irritated him to no end that he would have to walk all that way at this time of night. It was simply unacceptable to treat clients this way, and he made a mental note to add it to the list of things he was going to speak to Tyrone about as he started off into the darkness.

But it was a pleasant evening, and even though it was still stifling hot the humidity actually felt good as it soothed away the dryness in his nose. He slowly made his way to his car and his mood began to improve. The sweet smell of night-blooming jasmine soon brought back visions of the girls he had left behind. He was feeling better, and was having second thoughts about the girls when the blow sent him flying.

There was nothing he could do but stare helplessly into the night as he followed his watch up, and into the darkness. There would be no mercy.

Once again his cry shattered the silence as he felt the heel of a boot slam down hard on his side. The pain was excruciating, and he was about to pass out when he was jolted back to life as the man yanked him to his feet.

"I'll give you one thing, you are one stubborn son of a bitch," said the voice as Howell struggled to break free.

"Did we not have this discussion once before?" asked the man as he came into vision.

"I thought I had made myself perfectly clear that you were going to stop all these bullshit accusations against our boss." His voice began to escalate. "You should have kept your big mouth shut and taken the money and run, but instead you went beaking off to anyone who would listen. Need I remind you, you are a guest in our country, Mr. Howell, and no one gives a shit about what you have to say."

"No! Please, I am leaving.......I promise," Howell stammered through his bloodied and swollen lips.

But he knew his words were futile.

He felt the bile burning up into his throat as he took in the size of the man centered in front of him. He was searching now, desperate to find a place to run as he dangled firmly in the grip of his captor. Was it instinct or self preservation? he wondered, as he felt himself drifting to a place deep within. A place where no one could hurt him.

The voice was barely audible now. He heard them laugh, and then watched as if it were all in slow motion as the one who had been doing the talking nodded.

1:47a.m.: The text message simply read; "Message delivered."

It was a message that would not only leave a man clinging to his very life, but would soon set in motion a chain of events that would rock the very foundation of the seductive and shady world of off-shore banking.

CHAPTER 1

Vancouver, Canada

"As I was saying, it seems the regulators are hell bent on putting us out of business and the sanctimonious bastards are hiding behind the interest of national security to do it. But I say it's bullshit. Pure and simple," bellowed Morton as he settled into his chair at the head of the boardroom table, his trademark worry beads clattering around his massive hands as he opened the morning meeting.

"It's all about taxes and covering the ass of those who are willing to pay, nothing more and nothing goddam less."

Morton Feinstein was the founder and CEO of Feinstein Bank and Trust, and had spent the better part of his sixty-nine years in the banking industry. He had risen through the ranks within the major institutions at an early age, and by the time he was thirty he was running his own trust company.

At six-foot seven-inches and a solid 235 pounds, he could easily have passed as a former pro wrestler rather than self-made billionaire banker. He often used his size to his advantage, and today was no exception as he vented his disgust with the regulators, whom he felt were now directly interfering with his business.

Morton's entire senior management team were all seated in the boardroom at 1027 Hastings, along with Michael Darrington, the managing partner of Darrington, Moskowitz and Calder. Michael was the founder and managing partner of the firm, which now occupied the top four floors of the building. It may have been his building, but it was Morton's show, he thought, as he listened to him crank it up a notch.

Michael was a seasoned pro with over twenty years experience in off shore banking and he'd helped write many of the regulations that were now being repealed. But then Morton's crew were also veterans, and had all the bases covered: global taxation, corporate and personal banking, insurance, investments and securities and compliance and any other myriad of services a private banking client may require.

He had known Morton by reputation only, so when Morton called in person less than a week earlier asking him to represent his bank he had jumped at the chance. Having no real idea what they would be up against, he had brought in five of the firm's top lawyers including Brian Fielder, who would be charged with overseeing the project and the one to whom they would all eventually report. It was a virtual "Who's Who" of the private banking and legal world all rolled into one.

No doubt the man was passionate about his business. Michael opened up his notepad and was about to start writing when a young woman entered the room. He could see a look of fear on her face as she headed straight toward Morton, who held up his hand in protest as he saw her approach. But to Michael's surprise, she side-stepped the huge arm blocking her way and leaned in close beside him.

"It can wait," barked Morton, the look of annoyance clearly evident as he abruptly waved her off. Mike could see a slight tremble in her hands, but she held her ground and leaned in even closer.

Then Morton's expression changed, and a grim look washed over his face as he slowly nodded his head and began to rise out of his seat.

"You will have to excuse me," he said as he followed her out of the room.

Michael did not know what to make of it, and neither did the others. But they did not have much time to think about it before Morton strode back into the room, his face now void of concern as he took his place at the table.

"As I was saying, our window of opportunity is closing a lot quicker than I thought," he said, "and as usual our overpaid friends in Ottawa and Washington have proven to be all but useless in talking sense into these goddamn bureaucrats." He then paused for effect as he took in their expressions.

"So ladies and gentlemen, it looks like we are on our own. In other words, we are going to have to move a whole hell of a lot quicker than we thought if we are to complete our program on time."

The "friends" he spoke of with great disdain, were the high paid lobbyists he had contributed vast sums of money to over the past few decades. These contributions were made based on the promise that they would deliver favorable rulings with the regulators, but now that the shit had hit the fan they were all running for cover.

He was still speaking when one of the junior lawyers leaned over to his assistant and muttered just a little too loud, "A little melodramatic don't you think?"

Michael heard the bomb go off in his head, even before Morton's palm hit the table with such force it felt as though the room had quaked. Not a good way to start the day. He watched the more junior staff recoil in their seats. There was nothing he could do but watch as Morton slowly stood.

His voice was cold, and his eyes flared as he stared at the young lawyer, "Pick up your bags and get your pimply ass out of here, *now*," he snapped.

"I'm sorry, Sir, I meant no disrespect....." but Morton cut him off as he pushed his chair back from the table with the back of his legs.

"Pick up your things and get out, or so help me god I will throw you out," he bellowed.

Painfully aware of his mistake, he quickly scooped up his binders and headed for the door as the rest of the occupants sat quietly and watched him leave.

"As for the rest of you, if you think this is some kind of goddam game you can all pack up your shit and follow suit."

The associate's new assistant sat frozen for a moment not knowing what to do. But she quickly composed herself and was about to stand and follow her now former boss out when Morton addressed her.

"Easy young lady, no need for you to leave just yet." His voice was surprisingly calm, almost soothing.

"The man made a mistake," he said, staring directly at Michael. "And I am sure," he said as he cleared his throat, "that his actions do not reflect that of the rest of you."

"Jesus," Mike said to himself as he watched the drama unfold. It was not only giving him some insight and perspective into his new client, but it was also becoming clear that Morton was under a lot more pressure than he let on. And now, for some reason he had a sudden, uneasy feeling that there was more at play here than just a simple bank restructure.

An uncomfortable silence hung over the room when Morton finished, and it seemed no one wanted to speak for fear of unleashing the wrath of Morton's ill temper.

Finally John Farrington broke the silence, "Ok, if we need to move up the schedule, how much time are we talking about?"

John was in charge of the North American Bank and Trust division and had been with the bank for the past fifteen years. Morton had taken a liking to him from the first time they met and John had not disappointed him. He had exceeded even Morton's high expectations, risen quickly to CFO, and was now second in command only to Morton.

He was seated midway down the table, flanked by two compliance officers, who were well prepared and ready to answer questions.

"Let's just say we are shaving a little off the back end," replied Morton with a calculating look as he settled back into his chair and took a gulp of coffee.

"Just how much shaving are we talking about?" asked Jim Williamson, as he sat forward and stared back at Morton.

Jim held one of the most challenging positions in the company as head of the European, Principality of Liechtenstein, Ireland, and Channel Islands divisions. He was a stickler for detail and any change of plan or routine was never a good thing in his mind. From the expressions on his colleagues' faces, he got the sense he was not alone in his thinking.

But Feinstein ignored his question and continued, his voice growing ever louder, "The proposed changes these assholes are making will go into effect far faster than we had expected. And now, the IRS has either enacted, or is damn close to forcing full disclosure by all banks back to the country of origin. That is, any holder of a bank account, personal or corporate will be required to report back to the country of citizenship."

"Have any of the new regs taken effect or are they still on the floor for debate?" asked Jim.

"Consider them in effect by the time you leave here today," snorted Feinstein.

"Ok, so if you add that to the fact the IRS has just announced new incentives for the owners and inheritors of foreign bank accounts to disclose them, the noose has gotten pretty tight. And there have been major changes in both the offshore voluntary compliance program (OVCP), which has gone through several iterations since 2009, and the streamlined compliance procedures announced in 2012," replied Jim.

"Does this mean that if you come clean now they will give you clemency?" asked one of the compliance officers.

"Not exactly," Mike answered, "failure to report the existence of offshore accounts or pay taxes on these accounts can lead to civil and even criminal penalties. And there is an ever-increasing risk of getting caught. Since 2009, government investigators have been relentless in their pursuit of foreign banks and have been pressuring them to turn over the identities of their U.S. clients. That's both corporate and personal.

"And of course the Canadian Revenue Agency is rushing to catch up," added Morton.

"Don't want to be left behind Big Brother," replied John, lightening the mood and drawing a laugh even from Morton.

The ice was finally broken.

"Sadly you are ever so right. We know that many of our clients have kept their accounts secret, and in most cases have not paid taxes on them. But that's of no concern to us. We are not tax collectors, we are simply custodians of the accounts."

"So, I assume we need to get our houses in order, and quick," said John.

"Yes, we do, because as we race to get our new structure in place, the government continues to get more offshore records and leads that are now more far-reaching than just Switzerland. They are now snooping into banks in Israel, Hong Kong, India and the Caribbean specifically, but broadening the net to cover all off shore banks and trusts," replied Morton.

"Mr. Feinstein is correct, Under the Foreign Account Tax Compliance Act (FATCA) which goes into effect shortly, all foreign financial institutions will be required to report to the IRS all overseas accounts held by U.S. persons," said Ken Chaplin, head of the Cayman Islands and Bahamas divisions.

Ken had spent most of his time recently in the Bahamas and wanted to ensure that Mr. Feinstein knew he'd done his due diligence, "There is a far more punitive component to this as well, the offshore penalty percentage will increase from 27.5 percent to 50 percent if it becomes public that a financial institution where the taxpayer holds an account or another party facilitating the taxpayer's offshore arrangement is under investigation by the IRS or Department of Justice."

"How do we get around that one," asked one of the compliance officers as he turned to Ken. But it was Morton who answered, "We are working on it, but it may mean some of the clients will simply have to move offshore."

He paused for a moment and then continued, "In other words, as of now, and I mean right now we will start the process of moving the majority of our client accounts to the Bahamas."

And then noting the looks from around the table, he leaned back and put his palms to the air, "It will ultimately be their choice, but in some cases simply unavoidable; move and avoid penalty or stay here and face the consequences," he said matter-of-factly.

"And it's been their choice from the outset. Up until now they have kept one foot on the dock and one in the boat, but now the boat is sailing and they either need to get on board or face the music. If they stay, they could face substantial penalties for not filing or disclosing all their offshore holdings."

The room was now abuzz as he sat back in his chair and gave them time to digest what he had said before reeling them back in. It was going to be a tough haul and he needed the entire team on board.

"Look, I'm no happier about changing the game plan at this stage than any of you. But it's the nature of our business, ---and it's what I pay you for. So let's get to it. We have always known new rules would be coming into effect; we just did not know the extent to which the governments were going to take it."

There was a tremendous amount of money at stake, and undoubtedly there would be people out there watching, ready to take a run at them. When Morton first came up with the plan it seemed brilliant and relatively straightforward. But now, as he considered the prospect of moving the majority of his company offshore, he was no longer sure he had made the right decision.

Providing security for his people, both here and abroad as they managed the transfer of the massive sums of cash and securities would be a real threat. Not to mention rolling the multiple financial institutions all into one, with their client accounts as well. He felt as though he was all of a sudden losing control, and he didn't like it.

One of their larger clients was locally based, their operations spanning from Vancouver to Amsterdam with multiple offshore banking centers which included the Channel Islands, Ireland and Liechtenstein. For tax purposes, their base had been set up in Liechtenstein, and the majority of their cash reserves were there on account with FB and T. They would be the first to be moved to the Bahamas.

For a brief, rare moment, Morton tuned them out and found himself thinking about the small storefront office he had first opened so many years ago. It was a simpler time, the clients were different back then and he knew almost all of them on a personal level. They were good and decent hard-working people.

But times had changed, and he found it easier to think of them as numbers rather than persons, and found himself doing what he could not to remain in the same room with many of them. But now he was moving the very core of his business offshore just to accommodate their needs.

And then he heard Ken as he continued in his attempt to impress him, "We can do it, Sir, the banking arm is nearly set up in Nassau and we have already moved most of our key staff from Cayman. We will be ready within the next ten days to start moving their companies and holdings to Nassau."

At twenty-eight, he had already been with FB and T in the Caribbean nine years and was looking forward to finally being based permanently in Nassau. For him, the news could not have been more welcome.

"He's right," Morton heard someone else say, "the timing

could actually work in our favor. Anyone who takes advantage of the streamlined procedures just needs to certify that previous failures to disclose an account were not willful.

"But once they move offshore and become resident it's a non-issue. Correct?"

"Correct. Once the act takes effect, offshore trusts will become redundant, at least as we know them. So the only option is to become resident."

"Which is why we have to get our clients safely offshore now, and then we can address the issues you have all raised," said Morton. "We have to move now, because not only are the accounts and individuals exposed, but they will essentially be shut down through these new regulations."

At that point Morton hoisted himself up and out of his chair, "I don't know about the rest of you, but I could use a break," he said and was about to leave the room when Michael cut him off.

CHAPTER 2

Max was still half asleep as he lay in bed listening to the rain hammering down on the patio outside. He knew he needed to get up, but even the mellow aroma of fresh brewed coffee drifting from the kitchen could not coax him out of bed quite yet. He let out a yawn, rolled over, and grabbed the remote off the bed stand. As he clicked on the seventy-inch flat screen he heard a deep guttural growl and looked down just as a dark nose appeared from under the quilt.

As usual, his dog, Phil, was sound asleep beside him and showed no particular interest in getting up either. The growl showed his obvious annoyance at the unwanted movement.

"I'm sorry, am I bothering you?" said Max as he navigated the channels to the local weather station. But after finding nothing but commercials, he hopped out of bed and headed into the bathroom.

Phil maneuvered himself to the top of the covers and seeing his master emerge in his running gear he jumped off the bed, and less than ten minutes later they were standing on the seawall looking at the boats and taking in the cold salt air.

Max lived at One Ocean Drive, one of the most sought after addresses in Vancouver. The building was a waterfront masterpiece that had been conceived by one of the most renowned architects in the city. But aside from the architecture, he had chosen it for its proximity to Stanley Park, and the fact that it was very near where the seaplanes operated dozens of daily flights to a multitude of island destinations.

He had a passion for planes and could not help but think of his father as he saw a Twin Otter race across the choppy waters of the inlet, struggling to break its floats free of the icy grip of the Pacific Ocean. He watched it bounce a couple of times, and then clipped on the lead as the plane disappeared into the distance.

He hated using the leash, but had recently lost a fight with a local enforcement officer who had given him a fine and final warning "to comply or lose the dog."

They fell into an easy pace of about six and a half miles an hour, one that Phil could keep up with and a nice warm up for his morning workout. The rain had appeared to let up and it was turning into a decent morning as they passed through the massive first growth forest in Stanley Park.

But as was typical for this time of year, they were only about halfway through the run when the rain started to pick up again, and he decided to take a shorter route and cut across the cricket pitch to the east of the park, which would cut their time by about fifteen minutes. They saw few other joggers, and aside from the freighters looming in fog they had the sea wall to themselves.

Max could see the skies darken as he picked up the pace, and they just made it back to their building when the clouds opened up with a deluge. Phil led them under the front entry and was shaking himself off when Max felt a sharp jab in his side.

He heard Phil growl, and as he spun around he felt an iron grip on his right wrist, "Easy boy," said Thomas, his good friend and mentor. "Don't hurt yourself."

"Thomas, what the hell are you doing here?" he replied with a slight look of embarrassment at having been snuck up on.

"In town to give a seminar at the Justice Institute, but it's not until this afternoon. So I thought I'd drop in and say hello and maybe get in a little workout."

Max had already scheduled his morning, but was always willing to take the opportunity to work out with his buddy when he was available.

"Sounds good to me," he said as opened the lobby door and headed to the elevator. They came to a stop, and as he turned his key the doors opened into his private foyer which had a breathtaking view of the harbor and North Shore Mountains.

"I still don't know how you manage to keep this place," said Thomas as Max threw him a towel he pulled from the basket by the door.

"Don't hurt your head thinking about it," he replied evasively as he dried off Phil and then watched as he bounded off down the hall.

The two of them followed, and soon emerged from the kitchen with glasses of fresh juice in hand as they headed to his gym one floor below. Max had purchased the top two floors of the place after the builder had first broken ground, and had designed a private stair into the plan when it was still under construction. It occupied two thirds of the 2500 square foot area, and would be the envy of any professional athlete.

The centre piece was a regulation-sized boxing ring, with the balance of space taken up with elliptical machines, a heavy bag, a full range of free weights and almost every other piece of equipment one could possibly want.

They had met several years earlier at a self-defense seminar that Thomas had organized for some of the firm's executives where Max used to work. As it turned out, Max was a natural when it came to tactical fighting and began spending all his spare time training. Thomas was so impressed with his abilities that he soon had him assisting with his seminars with the Justice Institute at some of the highest levels.

It was a great surprise that he had shown up, and it gave him a good excuse to delay the project he had been avoiding and give them time to work on some of the Krav Maga training they had been studying.

But little did he know the day would soon be cut short. He had just finished stretching and was warming up on the heavy bag when the gym door flew open and his live-in maid, Beatrice, came rushing in.

She rarely entered his inner sanctum, so he knew it must be important and was already peeling off his gloves as he headed toward her.

"It's Mr. Darrington on the phone, he says it's urgent."

CHAPTER 3

For as long as he could remember, Max had dreamed of becoming a pilot. And although his father had always been supportive of his needs, he did not want him following in his footsteps. Instead, he had encouraged him to pursue a career in law. It was much safer and far more lucrative he had argued, and soon Max was accepted into law school at the ripe young age of eighteen.

University had been a breeze for him, and despite spending far too many nights in the Bear's Lair Pub drinking beer and shooting pool he graduated top of his class. It was no surprise to his professors when he was offered a position with one of the most prestigious firms in the city at a starting salary of over six figures.

His father could not have been more proud, and Max was thinking that maybe his dad had been right after all.

He had been assigned to the corporate finance department in charge of overseeing the small cap initial public offerings which was not only exciting, but gave him a firsthand look into a whole new world of wealth. And soon he found himself socializing with clients who were barely thirty and living in waterfront mansions and flying around in private jets.

But being on the inside exposed him to an ugly side, a side where the corruption and the arrogance of the players began getting on his nerves. He had lasted less than three years when he hit a point where he'd had enough, and was seriously considering quitting when a strange twist of fate would ultimately make the decision for him.

He had been working late as usual, trudging his way through a painfully boring IPO for two clients whom he held a particular disgust for when an old friend called him from out of the blue. An offer of a few pints of beer and a plate of hot wings was more than enough to entice him out of the office. It was an offer that would change his life forever.

His friend had seemingly stumbled across a situation where the shareholders of a publicly traded company on Canada's Toronto Stock Exchange were joining together to sue the company and its directors. It had class action lawsuit written all over it, and if the information his friend provided proved out, he knew it was a winner with tremendous upside.

The company, KLG, had acquired claims in an area of Eastern Canada known as Kirkland Lake. And their public relations machine had been working overtime touting the fact that this had the potential of being one of the biggest discoveries since Harry Oakes struck it rich in the same area over one hundred years earlier.

Oakes was one of Canada's early and very flamboyant prospectors who became fabulously wealthy in the early 1900s when he founded the second largest gold mine in North America. By the 1930s he had become one of the richest men in the world, but by then the Canadian government was taxing him at a rate of almost eighty five percent and so he packed up his family and took up residency in the Bahamas. This would prove to be ironic, as Max would soon track one of KLG's directors to Nassau, the main island of the Bahamas.

The company had been well into their exploration program and the results looked almost too good to be true. There were rumors that a takeover bid was in play with a large multinational mining conglomerate that had the cash to turn it into a real mining operation. And all the while the stock was climbing.

But despite the good news, two of the directors became impatient and soon greed got the better of their good judgment. Not wanting to risk failure they began falsifying assay reports in order to keep driving up the stock prices. Their plan worked, and before long the results they had cooked sent the stock soaring and the company had a staggering market cap of over two billion dollars.

The stock continued to climb as Investors anxiously awaited confirmation of the takeover, and while some of the more aggressive players continued to buy, the directors were dumping their positions through numerous offshore accounts.

It was a cold, wet Tuesday morning when the heavily anticipated press release hit the wires, but the news could not have been more devastating. The SEC announced suspicions about the recent ASAY reports, and trading was suspended without further comment.

Several months passed, and the investors agonized over the future of their investment before the SEC finally lifted the suspension and trading resumed at just over seven dollars, the price at which it was halted. Shares immediately began trading higher on moderate volume until it promptly crashed to under a dollar and the SEC suspended trading once again.

Formal charges were finally filed against the two directors who had long since fled the jurisdiction, and investors were left twisting in the wind. The broker handling the takeover, when interviewed on Stock Watch, had referred to the resumption of trading and ensuing collapse in value as "The Dead Cat Bounce."

The investors were out for blood, and that's when Max got the call.

They talked late into the evening, and by the time the bartender announced last call, Max was vibrating with excitement. He barely slept that night, and was in the office before 5:00 the next morning, pulling all the information he could on KLG and its directors. He knew time would be of the essence, and all but ignored the files stacked on his desk. Instead he dedicated every spare moment he could to researching his case.

If Max was anything he was thorough, and by the time he brought the file to the managing partners of his firm a week later he had it all laid out and it took very little to convince them to take on the case. It did, however, require some serious negotiation for them to allow him to take the lead. And for him to do it on a contingency basis. But he knew Michael Darrington, the senior partner, had a soft spot for him and after hitting all the right buttons he not only had their blessing, but had negotiated an unheard of split of the fee in his favor.

The trade off was that he would not be compensated for any of his billable hours for time spent. And, if they were successful the firm's share would come off the top and his fee would be at the back end. It was a deal the partners would soon live to regret.

With the blessing of the firm behind him, he worked non-stop and virtually around the clock to get his paperwork in order, as he knew he was up against some stiff competition. He filed the action and had it duly stamped just one day before a big East Coast firm made its application and was turned down.

He had his class action suit and was off and running.

It was one of the most high profile cases ever involving a publicly traded Canadian company, and soon made the front page of all the major papers. It was a case that had the entire investment community on edge, and they watched with grave concern as the case dragged on. A settlement in favor of the plaintiffs would not only be devastating, but potentially curb their rather unregulated and lucrative market.

Max worked around the clock for several months, and was ready for trial when he and the opposing counsel were summoned to the judge's chambers. During the meeting the judge all but berated the defense counsel for their lack of evidentiary substance, and advised them they needed to "seriously consider settling the matter and not waste any more of the court's time."

Everyone, including the firm's senior partners were at first stunned by the news, then soon elated with the outcome.

As it turned out, the directors had not only been trading heavily in their offshore accounts while dumping millions of shares into the open market, but they had also been trading the stock in the companies locally held accounts. And while they had stashed away close to one billion dollars in their offshore accounts, the company was sitting on over $250 million in cash.

So they had not only screwed their investors, but had also racked up a huge debt to the Canadian Revenue Agency and found themselves facing multiple counts of fraud, money laundering, racketeering and tax evasion. And when they were presented with an offer to settle, they had rolled over and cooperated fully.

The total amount of the cash award to the shareholders was just over $700 million.

It was a sweet deal. In exchange of forfeiture of their profits, and a healthy payment to the tax department they received no jail time. But on sentencing, the judge imposed a lifetime trading ban and restricted them from ever holding positions as directors of a publicly traded company.

Max's firm took forty-five percent of the settlement, of which he received half. His share after expenses and taxes was just over a whopping $110 million dollars.

But by now he was all in. He knew KLG was a solid company and as soon as the case was settled he took a chunk of his share of the settlement and put it back into the stock. The shares were at an all time low of .35 cents when he began buying, and at the time the takeover was completed they were crossed at almost $5.15.

At the end of the day he was left sitting on over $350 million in cash and stock. And it was all within a year of his receiving a call from his old friend.

The terms of the settlement were complex, and one of the many conditions of the settlement was strict non-disclosure agreements.

Aside from the senior partners of the firm, no one was privy to his compensation package. And although he had not spoken to his old friend since taking on the case, he suspected he had done very well on the deal as well.

But his real debt of gratitude was to his father. If he had not pushed him into law in the first place, he would never have been afforded such an incredible opportunity.

Max kept the paperwork in the safe at the office for over a

week, and each day he would read over the settlement agreement and look at his check before carefully locking them back up. He had no idea what he would do with such a vast amount of money, but he did know two things for sure. One was that he would be tendering his resignation, and two he would never share the information with anyone other than his father.

A month passed and he finally started making plans for the future. His first priority was to press his dad into retirement so they could go travelling in their own plane. He had put a deposit down on his penthouse, which was still under construction and he was looking at buying a ski-in, ski-out home on Whistler Mountain. Life could not have been more perfect, and then it all came crashing down around him.

The call came late one afternoon, and as soon as he answered and heard the voice on the other line identify himself as being with the Florida State Police he knew it could only be bad news.

His father had died. The plane on which he was a passenger had gone down in the Gulfstream in heavy weather just off the coast of Florida, the officer had said.

And just like that, the dream was shattered. His sense of loss was overwhelming.

With his father gone he at first found himself bitter and angry at the world. And as time passed he began to somehow feel responsible for his death in some perverse way. Had his success come at the cost of his father's life? It was a crazy thought, he knew, but he could not shake the feeling.

Michael, having reluctantly accepted his resignation, did his best to comfort him. But in the end, he knew only time would heal the wound.

It was a bright and clear afternoon when Max rented the small

Cessna 176 and flew north. And as he flew high over the Strait of Georgia he opened his window and freed his father's ashes. When he felt the urn was empty it was as though a weight had been lifted, and he finally felt some closure as he turned and headed back home.

A week later he strode into the office of the broker handling the Piaggio and laid a cashier's check in front of him for $4,595,000. They had spoken briefly on the phone the week before, but had never met, and as the man slowly picked up the check and held it in his weathered hand, he took a moment to study the man dressed in jeans and cowboy boots sitting in front of him with the dog at his side.

"You don't mind my asking, are you ok, son?" he asked in a slow Southern drawl.

"Just fine," replied Max, his voice devoid of emotion. "I assume it comes with the twenty hours of training we discussed on the phone?"

CHAPTER 4

Max stood for a moment and took in the view from his office. The fog had begun to burn off, revealing jagged bits of deep blue high overhead. And he could see the lights of Grouse Mountain as they reflected off the fresh layer of snow that had fallen overnight. He watched the tram packed with skiers as it pulled itself up the cables that rose high above one of his favorite hiking trails, the Grouse Grind. It was a grueling 1.8 mile trail with a vertical rise of over 2800 feet, and a path he knew well.

"It's an amazing city," he said to Phil as the dog came sauntering in and plopped down beside his desk. Still standing and fixated on the mountain, he picked up the phone and dialed. He had not spoken to Mike in a very long time, and, as he waited for his friend to answer, suddenly felt guilty for not having called sooner.

"Thanks for calling back, Max," said Michael Darrington.

"Not a problem, Mike. I've been meaning to call," he said a little awkwardly.

"No need to apologize, Max. In fact, maybe I'm the one who should be apologizing."

"Hell, Mike, you know I will do anything I can for you."

replied Max warmly. But he could sense a weariness in his friend's voice. He was not the same old Michael he knew so well.

"Unfortunately it's business, the firm's business," he said flatly.

"Well, you know I've been out for some time and I can't think of anything you could possibly need from me. But what the hell, it might be worth a beer or two."

"It's true, I do have more talented legal minds than yours on staff, no offence to you."

"None taken," he said laughing, and somewhat relieved to hear a little humor creeping back into his friend's voice.

"But that's not why I'm calling," he said after a pause.

"I think I may need someone with not only a solid legal mind, but also someone with the particular set of talents you possess, Max."

"And just what particular talents are we referring to?" he replied, suddenly feeling a need to drop into the seat behind his desk.

There was silence on the other end of the line for some time, and Max was about to say something when Mike finally continued, "I think I need some advice on personal security."

"Hell, and that's your problem? Hire a security firm. Case solved," he replied, laughing.

Again, no response, so he tried a different approach, "Come on, Mike, what I do is a hobby for god's sake, I'm no professional. Why don't you just hire a security company? There are a zillion of them in the book. And, as I recall you already have a very reputable one on payroll, do you not?"

"I can't go to them. Not for this, it's..... complicated, Max. Besides, I believe the situation is isolated and I know what you are capable of, so indulge me, will you?"

Mike was referring to an incident that had occurred a few years earlier--one that had nearly cost Max his life. It was an incident that he had long since buried, but now it felt as though it were yesterday as the memory came flooding back. He could not help but wonder what his friend could have possibly gotten himself into this time. But whatever it was, he would find out soon enough as he agreed to be at Mike's office at 10:00 a.m. the following day.

He was left with a very uneasy feeling as he hung up the phone and headed back to his gym.

CHAPTER 5

Max strode into the offices of Darrington, Moskowitz and Calder a few minutes before ten. And although it felt a little strange walking into the giant reception area, it also somehow felt right. He had not been back since he packed up his desk and walked out just over a year earlier, but when he took in the familiar sight and smells it was as though he had never left.

He was delighted to see that Katlin, the beautiful young receptionist, was still with them. She had joined the firm just before he had left and he'd always felt bad about not saying goodbye, but clearly she had not held a grudge.

"Max," she shouted with a big smile. She actually jumped up and ran out from behind the desk and gave him a big hug.

"How are you? Max, I was so sorry to hear about your dad but you just up and left and I never got to say goodbye."

"I know, I'm sorry for just leaving but it was a pretty tough time. But look at you, I swear to god, if I was twenty years younger," he replied laughing. It was really good to be back.

"Well, thanks, have you finally come to your senses? Are

coming back to work?" Then she lowered her voice and looked over her shoulder, "or are you here about the new client?"

"Maybe, maybe not," he said with a wink.

"You, Sir, are impossible," she said as she jabbed him in the side. "Shall I page Mr. Darrington then?" she asked as she reached for the keyboard.

"No need," he said as he started down the hall. "I want to surprise him."

He noticed right away that Mike was not dressed in one of his many tailor made three-piece suits, but rather black slacks and a linen monogrammed shirt with paisley detailing on the cuffs. It wasn't often you'd see him in anything other than a suit, and it was a change worthy of notice. However, it was his overall demeanor that caught Max off guard.

Although he was sixty-two, Mike could have easily passed for fifty-two on any given day. He had kept active in sports, lived a healthy lifestyle, and had kept himself in excellent shape. But today he looked tired, and even through the golden tan his eyes were underlined with dark circles. His shoulders hung heavy as if he alone were carrying the weight of the world.

"Good to see you, Max, really. I wasn't sure you were going to come," he said enthusiastically as he stepped around his desk.

"It's hard to believe it's been over a year since I walked out of here for good," Max said as they shook hands and embraced each other.

"We were all truly sorry to see you leave so soon, Max. Your presence here has been missed."

"I see you're looking rather casual today," Max replied. "And if you don't mind my saying, a little tired."

"Times are changing, Max," he said as he ignored the

observation and gestured toward one of the big armchairs. "I'm just making an effort to keep up with it all."

"If you say so," Max said as he settled into a chair and got comfortable. "So, tell me about this,--problem of yours."

"Where to start?" Mike replied slowly. "We have a new client, a private bank with a very powerful and wealthy client list. I'm still trying to sort it all out, but something just isn't sitting right with the whole deal."

"And just who is this mystery client?"

"Feinstein Bank and Trust, or better known as FB and T. The founder, Morton Feinstein, is the majority shareholder and really the client when it comes down to it. They are a large private banking firm specializing in offshore structures. Don't suppose you've heard of them?"

"Can't say that I have, but then again I've been out of the loop for some time."

"Well, suffice it to say they are not your average bank and trust. They only represent high net worth clients from around the globe, and they recently brought us in to assist in their worldwide corporate restructure."

"Ok," replied Max, "but are there not dozens of these kinds of operations already operating in god knows how many tax jurisdictions?"

"That's true. But this particular bank represents some pretty big clients, some of whom, are --- how should I say, on the fringe."

"Just how on the fringe are we talking? A little tax evasion here and there or full blown wall-street scum?" asked Max as he began to wonder just what Mike had gotten himself into.

"As far as I know, we are not dealing with outright criminals if that's what you're asking. At least I never thought so at first, but now I'm not so certain."

"You're not telling me much; can you be more specific?" replied Max.

"Yes, some. A few of the clients are not people we would necessarily want to represent. And we don't, at least not directly."

"Right, you represent the bank who represents the clients. So what? It's what lawyers are paid to do. I still don't see the problem here." But he could see Mike was clearly uncomfortable, and appeared as though he was searching for an answer for him right then and there.

"In retrospect, it's a major oversight on my part," he said as his voice trailed off. "I would not have taken them on as clients had I known what we were getting ourselves into. But as you would say, the horses have already left the barn and if we back out now we would be opening ourselves up to some serious liabilities."

"With all due respect, Mike, get to the point. I've never seen you beat around the bush like this before," said Max somewhat impatiently. "So what if you represent criminal clients directly or indirectly--It's what we do. But then corrected himself, "Sorry, what you do."

"Shit, it's not the fact that they may be criminals. And don't patronize me; I'm still your mentor," he said as though he were a teacher reprimanding a student.

"I just have the sense there is something more to this so called consolidation than I have been told. And that's what's bothering me."

"Ok, now we're getting somewhere," replied Max.

"Look, your concerns are my concerns. So let's start from the beginning and see where it leads us."

It took almost two hours for Mike to navigate his way through the chain of events that led them to where they were today, and it now seemed pretty clear to Max that it was a mess, no doubt about it. He was a little overwhelmed and still trying to digest it all when Mike suddenly got up and stretched, "I don't know about you, but all of a sudden I'm starving. Let's hit the dining room."

"Dumping your troubles onto others will do that to you," said Max sarcastically.

"Do what?" replied Mike absently as he scooped his cell phone off of the corner of his desk.

"Never mind, just lead the way."

CHAPTER 6

The food in the private dining room was always top notch, and they both ate more than their share as Max recounted stories of his travels over the past year. Max had always been an engaging storyteller with great animation, and it was a welcome respite for Mike as he listened with fond interest to his exploits. Although he had never admitted it, he admired Max for his decision to get out early, now even more so, given the present circumstances.

But Mike soon became conscious of the time, and he had much more to cover before tomorrow's meeting and called an end to what had been a thoroughly enjoyable lunch. Just as they were leaving, he gave instruction for some after lunch "goodies" to be delivered to his office.

"Good to see you haven't lost your appetite for the sweets," Max said enthusiastically when Mike's secretary followed them into his office moments later with two steaming espressos and a plate of fresh chocolate chip cookies.

"Tell me about the board meeting yesterday," said Max as he twisted the lemon skin on his espresso.

"Right," replied Mike. He leaned forward and continued as

though he was about to tell some deep dark secret that he did not want anyone to hear.

"We had just gotten started when old man Feinstein was interrupted by one of his aides, and then just got up and left. Obviously the matter was urgent enough for him to interrupt the meeting but---"

"And I take it to be highly out of character for him to leave a meeting once it got started?"

"According to his CEO it had never happened before. And, I would not have paid it any mind but the look on his face was well, I don't know, he was shaken. It just gave me cause for concern. I mean, this is a man that built a substantial empire from nothing and has a raft of people who are handling his daily affairs."

"So why would he interrupt a meeting to go and deal with some menial problem?" said Max.

"It seemed odd to me too, so I confronted him on it afterwards. At first he was evasive and tried to brush me off, but when I persisted he finally told me that one of his key people on the ground in Nassau was nearly beaten to death two nights ago."

"Jesus," Max said, as he let out a long sigh. "Did he tell you anything more, or was that it?"

"As I said, he tried to brush it off. But as you know, I can be very persistent when I want to be."

"And?"

"Well, it turns out Morton had just purchased the guy's company, a small investment bank and trust less than six months ago."

"Really, so Feinstein already has business in the Bahamas."

Interesting. He began pondering the multitude of scenarios that could be going on within the Feinstein empire.

"Yes, it's really just a small trust company which manages a portfolio of about fifty million."

"Only fifty million," replied Max with light sarcasm.

"Funny how easily that number just rolls off your tongue. Man, I remember when a million seemed to be all the money in the world."

"So why would he buy a puny little bank at a time when they are opening their own billion dollar operation?"

"My thoughts exactly. It turns out this guy who was beaten has a local partner who's closely connected with the government, and can supposedly expedite the old man's program."

"That makes no sense at all. Why would a guy like Feinstein screw around with some low life bank when he could just walk into the prime minister's office and work out a heads of agreement? Wouldn't an intermediary just get in the way?"

"Come on, Max, it's the Bahamas for Christ's sake. I mean, notwithstanding the inefficiencies in their system, corruption is at an all time high. And with the present government, banking licenses are almost impossible to get, especially since the Patriot Act went into effect."

"And if you don't pay, you don't get. Is that it?" asked Max.

He sensed the conversation was heading toward a rocky precipice, and he was for the first time beginning to feel Mike's concerns.

"Ok, so give the man credit where it's due, but you mean to tell me a billionaire walks into the P.M.'s office wanting to open up a new banking operation and employ a bunch of people, he isn't going to get what he wants?"

"Not anymore, but I get your point on the timing which has been the burr in my saddle through all of this. I don't get it either. And you think that's strange, here's where it gets even more interesting; the Bahamian partner of the guy who was beaten to a pulp last month walked with over fifteen million of the trust's money."

"No wonder you look like shit," said Max as he got up and plucked a large rubber band off Mike's desk and began spiraling it in and out of his fingers as he walked over to the window and stood staring at the street below.

"I really don't like where this is headed. What do you think happened? Feinstein's man tries to collect and so they do a number on him to shut him up?" he said without turning around.

"That was my thought. But when I pressed Morton he said absolutely no. The word is the guy is a serious player with a habit of dipping the local gals."

"Dipping the locals, that's a new one," Max said as he shot the rubber band across the room. "I take it you didn't buy that theory."

"No, I didn't. And I don't. So, I put a couple of people on it and after some digging we found out the trust company only really has two big clients. And they account for about eighty percent of the bank's capital.

"Do you think one of these companies is what's giving Morton indigestion?"

"Unfortunately, yes. The larger of the two appears to be a front that is moving a lot of stock through a number of accounts. But we really have not had enough time to flush it out."

"And the other?"

"Don't know. But in researching the two companies I found

that we represented two of the key directors of the company in question in two separate IPOs that we handled a while back."

"Shit, Mike," Max sighed as he walked back over and stood staring down at him. And then it hit him, "Do I know these guys?"

"I'm afraid so, they were two of your least favorite clients."

"It just keeps getting better," he said as he sat back down.

This wasn't just about a partner stealing fifteen million. He reflected back on the two hotshots he had been working with prior to leaving the firm. They were first class creeps that left you feeling the need for a shower after being in the same room with them. He had been more than happy to put them in his rearview mirror.

"I'm afraid that's not the worst of it; when my people were doing background checks on the two directors your father's name came up."

"Ok, now you're beginning to scare me," Max shouted as he jumped up, sending the small table beside his chair flying.

"Just what do you mean, his name came up? What's he got to do with any of this? He's dead for Christ sakes."

Mike could see he was furious and realized he needed to put a lid on it, and quick. But Max was on his feet, and there was a tremor in his voice as he stood staring down at him.

"Speak to me, Mike. Have you lost your fucking mind?"

"Sit down, Max-- Please, just sit down and listen to me," replied Mike in as calm a tone as he could muster.

"Your father was the pilot on a flight that took a group of these guys down to the Bahamas. It's how he ended up on the commuter flight from Nassau to Palm Beach."

"Bullshit," he said in disbelief.

"Look, I don't have all the details. But from what we can

gather, the day after they arrived in Nassau two of these geniuses took the Citation over to Palm Beach with the co-pilot, and left your dad back in Nassau with the others. They probably never even told him they were going."

"And what was so goddam important in Palm Beach?" Max said as he tried to understand what Mike was telling him.

"It seems one of them has a hard on for a gentlemen's club in West Palm Beach, and went over for a visit."

"So they went to a titty bar; I don't see what that had to do with my father," Max replied coldly.

"One of the idiots lost his passport in the club, and could not get back into Nassau, some dancer probably stole the damn thing. In any case, your dad was on the commuter flight the next day so he could take them back to Vancouver."

Max was beginning to shake, and his mind raced as he paced around the room and tried to take it all in. How could Mike know this? Did he really just find out? And why was he only telling him now?"

"So what you are saying is: if one of these assholes had not taken the jet to Florida my dad would still be alive?"

"I'm afraid it looks that way," he replied as he thrust up his palm in protest. "And before you even go down that road, the answer is absolutely no. You know me better than that, or at least I hope you do. I swear that I only just found out about this yesterday."

Max could see the look in Mike's eyes, and realized he needed to cut him some slack. It was clearly painful for him, and for what it was worth, at least he finally knew the truth about his father's death.

It had never made sense that he would have flown in bad weather, not with the thousands of hours he had clocked as a bush pilot. It was just too risky and his father was far too good of a pilot. Instead, he died at the hands of some piss ant commuter pilot with maybe a few hundred hours under his belt.

Mike's voice was just a faint murmur in the background as he tuned him out and thought about his father, and how his life had been cut short when he was in his prime. But for the first time since his death he felt real purpose in his life, because now he had someone he could hold accountable.

And make no mistake, they would be held accountable.

"Well, it looks like we have work to do," he finally said as he pulled out his cell phone and began hitting the keys. "I need all the files and documents you have on these creeps."

Max could almost feel the stress leaving Mike's body as a thin smile broke across his face, "You got it, and Max, thank you."

"You can thank me later--maybe," he replied. "I've sent you a private email address that you can send any of the electronic files to, and in the meantime give me whatever you have here and a quiet place to sit and think."

Max spent the rest of the day reviewing what he considered to be the most pertinent files, and prepared for the 9:00 meeting the following morning. It was just after 10:00 when he finally called it quits, and by the time he got home he was mentally exhausted and went straight to bed.

Phil, sensing his master's mood, hopped silently up on the bed and curled up beside him. Despite the devastating news about his father, Max slept like a rock. And when he woke at 5:30 the next morning he was feeling better than he had in a very long time. Maybe the truth about his father's death had finally brought closure to it all.

But unbeknownst to him, the real closure would come much later.

CHAPTER 7

The elevator bumped to a stop and Max stepped off, went out through the vestibule, and walked around the corner, climbing into his 2000 Mercedes 600SL. It was not only his pride and joy, but in his mind one of the best sports car ever built. It packed over four hundred horsepower, weighed in at just over forty five-pounds and handled like a dream. It was a classic, and although he had his choice of any car he wanted he was not about to change it.

It was a short drive to Mike's office and less than thirty minutes later he was pushing his way through the massive doors that opened into the boardroom of Darington, Moskowitz and Calder. The very same law firm he had resigned from just over a year ago. Everyone was just getting seated and he could hear what he was sure was Morton Feinstein's baritone voice as he walked in.

He couldn't help but smile to himself as he saw the puzzled looks on the faces seated around the table as he pulled up a chair and sat quietly at the far end of the table. After two hours they called a break, and not yet wanting to talk to any of his old colleagues he got up and was heading for the door when Morton cut him off.

"Max, --- Morton Feinstein," he said in a soft and measured tone as he extended a hand.

"A pleasure, Mr. Feinstein," Max replied. The old man had a firm handshake, and although Max stood six foot two and weighed in at 190 pounds he felt somewhat intimidated by his presence as he took a step back.

"Call me Morton. Michael speaks very highly of you, says you are the best security man around. I appreciate your coming on board."

"I'm afraid Mike has a tendency to exaggerate, but in any case it's my pleasure, Morton."

"Can we take a few minutes one on one? There are some matters I would like to discuss in private," said Morton as he looked around the room.

"Absolutely," said Max as he led them into a small conference room just down the hall.

Max closed the door behind him, and although Morton had an imposing personality there was a true genuineness to the man, and he didn't waste any time getting right to the point.

"I assume Michael has brought you up to speed on our company and that we are in the middle of moving our base of operations to the Bahamas?"

"He has," replied Max. "I have not had a great deal of time to do my research, but I am aware of the broad brush services your bank provides to its clients, and am also aware that some of your clients may not all be the most upstanding citizens of our community."

Morton chose to ignore the last comment for the moment, but knew it was something he would have to address.

"Good. Then you know the majority of our clients are north of fifty million and are generating substantial pre-tax profits--profits that they expect us to protect. And that is what this whole program is about, protecting assets and profits. But with the new regulations coming into effect we have had to change our focus completely."

It generally took Max some time before he could form an opinion of someone, but he had taken an instant liking to Morton and had an unusually good feeling about the man. However, he had a foreboding that he was in trouble, and wasn't even fully aware of the extent.

"As you heard, Ken has been working closely with the government to get permanent residency for the clients that we will be relocating. He also has several realtors securing properties that we will need to purchase on their behalf in order for them to meet the criteria for residency."

"Sounds like a windfall for the Bahamas," said Max as his mind worked overtime trying to find the weak points in Morton's plans.

"True, we are talking about moving vast sums of cash and securities, not to mention a large number of high net worth people onto a pretty small Island."

"And a relatively unregulated jurisdiction," said Max with a deadpan look on his face. "A move like this does not come without risk."

"Well, I assume that's why Michael brought you in. To make certain nothing happens to our people or their property while we complete our program."

Max sat quietly for a moment and gathered his thoughts before responding, "Mister Feinstein, Sir, if I may be frank. I am here because Michael is a close friend and has asked for my help. But then you already know that, don't you," he said as if speaking to an opposing counsel.

"So let's cut to the chase, shall we. So far you have told me what you want me to know. How about you tell me what you don't want me to know?"

People did not speak to Morton Feinstein this way, but although taken aback he found it to be a breath of fresh air. And although Max was uncertain how the man would respond, he really didn't give a shit. And it was all he could do to hide the thin smile as he watched Morton digest the rather direct assault.

"Fair enough," he finally replied. "I like your style, Max. No bullshit. And from here on, you won't get any more from me."

"Good, tell me about the problem in the Bahamas," said Max as he sat back in his chair and met the old man's gaze straight on.

"Yes, the Bahamas. Clearly I may have made a tactical error in that regard, but the truth is I am at a loss as to what the hell is going on down there," he said as he flipped the worry beads back and forth around his fingers.

"And yes, you are correct in your assumption that we attached ourselves to some less than desirable clients when we purchased that goddam bank. I have always prided myself in knowing my clients, but my team somehow missed these guys in the *know Your client* screening, and you can rest assured there are some sore asses because of it."

"I am sure there are," replied Max. "But the question now is, how to deal with them. Do you think they could have had anything to do with the embezzlement? Or the cut-ass that got thrown on your man, Howell?"

Morton's eyebrows lifted a good quarter of an inch as he let out a hearty laugh, "Cut ass, now there's an expression I have not heard in a while. But in answer to both your questions, I wish the hell I knew."

And then his eyebrows dropped as his tone grew serious, "So I guess this is where you come in. And I'm sure I don't need to tell you we have to use our utmost discretion in handling the matter. We simply cannot afford to draw any more attention to ourselves than we already have."

And then he reached into his jacket pocket and handed Max a card with a single phone number emblazoned on it, "I appreciate your commitment, son; god knows it's in short supply these days. I want you to know you can call on me at any time," he said as his face went hard.

"Anyone from my side throws up a roadblock you call me. You understand."

"You got it," replied Max. He flipped the card in his hand as Morton disappeared through the doorway.

He committed the number to memory, and not wanting to face the entourage just yet, he headed to a large outdoor patio just off the corner of the boardroom. It was the perfect spot to clear his head and think, not to mention the view over the city was fantastic.

Dedon, only the best for Darington, Moskowitz and Calder he thought as he navigated his way around the trendy outdoor furniture scattered about the roof top deck. He would have never considered such an expense, but after receiving the settlement he had outfitted his outdoor terraces with the exact same furniture. A simple lounge chair could set you back three grand and a patio set could easily run you $15,000, which was obscene no matter how you justified it. He stopped at the far corner where the view was unobstructed and turned his attention to the street below. He thought about the call from Mike, and sucked in a few deep breaths of the crisp cool air as he leaned against the glass railing. Although it had only been just over a day, it felt more like a week. He could feel his heart thumping against his temples as he reflected on the young clients he thought he had long since left behind, and how their lives were now inexplicably connected.

What would he do when the time came and their paths crossed once again? He stared at the street below and watched absently as an electric bus rolled to a stop. When one of the poles sparked at a connection of the electric cables, it made him think of something Morton had said in their brief meeting. He needed to get back to his office and look at one of the files, but then he noticed the time and cursed as he made a beeline for the boardroom. He just made it to his seat when Morton walked in.

Max certainly had to hand it to him--Morton had stamina. After three hours of his non-stop dissertation on changes to banking protocols Max was at system overload and needed a break. So, when Morton finally stopped talking and rose from his chair Max was about to get up but stopped when two aides broke through the boardroom doors with a mail cart piled high with binders.

And then one by one they dropped them on the table in front of each of them with a loud thud. The document had to be over four inches thick, but the cover page simply read "FINAL DRAFT" in bold letters.

"We are done for the day," Morton announced as he walked toward the doors and then stopped.

"I want every one of you to read the memorandum in front of you in its entirety and commit it to memory. It will serve as our road map to complete the restructure."

Thankfully it was Ken who said what Max was thinking, "Can we get this electronically as well?"

Morton did not turn around when he barked out his response, "No, you cannot. And I forbid anyone from scanning or making any other electronic copies of this document. Enjoy the reading, we will reconvene back here in the morning at ten a.m. sharp." And then he dissapeared through the double glass doors without another word.

Interesting, Max thought as he left the room, ten o'clock meant Feinstein had more pressing business to tend to before they met again.

CHAPTER 8

Frank Morano was stretched out in his chair with his size thirteen ostrich skin boots propped up on his desk and his hands clasped behind his head as he gazed absently out the window. His office was situated in a prime corner of the building in the old part of town and had a perfect view of the cobblestone intersection below.

He was in the process of lighting his first cigar of the morning, and as the tip of the Monte Cristo flared red he reached for the phone and hit speed dial. He drew hard as he twisted the cigar between his thumb and forefinger and waited patiently until he finally heard the familiar voice resonate through the speaker.

"Times up and we want the money," said Frank as he blew a large smoke ring at the handset.

"I understand, Frank, but there's been a little complication and I am going to need just a few more days, ten days max," replied the shaky voice on the other end.

"Horse Snot, I've been patient enough with you already," Frank shouted as he let his feet crash to the floor.

"Listen, --- I, I need a few more days, Frank, the funds are there but I just need a few more days. Just give me until Monday, okay?"

Frank could feel the desperation in his voice, and decided to temper it down.

"I'll tell ya what I'm going to do," he drawled. "I am not in a particularly good mood today, but I will give you until Friday. That's noon, Friday, you understand?"

"Fucking degenerate," he growled as he punched the handset with his oversized forefinger before the party had time to respond.

Frank, a former linebacker for the B.C. Lions, had by all accounts looked to have a very promising career. But his time was cut short when he had been forced to leave the league due to an unfortunate injury. He had let his temper get the better of him and hit an opponent who had pissed him off after a play had been called. The player suffered a broken collarbone, and the team owners had no choice but to reluctantly let him go.

He had always hoped he would eventually make it into the announcer's booth with a nice fat salary, so it was a rude awakening when the team fired him. But it wasn't long before an old friend set him up collecting money from deadbeat stock hustlers and degenerate gamblers.

It wasn't his first choice, but it was an easy gig and the money was good. He rarely had to get rough, and when he did it wasn't anything serious. Unless, of course, someone crossed him, and then all bets were off.

Frank was just south of forty, and although his thick dark hair had started to recede a little and his face was showing the slight lines of aging he was still a handsome man. Everyone liked him and he was fun to be around, but he had a reputation and everyone knew he was not someone you would want to cross.

Hearing the line go dead, the man on the other end dropped the phone back into its cradle and moaned as the throbbing in his head intensified. He had been in trouble before and had always managed to find a way out. But this was different; this time he had fucked up royally and was in way over his head.

In a drunken moment of weakness, and not thinking about the consequences, he had made a deal with the devil. It had been a last ditch effort to find a way out and the cards had gone against him.

"Shit, shit, shit," he yelled as he reached for the Percocet on top of the filing cabinet. His hands began shaking uncontrollably as he sat staring at the bottle. "If I take them all would it end the nightmare?" he wondered as he filled a glass with vodka and washed down two of the pills.

This past year had been a complete and total disaster and he was out of options.

He had lost over two million on Internet sports betting and that fucking Texas hold 'em game. He had not only hit rock bottom, but was digging his way to an early grave. His mind became foggy and he thought about his first meeting with Frank.

A fellow gambler had introduced them just over a year before. Frank was engaging and easy to talk to, and he took an instant liking to the big man. But he was clearly someone you wanted as a friend, not an enemy and now he needed to make this right.

The terms of the loan, at the time at least, seemed reasonable and they did the deal right then and there. The "Lender" had given him a letter of credit that he could borrow against, not cash. The LC, as he referred to it, would be used as collateral with the lending facility Frank would direct him to. It all seemed simple enough, and once the loan was repaid, the LC would be returned to Frank.

"Understand, the LC cannot be cashed under any circumstance. It is simply the collateral for your loan" Frank had told him numerous times during their meeting.

"But what if something happens and they need to cash it?"

"Trust me. You won't."

But he had cashed in the LC to cover the loan, and was in deeper than he could have ever imagined possible. The debt was now twice as much as before, and he needed to cover it or face the consequences.

Everything had been working fine, and in a matter of days he would have more money than any of them put together. He just needed to hold on and bridge the gap, but years of abuse were finally taking their toll and he was no longer thinking straight.

"Fuck it, why should I pay these assholes anything?" he said aloud as his courage continued to build with every drink. There would be more than enough cash coming to him to live out a life of luxury. And he was in no mood to share. No, this time it would be different and he would dictate the rules.

He poured a full glass this time, and downed half of it as if it were water as he lay back in his chair and went over his new plan. Soon, it would be all over and they could all go fuck themselves.

He actually smiled to himself as he took another drink, but then suddenly he began having trouble breathing. He could feel his heart pounding hard against his chest, and then his hand began to cramp and he lost his grip on the glass. He heard it smash to the floor as he felt his chest tighten, and then he lost all consciousness as he fell from his chair.

Frank, oblivious to what had just happened, was standing at his window watching the tourists meandering along the street below. It was a favorite pastime of his, and sometimes when he spotted a particularly pretty girl he would scoot downstairs to the coffee shop to take a closer look.

At the moment he was following a perky brunette when his personal assistant walked into the office.

"Busted," he cried out as he spun around and flashed her a broad grin.

At five foot nine, Gisella was a stunner. She had her long dark hair tied back in a ponytail, and the deep V silk blouse did little to hide her large firm breasts.

"Hey, it's harmless fun," he sighed as he went and sat back down.

"Whatever you say," she replied and then broke into a giggle. "Can I get you anything, Casanova?"

"Yes. Yes indeed. Would you be so kind as to bring me an Americano with four sugars, and one of those chocolate croissants from the Deli."

And then a devilish grin tore back across his face, "No, better yet, why not climb on and take big daddy for a ride. You know, for old time's sake," he said as she came close to his desk.

The aroma of her perfume was intoxicating, and just her presence alone made him forget about the call he had just made.

She toyed with him. "No, and absolutely not, but I will bring you one sugar and a regular croissant."

"Damn girl, you're no fun at all," he replied as he feigned his best sulky look.

She just laughed and tossed back her head as she sashayed away, "Stop sulking, you had your chance, big guy."

DALE BRONSTEIN

He was on the phone with his boss, Gino, when she came back twenty minutes later with his coffee and croissant, and he just motioned for her to leave it on the corner of the desk as he listened intently.

CHAPTER 9

"Listen Frank, I need you to get these accounts in order," said Gino as beads of sweat began to form on Frank's forehead. "How much is this guy into us for anyway?"

"A Buck, replied Frank sheepishly."

"Are you kidding me," yelled Gino as he shot up out of his chair.

"You mean to tell me this schmuck owes us a million bucks?"

"Don't worry. I just spoke to him, he's good for it."

"Jesus Frank, how could you have let this happen?" replied Gino as he began pacing the room.

He had a sense that this one would be trouble and he cursed himself for not getting on it sooner.

"You better get over here so we can deal with this," he said as he tossed the phone onto his desk.

Frank could tell Gino was pissed, and that was never a good thing. And now, realizing his mistake he picked the up phone and hit redial, but it went straight to the deadbeat's voicemail.

"This is not good," he said quietly as get got up and headed for the door.

Gino's office resembled more of a great room in a Westside mansion than an office in the old warehouse district. Persian rugs covered the floors and there were original artworks by some of Canada's top artists including an original Emily Carr, estimated at over $3 million dollars. There was also a Lawren Harris for which Gino had recently been offered over $2 million dollars.

His treasured Gretzky Warhol hung alone on the wall behind his desk.

He stood looking out at another new condo building going up across the street, and wondered how long it would be before one of the big guys came and made him an offer he could not refuse. The lands around him were being re-zoned into high-rise towers and he already had offers of more than ten times what he paid for the building that housed the head office for Global Enterprises Inc. His building took up over half the block and they had over 600 employees at this location alone working shifts twenty-four hours a day seven days a week.

He owned several other buildings around the city, including the one Frank occupied but this had by far and away been his best investment. Global was Gino's most successful venture generating almost $250 million a year in sales, but his real estate holdings were almost a match in pure profit. The building had already appreciated more than ten times since the invasion of the Hong Kong buyers, and the potential for redevelopment was enormous.

Gino loved his clothes, and was looking every bit the part of Henry Hill in Goodfellas as he listened to Frank and paced back and forth in his $1200 Croc Toe Cap Oxford shoes that he had bought on a recent trip to London. And with his $500 Brunello

MAX DUNCAN: THE DEVIL'S BACKBONE

Cucinelli shirt hanging outside his designer jeans he could have easily passed as a wealthy rock star and not a multi- millionaire entrepreneur.

As usual, Sal was sitting in the office and listening to the conversations. He was better described as Gino's consigliere than in-house counsel, but he was also therapist and long-time friend. And it wasn't that many years ago since he had also been the janitor who cleaned up the mess when some of Gino's men got out of hand. But those days were long gone, and they were now a legitimate organization.

Well, almost legitimate.

Private lending, more commonly referred to as loan sharking, had been one of Gino's first business ventures. He had come up with an ingenious way of lending money where he seldom if ever put up any cash. The interest rate, or vig as they referred to it, was 10% for the first month, and then 20% per month compounding after that. He would post a letter of credit rather than cash, and then the borrower would use it as collateral at a lesser known bank of Gino's choosing to procure a loan.

Frank had gotten on board when he had been forced to leave the league and the business had grown ever since. If someone got behind, he would pay them a visit and the loans got repaid. But now it was small time, and Global Enterprises was raking in over a hundred times what the lending could ever generate.

With the cash from his lending operation and the help of some "private Investors," he started selling lotto tickets by mail order to the United States, and then branched worldwide and soon was into gold coins and collectibles. And suddenly, Global Enterprises was born. It had been a huge success for many years, but mail order was now being replaced with infomercials and the

Internet, and he knew they would need to move into new markets in order to survive.

The company had over three million customers and an invaluable database; it was time to capitalize on it. It was time to branch out into Internet gaming, a relatively new and unregulated market where the real money was being made. And with an already established customer base it was a virtual gold mine just waiting to be tapped into.

"Problems with Bear?" asked Sal as Gino dropped himself back into his chair.

"Nothing we can't fix. But I swear sometimes I don't know if I'm talking to Frank, the enforcer, or Mister Rogers."

Sal howled at the thought. "Don't worry about Frank; he'll always have your back."

"Maybe, but he's gotten complacent, and it's not the first time," said Gino as he walked over and sat down on the leather sofa.

"And I can't afford that, especially now," he said as he looked across at him intently.

"I'm thinking of closing the lending operation and moving him back here. It's become a pain in the ass, and not withstanding the issues with Frank, washing that kind of money is becoming virtually impossible."

"The lending has been very profitable, Gino," replied Sal.

"True enough, but with all the new legislation and restrictions, they are going to be all over us, and I have a feeling we're going to need him close by while we make this transition."

"I don't know, like you've always said, Frank's not exactly management material. What's he going to do around here beside wander the halls and chase skirts?"

"Look Sal, he knows how we operate better than anyone and I can't just cut him loose. And besides, like you just said, he will always be there for us."

Sal sat back and sighed, "You're right. When are you planning on making the move?"

"Now," he replied as he stood and headed for the door.

"We'll discuss the logistics tomorrow, but right now I've got to head over to the marina and check on the boat before I leave."

"Big tournament this weekend if you want to go," he said, as he threw out a mock cast at the waste bin.

"Wish I could, but I got kids' soccer this weekend."

CHAPTER 10

The vertebrae in his neck made a subtle popping sound as Gino arched his back and dug the heels of his palms deep into his eyes. Even though he had a crew to take care of the boat, he was the only one allowed near his equipment and he had spent over three hours rigging his fishing gear.

If he was competitive in business, he was obsessive when it came to fishing. Everyone knew better than to bother him when he was on the boat, let alone during a tournament. So he knew it was not good news when his phone began vibrating its way across the bar.

"What's up, Sal?" he said as he stopped the phone and hit the speaker function.

"You best get back here, Gino."

"Can't it wait? I'm still on the boat," he said curtly as he snatched up the phone and held it to his ear.

But Sal was all business, "No Gino, I'm afraid it can't."

"Fine," he said as he slammed the phone down on the counter.

Sal heard the screech of tires less than twenty minutes later, and as he went to the window he saw Gino's car coming to a stop in the parking area below. He immediately left the office and sprinted for the stairs, hoping he could catch him coming in.

"Follow me," he said as Gino threw open the front door.

Sal led them through the maze of corridors to the back of the building and then took the stairs to the basement. Gino could feel the sweat beginning to drip from his forehead, and by the time they reached the bottom of the stairs he had to stop and catch his breath.

And then his jaw dropped when he saw the open door in front of him.

"Fucking Christ," he shouted as he stood staring into the wide open I.T. room that housed their computers and data processing equipment.

The IT room was a bunker that housed not only their computers and software, but also their master mailing list. The backup of the systems normally took place between midnight and six in the morning when the operation was limited to the phone room and call center.

Everyone was under strict rules to keep the room locked at all times, and a guard was supposed to be posted at the door. So when he saw the door open and people milling about he shoved past Sal and went inside. He quickly scanned the room, and when he saw the open door to the walk-in safe he flew into a rage.

The discs were gone.

"Mother Fucker," he yelled as he sprinted down the hall and back up the stairs in search of Alphonso.

Otto, the man in charge of his security, was nowhere to be found, and Gino was screaming into his cell as he heard the call go to voicemail. Alphonso was gone, and so were the hard drives for their mailing lists.

Gino was having a fit as he stormed down the hall kicking anything in sight, and was soon screaming at anyone foolish enough to be anywhere near.

He finally heard a voice on the other end of the phone after his fourth attempt, but was now standing at his desk now using a hard line. "Where the fuck are you?" he hissed.

"Gino? Is that you?"

"No, it's the fucking tooth fairy, you useless piece of shit. Get your ass down here, now," he yelled as he slammed down the phone and went to the bar cabinet and filled a tumbler half full of scotch.

Veins were bulging on his neck, and his face was a deep red as he tossed back his drink. He began to pace, and his nostrils flared as he drew in deep breaths and went and poured another scotch.

Otto entered less than thirty minutes later. "What's up, boss? What are you, a fucking comedian?" he yelled as he dove at him with cat-like speed, slamming one fist into the side his head as he drove the other deep into his solar plexus.

Otto never saw it coming, and a second later he was lying dazed on the floor with blood pouring from his nose. Slowly, his eyes came into focus and he could see Gino standing over him still in a fit of rage. And then he felt Gino's foot slam mercilessly into his ribs as he curled into a ball in a feeble attempt to avoid further attack. But Gino had already backed away and was now standing by his desk.

"Our mailing list took a walk tonight, you useless skank-eating piece of shit," he said, wiping the spit from the side of his mouth.

Otto made an attempt to get up, but his knees buckled and he fell back down as he struggled to steady himself. Gino was not a big man, but he was street smart and knew how to fight. Otto knew he was lucky that he had backed off when he did.

Gino went quiet, and then took a handkerchief from his pocket and threw it at Otto as he went and sat down on the corner of his desk. He seemed almost calm, as though nothing had happened and that scared Otto even more. It was hard for him to comprehend how a man could simply turn on and off like that, and he knew at that moment his time here was probably over.

"Clean yourself up. And go and get Vito, Jimmy, and Mickey, and find Alphonso," he said as his eyes bore down on him.

Otto was nodding in agreement and nursing his swollen lip as he spoke, "I'll get it back, Gino, you can count on it," he replied as he turned and started walking out.

He was near the door when Gino called after him, "I want my property back by morning. Understood?"

"Yes, Gino."

One of the original backers of Global Enterprises was a group well known for their connection to organized crime, and Vito, Jimmy and Mickey all worked for them. But when it came time to split the sheets and Gino had paid out his debt, they had stayed on with Global. No one at Global was totally sure what their role was within the company, and no one had ever dared to ask.

Gino took a seat on the sofa as he searched for answers as to who could possibly be involved in the theft of his mailing lists. And then he remembered his old partner, Shane. He had been the one who introduced Gino to his original "investors," and then years later brokered the payout to them.

A month after the buyout, Shane had been found dead in the walk-in closet of his waterfront mansion. His package had been cut off and stuffed in his mouth before a bullet went through the back of his head.

The crime had never been solved.

Was it paranoia, or were his old backers somehow behind this? If they were, he needed to find a solution to the problem and deal with it quick or else he was ruined. He had to get those discs back.

Otto was on the phone before he was even out the door, and less than half an hour later had collected the boys and was on his way downtown. Alphonso had a weakness for booze and young women and they had a pretty good idea where to find him.

The place was popular with the in crowd, a place where less than a month earlier a famous celebrity had been caught with two young dancers. He was a very married celebrity and the two dancers had been very young and very naked.

The tabloids had a field day.

Just as Vito had hoped, he found Alphonso sitting on a sofa with his back toward the heavy curtain that divided the private dance area from the stage. There was a hazy layer of cigar smoke hanging from the ceiling, and the smell of stale sweat and sex was thick as he pushed back the curtain and quietly slipped into the room.

He took note of the half empty bottle of Dom Perignon on the table, and then he smiled when he spotted the travel briefcase on the floor beside the sofa. It was the kind of case airline pilots used and large enough to store the discs in.

"Stupid fuck," he said to himself as he let the curtain fall closed behind him.

Alphonso could have made a clean getaway had he gone

straight to the airport, but instead was taking one last indulgence before his British Airways flight left for London. And he was now too stoned to even notice the big man who was standing directly behind him.

It would be his second and last mistake of the night.

Vito could feel the bass thumping off the walls as he watched the gorgeous brunette gyrating on top of Alphonso, and as he came around from behind he could see she had her hand deep inside his zipper. At one hundred bucks a dance she was giving him his money's worth.

At first she smiled when she saw him standing over them, but then her eyes grew wide and the smile slipped away when she stared into his hardened eyes. Flustered, she pulled her hand from Alphonso's pants and tried to get up but she fell back on top of him.

And before she had a chance to move she felt his iron grip on her arm as he lifted her into the air as if she were a doll.

"Alphonso, so good to see you," said Vito as he tossed her back onto the sofa beside him.

It took a second to register, but then he jumped to his feet just as Vito snatched the airline ticket from the breast pocket of his jacket.

"Going somewhere?"

He staggered as he grabbed for the ticket, and almost fell over the table as Vito slammed his palm against his chest, knocking him back onto the sofa. Vito could see the tears begin to form as the dancer stared up at him, fearing what was to come next. He hated this part of the job, and he knew he needed to get her out of there, and fast.

Alphonso's adrenalin was pumping and he was starting to

sober up, realizing he was in deep shit and desperately trying to figure a way out before it was too late. He could see the brunette was frozen with fear as she sat trembling beside him, but he felt nothing for her.

He was still searching through the fog, trying to think of something to say when Vito reached back inside his jacket and pulled out an envelope filled with cash. All the while keeping his hand on Alphonso's chest, he tried to hand her the envelope but she recoiled and it fell to the sofa.

Seconds passed as the music from the main stage shook the room, and then just as the Deejay introduced the next dancer in the nightly line-up Alphonso found his voice.

"Are you out of your fucking mind? There's over ten thousand dollars in there."

"That's what I thought, but you ain't going to need it where you're going, sport," Vito growled. Realizing he was letting her go, the brunette grabbed for the envelope and without a word, snatched up her clothes and made for the curtain.

Vito was a big man, skilled and quick. And as he watched her go he brought his fist around in an arc, and slammed it hard into Alphonso's jaw, sending him clear over the back of the sofa.

Vito came around from the side and had a hold of Alphonso's shirt in his left hand when he noticed the girl frozen in the corner as she stood staring back at them.

"Get out of here," he shouted at her.

The sound of his voice snapped her out of it, and as she disappeared through the side door Vito turned and drove his fist down hard into Alphonso's face. Seconds later Jimmy and Mickey burst into the room; they would have had other ideas about how to handle her. And that would have resulted in an even bigger problem for him.

Vito bent down and picked up the travel case, and seeing the discs were safely inside, he nodded to the other two and then closed the case and headed toward the door. He waited until he was sure the stairway was clear, and motioned for them to follow as the two picked up the limp and bleeding Alphonso and carried him out.

An early morning jogger found the body beside the seawall near a pub in Stanley Park and called 911. It could have been a mugging, or a victim of Gay bashing, the police officer told her as they loaded the body into the ambulance. The police found no identification as the first class ticket to London along with his wallet were now at the bottom of a dumpster off East Hastings Street.

It would be days before they eventually identified John Doe, and the taxpayers would have to pick up the tab for the reconstructive surgery to his face and the ensuing two month stay in the hospital. After which, no one would ever hear from him again.

They were all sitting in the office, waiting quietly while Gino looked through the briefcase. They were praying that the discs were all there.

"Well done, guys," he said as he sat back and closed the case. "It looks like they are all here but I need to get this down to the data processing room to be sure."

"Anything I need to know?" he asked as he came back into the office and sat down behind his desk.

"He'll live, but I doubt he'll play the sax again anytime soon if that's what you mean," replied Vito as he rubbed his right fist.

Gino knew that killing him could have been a problem, but given his frame of mind he could have cared less either way.

"Good," he said as he glared over at Otto, "go and wait outside."

Once he was out of the room, Gino swung his chair around and grabbed the corner of the Gretzky picture and swung it to the side revealing a large safe door behind. He quickly spun the dial back and forth and then pressed his thumb on the print recognition lock and waited until it clicked. He pulled out three stacks of fresh hundred dollar bills.

"I'm sorry, guys, I had hoped that by now we would have left this shit behind us," he said as he threw each of them ten thousand dollars.

"It's all good, Gino, ya gotta do what ya gotta do," said Jimmy.

But Gino just nodded, "Send in Otto on your way out."

Gino could be a very generous guy, but he could also be a real son-of-a-bitch, and they were very thankful they were not in Otto's shoes as they left him standing at the door to Gino's office.

CHAPTER 11

Max took a break from reading, leaned back in his chair, and loosened his tie as he set his feet up on the corner of the desk and stared at the cold mug of coffee beside him. Michael had set up a temporary office for him on the reception floor in a client conference room that was rarely used. But as was customary in the firm, it was adorned with fine furnishings, and a decently stocked bar and beer fridge.

He decided to take a pass on the coffee, and went and dug around in the fridge for a bottle of organic juice. He twisted off the cap and tossed it into the waste bin as he considered the FB and T financial reports he had just finished reading. By all accounts they looked pretty damn clean.

The bank had several hundred clients, but only a few that he felt were notable. Not a lot in the broader scheme of things. He sat back down and picked up another file and began thumbing through it. He was still not certain what he was looking for, but was convinced the answers lay within the files in front of him.

The restructure not only involved dozens of banks and trust companies, but also the clients themselves. FB and T had been in the forefront of offshore banking and tax planning for some time, and had grown from a small family bank and trust into an international powerhouse that now controlled over $100 billion in assets.

But with the recent changes to the global banking industry, Feinstein had seen the need to consolidate their business offshore. He had masterminded the mechanics of the restructure, and although it was a brilliant and ballsy move, Max was becoming ever more skeptical of the motives behind it.

Until now they had been working within a heavily regulated environment that was admittedly a nightmare in which to operate. But it provided an umbrella of protection that they would soon leave behind as they moved into the relatively unregulated jurisdiction of the Bahamas.

From here on they would be on their own.

He checked his watch and groaned as he realized it was only 8:30 a.m., but he'd already been at it for over two hours and his eyes were beginning to get sore. He felt restless, and was not thinking straight so he tossed the file back onto the desk and went in search of a fresh coffee.

Kate was standing in the reception area and smiled when she saw him walking toward her.

"Max, you look terrible. Were you here all night?" she asked with a look of concern.

"Good morning, sunshine, follow me," he replied, ignoring her comment.

He led her down the hall and into the staff kitchen, stopping in front of the cappuccino machine.

"Looks like you and I will be attached at the hip for the next few months, kiddo," he said as he dialed the settings and chose a double shot for himself.

"It's about time," she said sternly as she leaned back against the counter, "I was starting to feel like a charity case with nothing to do. And now poof, here we are. It's just like old times, with our own office and everything."

"Be careful what you wish for," he said as he picked up his mug of cappuccino and tilted his head for her to follow him back to the office.

"How's Phil been doing?" she asked as she caught up with him. "He's good--I'll tell him you were asking," he said with a chuckle.

"But seriously, I'm not sure either one of us will be too happy with the change in routine."

At twenty-eight, Kate was in excellent shape and he could not help but notice the conservative, black knee length dress that struggled to conceal her near-perfect body. And then he almost flushed when he realized he was looking at her in a way he had not looked before.

He had always admired her for her love of life, and how she had overcome the odds and put herself through school, eventually landing a job with Mike. They had a lot of good times together when they were still with the firm, and he had to admit he was looking forward to having her around.

Maybe Mike was right, maybe he was spending too much time alone since his father died. But now was not the time and he forced himself to dismiss the thought.

"Looks like we're in for a few marathon months with FB and T," he said as he set his cappuccino down and began reading the file he'd left on the desk.

He never noticed Kate had left the room and lost track of time until he heard her come walking back in. But as he looked up and saw the tears rolling down her cheeks he knew something was terribly wrong.

"What is it, Kate? What's wrong?" he said as he jumped up and rushed toward her.

"Trent Jordan. He's--- dead."

"What do you mean he's dead?" he said almost dismissively as she stood there in the middle of the room with her arms hanging at her side.

Not knowing what else to do, he gently pulled her into his arms. Her head fell softly onto his shoulder and she began to sob. Her body jerked as she tried to control her breathing, but it came in fits as she choked back the tears.

It had been a simple fling for him, but she had fallen hard and was devastated when it had ended almost as quickly as it began. But she had managed to maintain a relationship with him and now, the news of his loss brought back all the painful memories as she struggled to compose herself.

After a few moments she finally pulled away, and then took some tissue from the box on the table and took a seat on edge of the sofa. Her eyes burned and there was an aching inside that was indescribable as she tried to shut it all out.

Max gave her space to breathe as he backed away and then sat down quietly across from her.

"It was a mistake. Us---I mean, Trent. You know?"

There was little he could do but watch as mascara streaked down her cheeks and fell in tiny dots onto her blouse.

"I was lonely, he was handsome and available and, --" then she stopped. "God, I'm pathetic, it sounds like a frigging soap opera."

"No, it's life," he said firmly as he took her hand into his.

His emotions were boiling, and as he felt her warmth he could also feel a door opening to a place he had sealed off long ago. It was a door he needed to shut, and fast.

Finally, he pulled himself away from her grip and went to the bar to get her some water, but then decided on a brandy instead.

"Do they know what happened?" he asked as he handed her the snifter from a safe distance.

"No, at least I don't think so. They just said he died."

Max was feeling uncomfortable and searching for something to say when he heard his phone buzz. The safe harbor had come into sight, and he headed straight for it as he crossed the room and answered the call.

"Max, I'm not sure you heard, but Trent Jordan is dead," said Mike. "I want you to go to his apartment as quickly as you can and check out the situation and report back. Get the address from reception; there's a car waiting for you out front."

"What about the meeting?"

"Don't worry about it, I will hold off Feinstein until you get back."

He was about to hang up when the thought hit him, "Howell connection?"

"Maybe, I don't know. I hope to Christ not, but who the hell knows," he replied.

"All I know is they found him dead in his loft, and I need you to look into it before the police get too far. I'll be here. Call me as soon as you know anything," and then Max heard the line go dead.

Max hung up and then looked over at Kate. No time to get weak in the knees. His adrenalin began pumping. The drama was finally beginning to unfold.

"Go home, Kate, I will check in on you later," he said softly.

"I'm ok. But thanks," she replied as she pushed herself off of the sofa and shuffled out behind him.

Max picked up the address on the way out and moments later was speeding down the street in the back of one of the company sedans to what would soon be referred to as "the crime scene."

He arrived at Trent's apartment less than fifteen minutes later, and was met by a plain-clothed police officer stationed out front. It took a few seconds to get by the sentry, but he finally got inside the apartment where he was met by a detective with whom he thankfully had a history.

"Stan, how are you?" he said as he thrust out his hand.

"Max, how the hell are you? Or more to the point, what the hell are you doing here," said the detective.

"Working contract for Darington, Moskowitz and Calder, where Mr. Jordan is,--I mean was employed. So what happened?"

"Didn't you used to work for the same firm?" asked Stan looking a little puzzled.

"Couldn't hack it so I took a leave, but they couldn't live without me," he said with a wink.

"Right. Whatever you say, fly boy," he said with a grin.

"So what about it?" Max asked again.

"The call said a robbery gone bad."

"Jesus, really bad, huh?"

"Yes, and you ask me, it ain't no robbery. But I'm reserving judgment pending a little more investigation. It's never clear, but it don't smell right to me if you know what I mean. Feel free to look around, but you know the routine, don't touch anything and get lost before the gong show arrives."

"Cool, how much time do I have?"

"Fifteen minutes tops, the guys are backed up with a shooting in Chinatown. Just make sure you are outta here, you got it?"

"Thanks, Stan, I owe you big," he replied as he placed his hand on his shoulder.

"My boss is all over this and I appreciate your letting me in."

Max quickly went through the apartment, committing every detail to memory as he methodically violated the dead man's privacy. The thought of him poking into a man's personal life after he had passed made his skin crawl, and he began wondering if someday strangers may be rifling through his personal and private life.

As he passed through the apartment from room to room, he thought about his father. There had been little left to identify him other than from his dental records. Maybe, in some deep dark perverse way it was a better way to go. No one slicing you open, taking out your liver to weigh it and debating your history of alcohol consumption. Or pulling out your insides as they analyzed your last meal.

He had left the master bedroom for last and for good reason. He prepared himself, but as he entered the room it hit him like a shock wave as the impact of a violent and terrible force filled the room. He could sense the fear, the smell of death emanating from every corner as he stood silently taking in the room. And then his eyes settled on the late Mr. Jordan.

He was lying on his side near the door to the bathroom with one arm twisted in a grotesque and unnatural way beside him. It had clearly been broken in more than one place, and his face looked like he had gone fifteen rounds with Mike Tyson.

No question Trent had put up a fight, and as he put a handkerchief over his nose and closed his eyes, he could see it unfolding in front of him. Stan was right, this was no robbery. Trent had suffered a terrible beating and he couldn't imagine what he had gone through, but he hoped he had gone quickly.

He needed to talk to Mike, but more to the point, wanted to talk to Morton Feinstein.

He found Stan less than ten minutes later, well within his allotted time limit.

"I have to agree, it doesn't look like a robbery to me either," he said as he approached him.

"The world's one screwed up place, my friend," replied Stan. "Look, it was good to see you, but you better skedaddle before the dog and pony show arrive."

"I owe you one," Max shouted over his shoulder as he rushed out of the apartment and jumped into the back of the waiting sedan.

CHAPTER 12

The car had barely come to a stop before Max threw open the door and hopped out of the back, but then he stood for a moment and watched as it pulled away from the curb. He failed to notice that the sun had broken through the clouds, and although he could feel the warmth on his back it did little to lift the chill that had settled into his bones.

The elevator was empty as it carried him to 22nd floor, and he was deep in thought with visions of Trent's battered body when the doors opened and he stepped off and into the lobby. He knew he had to get to Mike's office, but decided to go and check on Kate first in hopes that she would still be there.

He knew it was a diversion he could not afford and was relieved to find her things were gone as he did a quick check of his office. But when he entered Mike's office he was surprised to see several other members of the team crowding the space, and it took him a moment before he spotted Mike.

"Well?" asked Mike in a hushed voice as Max came up beside him and then took his arm and directed him off to a corner of the room.

"Don't know. They think it may be a robbery gone bad."

But Mike could tell by the look on his face that Max thought otherwise. "You're not buying it?"

"Look, I'm no expert on robberies, but ----- no, I don't. I can't put my finger on anything specific but it didn't look like a robbery to me. In fact, it was quite the opposite. His watch and an American Airlines ticket to Cabo San Lucas were sitting in plain sight on his desk, and there was over five grand cash in the top drawer."

Mike's expression turned to one of sadness as he looked out the window, "That's right, he was supposed to be going Marlin fishing."

"Marlin fishing? You mean to tell me he was planning a fishing trip with all this going on," Max replied in disbelief.

"It was a bone of contention to say the least, but he had it planned and, well, I gave him four days on the promise I had his full commitment from there on."

"Best laid plans of mice and men," said Max as he watched Mike move toward the center of the room.

"Gentlemen, and ladies. I'm sorry to advise those of you that have not already heard, that our young Trent Jordan passed away suddenly last night. I know that some of you were closer to him than others, and I know we all miss him."

"What happened to him?" asked a shaky voice from the back of the room.

"We are not sure of the circumstances surrounding his death, but rest assured we'll be in constant contact with the authorities and we'll pass on any information as it is received."

There was a brief silence as his words sank in, but then Mike was quick to do damage control as they all began to speak at once.

"Listen….. please, everyone just listen. Believe me when I tell you I am as upset as any one of you. Trent was a friend, and an important member of our family. In fact, I was about to announce that he was not only going to assist with the FB and T account, but was going to be the lead during the consolidation."

Mike's voice faded as Max tuned him out and started thinking about what he had seen in one of the files, and as his heart began to race. Was Trent's death really an accident?

"Now, as tragic as this all is, we have much work to do and we best get to it."

Max waited until the majority had filed out and was just about to leave when Mike stopped him, "We need a one on one with Feinstein," he whispered and then turned to face him.

"I agree," replied Max as he followed him out.

They were almost to the boardroom before Mike finally spotted Feinstein and quickly intercepted him, "Mind if we have a word with you, in private?"

There wasn't much that got by Morton; he had already heard the news and his steel blue eyes bored into them as he spoke.

"Is this Jordan incident something we need to be concerned with?"

"You mean is it somehow connected to Howell?" asked Max.

"How about you tell us?" said Mike in a rather aggressive tone.

Morton looked toward the boardroom, "John, have everyone take an early lunch, and we will convene back here in one hour," he said in a raised voice.

He then turned to face Mike, "I do not appreciate your tone, but lead the way," he growled.

"Alright, let's just all take a deep breath and calm down," said Max as they crowded into the tiny office."

"Look, Morton, I don't know what the hell is going on or what you have gotten us into, but the bullshit stops right here, right now," fumed Mike as Max quickly pushed the door shut.

To Max's surprise, Morton remained cool and let Mike continue. He was used to far more aggressive attacks than this, but he also knew Mike had a right to know what had happened.

"We've got one of our staff dead in his apartment, and one of your executives beaten to a goddamn pulp in Nassau, and I want to know what the hell is going on," Mike continued as he took a seat at the table.

"When I first heard about the situation down South, I figured it was the age old problem of a jealous boyfriend or husband," said Morton. "But I now believe there were far more serious problems between Howell and his Bahamian partners."

"And the fifteen million was just the tip of the iceberg," Max said, as he watched Morton flash a faint smile, "Good to see I'm not the only paranoid one around here."

"To be honest, I no longer know what to think. But since all of my problems started right around the time we purchased that goddam bank, it's a good place to start."

"Finally," replied Mike in an I told you so fashion. "Now, can we go some place a little more comfortable and talk about what we do know?"

"Yes, we can," replied Morton. "But can we do it over some lunch? I haven't eaten since early this morning."

CHAPTER 13

"Alright folks, listen up," said Michael as he took a spot at the podium in front of the screen.

"The unfortunate passing of Mr. Jordan has left us with a large hole to fill, and it looks like you are going to have to step in and take over for him," he said as he stared over at Brian.

"No, problem," Brian said as though he had been expecting the news.

"But I will need time to review his files and get brought up to speed," he added.

"Take as much time as you can now, because we've got to be ready to move within twenty-four hours," said Michael. "His files are already on your desk."

Brian was second generation with the firm, had plenty of experience in the banking division, and should have been the first choice for the job. But they had decided to give it to Trent in case they needed him to step in on other matters that his father Brenton had been working on. But it had been a point of contention for Brian, and he'd made sure to let everyone know.

Brenton was one of the founding partners in the firm, and had been the real driving force in the early days. But personal issues recently caused the partners to ask him to step down and take a more passive role. He'd seemingly done so without a fight. Brian had been mortified when he heard the news, but did his best to take it in stride. And while he tried to maintain his relationship with his father, his focus was making partner. And he wasn't going to do anything to jeopardize it.

The rest of the meeting felt as though one hour just flowed into the next, and Max was no more the wiser when Mike brought the meeting to an end just before midnight. There was little exchange of pleasantries. Everyone rushed out hoping to squeeze in a few hours sleep before returning in the morning.

Max was of the same mind but on the way to his office to collect his things he felt his phone vibrate and then read the text, "Did U hear wat hapnd to TJ?" His first thought was to ignore it, but then he quickly punched back a response, and seconds later his phone rang.

"So, pretty shocking, hey," said a familiar voice as he took a cold beer from the fridge, and then downed half the bottle before dropping into one of the oversized chairs. Janet worked in the firm's securities division, and they'd been friends as far back as college even skiing together on the university ski team.

"I never really knew him, but it's very sad," he said wearily as he thought about Kate.

"I know, it's crazy. I mean I saw him just yesterday when he came into our office and started hitting on me--can you imagine?"

"Yes, I can imagine."

"Yeah right, thanks for the compliment," she said sarcastically. "Anyways, did you hear the rumors about him being involved in one of the recent public company scandals?

Max was tired, and, although Janet was a friend, he was not in the mood for this conversation, "Listen, Janet, I'm not trying to brush you off but it's late and I've had a really long day. I promise I'll call you in first thing in the morning."

He could tell by her tone that she was hurt, but he needed to get some sleep, "Fine, I was looking forward to a drink but I guess coffee will have to do," she said.

"Call me after eight," she said. "I have a cross training class at six." Then the line went dead.

Had Trent been hustling stocks, or something even worse? he wondered, collecting his things. As he closed the door to the office he stopped and yanked out his cell phone.

"Is it morning already, or did you reconsider the drink," she said wistfully.

Although they had come close, they had never crossed the line and he knew that it was best for everyone if he kept it that way, "Sorry sweetheart, no such luck. What I need is for you to look into something for me before we meet in the morning." he said as he rattled off his instructions.

Max slid his key into the lock and quietly pushed the door open, not even switching on the light as he stepped inside. He had just hung up his coat and was fumbling in the dark when he was knocked to the floor.

"Damn it," he whispered as Phil climbed on top of him and began licking his face. And then he squinted as the hall light came on and he saw Bea standing at the end of the corridor in her nightgown staring back at them.

"Goodnight you two," she said and then disappeared back into her room.

"So much for not waking up the neighborhood," he said as he picked up his briefcase and set it on the table. He was tired and should have gone to bed, but he was wide awake now and decided he could use a cold beer. He went and fished an ice cold Boddingtons Pub Ale from the fridge.

What a concept, he thought as he popped the top and listened as the plastic ball inside released the gas, causing it to form a nice head as he poured the contents into a frosted mug. "Someone probably made a few million bucks with this one," he said to Phil as he drained half the glass.

Feeling how well it went down, he grabbed a second can and headed for the bedroom, stripped naked, went outside and dropped into the hot tub. He settled back into the lounge seat and let the jets work their magic as the stress of the day slowly began to melt away. By the time he had finished the second beer he was ready for bed.

He woke to the sound of the alarm, disoriented and not sure where he was. He saw his father standing beside his bed and as he lay still, unable to move he could see his dad smiling down at him. He felt his heart hammering against his ribs as he strained to move, and just as he reached out to grab hold with his hand, his father vanished.

Max sat bolt upright and switched on the light, but realizing it was just a dream, he fell back down. The rain was pounding the patio deck, and he heard the faint sound of foghorns roll through the room as he pulled the covers up to his chin. His pulse had slowed back to normal, and as he squinted at the clock he could see it was only 5:30 a.m. Only four hours sleep. He reached down, rubbed his dog's head and began rethinking his conversation with Janet. Realizing he wasn't going to be able to go back to sleep, he tossed back the covers, went back, and plopped into the hot tub.

The 102 degree temperature felt good, and as he closed his eyes he could see Kate. She was standing in front of him and as he took her into his arms and held her close he could feel the moisture of her tears against his neck. The smell of her perfume seemed to linger as if she were right here with him, and he felt himself shiver as the jets timed out. He knew it was time to get moving.

He slowly lifted himself out of the tub and sat silently on the edge as steam radiated from his body in the cold morning air. He needed to get to the office. He needed to speak to Janet.

Quickly showering and dressing he headed for the kitchen where he smelled the aroma of fresh brewed coffee. Beatrice was standing beside the island, and handed him a mug as she motioned for him to sit.

"I don't have time," he said apologetically as she placed a toasted bagel with cream cheese, lox, onions and capers in front of him.

"Eat," she replied, as she shoved the plate closer.

"Sorry about last night," he said as he took a sip of coffee and then bit into the bagel.

"No problem at all, you know how he misses you," she said with a smile.

"Sure do," he said. He sucked a chunk of cream cheese off of his thumb, stood up and poured coffee into a go mug, and headed for the door.

"Gotta go, Bea, but I should be home early."

"We'll see," she replied as she picked up his plate.

He knew as soon as he left she would do a quick clean-up of

the place and then Phil would find her and the two would climb into bed and watch movies. What else was there to do on a rainy day in the city?

He thought about walking but considered the rain and decided to drive. He had just left the parking garage and was listening to the security gate as it rattled closed behind him when he hit the brakes, narrowly missing a petite young blonde as she fought her way across the entrance. The wind had caught her purse-sized umbrella and blown it inside out, and she did not see him as she struggled to get it back open. The storm was brewing.

He arrived ahead of everyone else, and was seated in his office going through the files when Kate walked in. She showed little signs of the effects of yesterday, and he felt his heart skip as she came toward him.

"Good morning," she said with a big smile as she set a cappuccino down in front of him.

"I wanted to thank you for yesterday; it's almost embarrassing to have behaved so irrationally."

"Hardly," he said as he got up and motioned for her to sit on the sofa.

"Listen, I'm sorry he's dead." She came and sat down beside him. "But it had been long over between us, and I guess that maybe, well, I don't know. Maybe I was hanging on to something that just wasn't there."

"I know how hard it can be. When I lost my father it was like someone had driven a spike through my chest, and every time I moved it just dug in deeper."

"But that was different, he was your father. And he was your best friend. Next to that damn dog of course," she said jokingly.

"For me, this had gone from a potential relationship to just friends with benefits in a few short weeks. And to be honest, it had become an uncomfortable working situation by the time I left to join you."

"All the same, if there is anything I can do, anything at all you let me know," he said as he put his hand on hers. "If you are up for it, why don't we have brunch on Sunday?"

"That would be nice, Max, I'd like that," she said as she got up and walked toward the door.

He waited until she'd left before reaching for his cell, and then sent a text to Janet; cal my prvt line.

"Can we meet for coffee?" she said as he answered the phone.

"Good morning to you too," he replied. "How about my favorite on Hastings, say twenty minutes."

"See you there."

Max found Kate in the hall near reception, "I have to go to a meeting, but in the meantime I need you to do something for me."

"Lay it on me," she said.

He could see she was going to be ok, and that made him feel a whole lot lighter as he described in detail what he wanted her to do. Once he had given his instructions he grabbed his overcoat from the closet and headed for the elevator.

The rain was bouncing up off of the sidewalk and the wind buffeted the oversized umbrella as he ran across the street, dodging the puddles that were now ankle deep. The coffee house was just around the corner, and would have normally been packed this time of the morning, but as he stepped inside he found the place was nearly empty.

He stood for a moment and shook the rain off of his umbrella before placing it in the stand. He placed his order and was still waiting at the pick-up line when Janet walked in. Even from a distance he could see that not even the rain could dampen her enigmatic smile, and he marveled how she always managed to light up a room.

"Hello darling, what can I get you?" he said as he bent down and gave her a kiss on the cheek. "It's good to see you."

"Café Americano, and good to see you too, Max." She tossed back a strand of wet hair.

"Grab us a table," he said gesturing toward one in the far corner.

She was sitting with her arms folded in front of her, and then sneezed several times into the sleeve of her sweater as she took the steaming mug and wrapped her hands around it.

"Bless you," he said, handing her a napkin.

"Are you kidding? It's the closest I've come to an orgasm in months," she replied with a mischievous grin. Then she pulled a compact out of her purse and wiped away the mascara that hung in dark circles under her eyes.

"On a bit of a dry spell," he said as she sat staring at him with her big hazel eyes. She was a character, always willing to say something with shock value to stir up a room and Max was happy to see her in good spirits.

"It's been a while," she said with a wink.

"Ok tiger." He said laughing. "But more to the point, did your investigative talents turn up anything interesting?"

"Did I ever," she said as she pushed her mug aside and leaned in close.

"You were right, I took a quick look at some of the underwritings we were handed over the past five years, and cross referenced the two specific companies you asked me about."

"And?"

"Well, the one in particular was involved in at least three, and by the looks of the trading history it's a textbook pump and dump."

"And you didn't find anything on the other company at all?"

"Nadda, nothing ---- zilch," she said, but listen, I came across something that I would never have found if you hadn't asked me to do some digging," she said and then her expression changed.

Max felt uneasy as he saw her look around the room as if she were checking to see if anyone was listening. "Someone in the firm did have a position, and a big one. And if I'm right, he was probably involved in several more of them."

"How big of a position are we talking here? Penny ante or big time?" he asked as he thought about Morton. It seemed the more he learned, the more he was convinced the man had no idea what he'd gotten himself into when he decided to move his headquarters offshore.

She sat back for a moment and took a sip of her coffee and then casually took another look around the room before answering, "Best guess, at least fifty million."

"Damn, are you sure? I thought it would have been more."

"Yes, I'm sure," she replied defensively. "I am also sure I will have a name for you by the end of the day. I just need to follow the trail."

"What about Trent--Is there anything to implicate him in any of this?"

"Short answer is no. But like so many of them these days, he was living far beyond his means."

"So he wasn't sitting flush," Max said in surprise. And just then he noticed a young couple moving toward them.

"Not even close, he was maxed out on his overdraft," she said, "credit cards, club dues were in arrears. I mean, he was virtually bankrupt…"

But she had lost his attention as he was now focused on the couple. They appeared to be of Middle Eastern descent, and looked to be in their early to late twenties. The girl was petite and quite striking with stunning green eyes.

Her companion however, was hard looking, stood at least six foot two and was well over 200 pounds. He was carrying a tray with coffee and muffins and seemed to be headed right for them. But when he saw Max staring at him he turned and headed back toward the front and placed his tray on a table by the window.

"Do you know that guy?" Janet asked when she saw the look on Max's face.

"Never seen him before," he said dismissively. "Now, what about Trent."

"I told you, I did not find anything ---- but."

"But what?"

"Well, truth is he, or I guess I should say we, took a few positions in some of the companies we took public."

"Jesus, Janet, really! You could lose your job, get fined, even go to jail for God's sake."

"But it was nothing big…I know it was stupid," she said as she sat staring deep into her mug.

"Okay." He sat back and tried to collect his thoughts.

"I'm not judging you, Janet," he said as he reached over and placed his hands over hers.

"What do you know about the recent changes in the SEC rules? As I understand it, they are finally starting to crack down on these penny stock players."

"A little, and yes," she said as she stared at him. "From the sounds of it, the U.S. and Canadian authorities are getting serious about putting these guys out of business, permanently."

"So if I'm a penny stock hustler and feel the noose begin to tighten, where's the easiest place for me to head to," he asked before she could continue.

He watched her eyes light up, "The Bahamas," she chirped, as the smile returned to her face.

"Precisely," he replied, and then suddenly he had a sense the couple who had come by earlier were watching them. But as he glanced in the overhead mirror they appeared to be having a normal conversation. He gazed at them in the mirror. He thought he'd seen the man before, he just could not remember where.

"Listen Janet," he said as he turned his attention back to her, "I don't know what connection Trent had to FB and T, but I want you to be careful. If he was involved, you could be in harm's way."

"Now you're scaring me," she said as she withdrew her hands into the sleeves of her sweater.

"Look, there is nothing to be afraid of, just be aware is all I'm saying."

But then he noticed the quiver in her lower lip, and it pained him to see her this way. "Yeah, right," she replied as she stared at the ends of her sleeves where her hands should have been. "Easy for you to say."

She was right, it was time to end the conversation. He rose in the chair.

"There is nothing to worry about, I promise. I'm just being cautious, ok?" he said as he helped her with her coat.

She stood on her tiptoes and kissed him on the cheek as she buttoned her coat. "I promise to be careful."

He felt the rain pelting him as they stepped outside, "Take this, I don't have far to go," he said, handing her his umbrella.

And then he stood and watched as she disappeared across the rain swept street.

CHAPTER 14

Max hung his raincoat on the rack and then slipped into the executive men's room and dried his hair before heading to his office. He only had one message, it was from Morton Feinstein asking him to call immediately.

He answered after the second ring, "I have spoken with Michael and we have decided we want to get some boots on the ground in Nassau. You are leaving tonight on the company jet, wheels up by midnight," he said as though speaking to an employee.

"Everyone needs to be at the FBO by eleven thirty, Mike has the details," he said, not giving Max an opportunity to respond.

His first reaction was no way, but when he thought about the prospect of using the old man's jet, his position changed. He had read in the company filings that Morton had just purchased a Falcon 900, one of the most luxurious flying machines made and the envy of many private jet owners.

It also came with a hefty price tag of $35 million.

Not only would the flight be non-stop from Vancouver to Nassau, but they would be flying at an altitude well above the thunderheads that were notorious in the South for that time of year. And with eight luxury seats, two sleeper sofas, a washroom, shower and a full galley, it would definitely be a comfortable trip.

"Ok, but can we meet here first? There's been a new development I would like to discuss with you."

"Can't," he replied.

"But I think it's important and would really like you to hear what I have to say."

"It will have to wait," he said emphatically. "The people in Nassau are waiting for you and have been instructed to be at your disposal for as long as you are there. I will be leaving Vancouver within the hour, but I will arrange a conference call with you in the morning."

Max was not able to hide his annoyance as he replied a little too coldly, "You're the boss."

"Listen Max, do not underestimate how much I appreciate your coming on board, but circumstances dictate I be elsewhere right now. In the meantime, I would appreciate it if you could just trust me on this."

"I'll be there," he replied. But Morton had already hung up.

Since Morton was not available he dialed Michael's cell but it went to voicemail. "I guess it will just have to wait," he murmured to himself as he hung up the phone.

He was deep in thought with his back to the door and never heard Kate until she dropped a pile of files onto the desk behind him. The noise startled him and as he spun around she could hear the crack of his knee hitting the corner of the desk.

"Shit," he cried out with that painful laugh one gets from hitting their funny bone.

"Ouch," she said, giggling. "That sounded like it hurt. Michael asked me to bring you these files, and to go to storage and get two of the travel cases for you to pack them in."

"Thanks, don't know what all the cloak and dagger is about. The rest of the world has gone digital and here we are carrying half a first growth forest worth of paper around."

"Poor you, where are you off to this time?"

"Old man Feinstein is flying us to Nassau tonight on his private jet."

"Nassau," she said scrunching up her face. "Poor little you, in a private jet no less."

"I know, it's rough and how do I handle the stress of it all? Sun, sand, nearly naked women with awesome tans and…."

"Alright already, I get the picture. The least you could do is leave the women out of your delusions of grandeur," she said with a pouty look.

"Relax, I was joking. At least about the women, that is," he said with a wink.

When he saw she wasn't softening he tried another tact, "How about lunch? I'm buying."

"Better," she said.

"Great, why don't you scoot over to Max's and get us two double smoked meat sandwiches and some of those crispy truffle fries they make," he said as he handed her a one hundred dollar bill.

"First, I don't scoot," she said as she crossed her arms over her chest. "Second, that's hardly a lunch date. And thirdly, are you nuts! Do you see how hard it's raining?"

He couldn't help but smile as he sat back staring at her, "Is that any way to talk to your boss? And besides, you need to give me more credit than that. They just opened a new location across the street and you can get there through the underground mall."

He felt his stomach rumble to the aroma of smoked meat as Kate walked into the office.

"Smells awesome," he said as he dropped his papers onto the desk and went and took two beers from the fridge.

"Benefits of being on contract," he said when he saw her looking at the beers.

They had spent a lot of time together when they were both at the firm, but since he left he had really not seen much of her. As he cleared space on the coffee table he realized just how much he missed their time together.

"Listen, I know it's none of my business, but why did you leave the firm in what was it, just over three years? I mean, it looked like you had such an incredible future here, especially after the settlement of that big class action suit."

Max couldn't help but smile as he watched her negotiate the three-inch-thick sandwich into her mouth. Then without thinking, he leaned over and wiped mustard from the corner of her lips and was about to lick his finger when he caught himself and wiped it onto the napkin.

"Ah yes, I wondered when this was going to come up. The simple answer, I was sitting in my office one afternoon looking at the people in the building across from us, and it occurred to me," he paused.. "Now bear with me as there is method to my madness. If we spend thirty years of our life working, that's eight thousand days of work and eight thousand hours commuting. Think about it, that's one thousand additional work days spent in a car, bus, train or any combination thereof. Now, here's where it really begins to get painful," he said as he stood up and walked over to the window. "Eight thousand work days, and that's no overtime mind you, is about six thousand hours spent in some tiny cubicle in the hopes of someday retiring before you drop dead."

"God, you can be depressing sometimes," she said as she set what was left of her sandwich onto the table and picked up her beer.

"Depressing, no, my dear. It's just a fact of life. And when I realized that I only had maybe thirty seasons left at best, to do the things I really wanted to do I decided to check out. I mean, can you really justify sitting at a desk for a year and a half of your life just so you can buy a new porsche?"

"You know, Max, maybe you're right," she said defensively. "But people have obligations and responsibilities and it's just not that easy to walk away and go live in a tent someplace."

"Look, I didn't mean to upset you, but you asked the question."

Kate sat for a moment and could feel an emptiness inside that she had not felt for some time, "You're right, Max. Maybe we do take life all too seriously."

And then seeing an openness, a side of him she had not seen before, she decided to keep him talking, "Tell me about your dad."

"My father?" he repeated, caught a bit off guard. "Well, let's see. After the farm he started life as a bush pilot, and while I was growing up I would fly for hours with him into the middle of nowhere. Sometimes, he would land on a lake and we would sit and fish from the pontoons while he told me stories of the places he'd been."

"I never knew," she said, surprised. "I guess that explains the theory of office life, by Max Duncan."

"Guess it does. Anyway, turns out he was an excellent pilot and it wasn't long before he was hired on with a large lumber company and began flying mid-range jets."

"Sounds like you had a great childhood," she said as she studied his face. She could see the pride in his eyes, but she also could feel his loss as she listened to him tell his story. It was a vulnerable side of Max she had not seen before.

"It got even better when he took on a job as the chief pilot for James Whitmore, at least for a while anyway. I did not see much of him once he started the overseas flights, but Whitmore was a great boss and he let him take me along whenever he didn't have clients on board."

"Why do I get the feeling the Bahamas somehow plays into this?" she asked.

"As a matter of fact it did. Whitmore had a small insurance business in Nassau, and he went there frequently. So I got to spend quite a bit of time there learning how to spearfish and sail."

"Well, that all sounds really great, but you don't seem to be breaking any income records these days. In fact, I've been thinking about resigning just to give you a break on your overhead."

"Stop right there, Kate," he said as he walked back over and sat down across from her.

"I am doing just fine, and this job alone will carry us for the year. Besides, Phil isn't planning on going to university any time soon, so I don't have any hefty tuitions hanging over my head," he said just as his phone began to vibrate.

The message read, "urgnt, meet at Cactus 4p?

He quickly replied, and then turned to Kate as she cleaned up the remnants of their lunch, "Listen Kate, I appreciate your concern about my financial health and am sorry about the weekend.

I know it's a tough time for you and that I promised you a real lunch this weekend, but I had no idea I was going to be leaving."

"If you have to get out of a lunch date, it's not a bad way to do it," she said. "Don't worry about it, we're good and we can do it when you get back."

And although he could tell there was more to her questions than curiosity, he just could not afford to think about it right now. They were good friends, and he wanted to keep it that way. At least for the time being.

She was almost out the door when he called her back, "Look, this may sound strange but this is the second time today I've said this: just be careful. This business with FB and T has me worried, and I -----,".

"Worry," she replied with a puzzled look on her face. "You just take care of yourself," she said as she disappeared into the hallway.

Max took a quick pass through the bar, and was almost back to the entrance before he spotted Janet sitting at a table in the corner with two pints of draft beer in front of her.

"The company I told you about was run by a group of East Indians, three brothers named Singh, and they are a bunch of scam artists," she blurted excitedly before he even had time to sit down.

"Hello to you too," he replied as he held up his hand and then climbed onto the stool and took a drink of his beer.

"Listen, I think we're really onto something here. I looked at the files again, you know, to see if there was anything out of the ordinary, but there wasn't. We covered every step, completed the filings, got the registration with the public company accounting oversight board. They did their audit and passed it with no red flags. The company was issued its symbol and they were up and running."

"First, thank you for the beer," he said. "And second, slow down and get a little more specific. Because I'm having a very hard time trying to follow you."

"Then pay attention, mister. Despite what the SEC says, the over the counter and bulletin board companies are still pretty unregulated, and the listing requirements are lax. Looking back, I don't think they even paid much attention to our filings."

"Jesus, are you telling me our firm was involved in an OTC swindle?"

"Yes and no," she said as she took a drink of beer. "The last filing we did had one hundred and fifty million shares issued between five and ten cents. A large chunk, and what was not issued to the insiders, had been bought through a Liechtenstein Bank, which holds an offshore account called Abitibi Holdings in the Cayman Islands.

"Who's the registered office for Abitibi?" asked Max.

"Andorra Bank."

"Bingo," he said as his heart began to hit high gear. Andorra was one of the names that had caught his attention when going through Morton's files. Andorra is a tiny principality between Spain and France, and although eighty percent of their GDP comes from tourism, they are also a well known tax haven.

When he was still at the firm, he had some Canadian clients who were working in Saudi Arabia and did their banking in Andorra for tax purposes.

"Well done, Janet, you have my attention," he said staring her in the face.

"What?" she said dryly. "Do I have something on my face?"

"Nice tattoo," he said as he lightly touched the miniature bird on the side of her neck. "Bluebird of happiness?"

"Very funny mister straight laced," she replied. "Never mind the tattoo and pay attention--there were nominee shareholders of the company on the register in Cayman, but someone fucked up when they opened their account with Andorra Bank in the Bahamas."

"Shit," said Max as he let out a whistle. Andorra Bank was the one and the same that FB&T purchased. And it now looked as though it was the one who had facilitated their stock trades.

"How was this a screw up, using Andorra, that is?"

"For shit's sakes, aren't you listening? The Bahamas has standard know your client reporting and one of the clerks at the foreign investment review board inadvertently sent the registry to the SEC.

"Anyway, from what I can gather, these guys were going to run the stock and unload the shares through their broker dealers. And as best I can tell, after paying the brokers and promoters they would have walked with a cool thirty million. Maybe more."

Then it finally hit him: the guy in the coffee shop. Max had seen him earlier that day in the elevator in Mike's building, and he suddenly had a bad feeling in his gut. He had only ever met two of the shareholders, could he have been one of the three she was talking about?

"So these guys, the three you speak of. Are they still clients of Mike's?"

"Not that I know of. But in any case, hold on to your ass because you haven't heard the best part."

She paused dramatically. The stock went to five bucks! Do the fucking math. The geniuses walked away with about four hundred million."

Max sat back in his chair and closed his eyes for a moment as the pieces all began to fall into place. He was no wiser as to the problems that had Morton so worked up, but this was a start. And not at all what he had been expecting.

"And the inside man?" he asked slowly.

She hesitated for the first time since he had sat down, the color drained from her face, and her voice was barely an audible whisper, "It was Brenton Calder."

At first Max couldn't believe what she had said.

"Brenton? Come on, there must be some mistake."

But the look on her face told him otherwise.

"I didn't believe it at first either, but look at the man," she said sadly. "He's had a string of divorces with huge alimony payments, and it's no secret that he's had a drinking problem. His billings have been substantially reduced, and from the little poking around that I did it looks like he's broke."

Max really did not like where this was going. Up until now he had only been focused on FB&T. If she was right, and there was a direct connection between them and the firm, this would add a whole new level of complexity. And he was caught squarely in the middle of it all.

"Do you think this is somehow connected to Trent's murder?"

He could see she was giving it a lot of thought as she took another swallow of beer, and then sat back. "No, I don't. But Brian was the one who handled the file and took the company public. What if he let his father in on it? God knows the old man has been a fuck up for years."

"No way. No way in hell. He's gone through too much shit with the old man to screw up now," replied Max

"No. I'm sure of it. Listen, it makes sense. Brian has been

living the life, new condo at Whistler, just bought the new Mercedes and look where he lives."

"Yes, but he is also making a pretty decent income. From what Mike said, his billings last month alone were over three hundred hours," he replied defensively.

"Believe it, don't believe it, Max, but I'm right about this." That smile he loved magically reappeared. "I'll get you all the proof you need, and I'll tell you something else, if the SEC gets hold of it the shit will hit the fan big time."

"Look, let's say for a moment you are right. Nothing good is going to come of this now that they have already run their scam, especially when there is nothing in it for you. So I am asking you to leave it be, at least until I get back."

"I appreciate your concern, but you're the one that got me into this in the first place, and I for one do not want to see these guys get away with it. A lot of people got hurt when the stock crashed, or don't you care?"

"Of course I do, but there are bigger issues at play here and I don't want to see anyone getting hurt. Especially Mike."

"No one is going to get hurt. Go to Nassau, have a good time and I'll get you your proof."

He knew there was no stopping her now. All he could do was impress on her the need to be careful. "Fine, but with what you have told me, I find it hard to believe Trent was not connected. And if he was, and with the kind of money we are talking about, you need to watch your back."

It was bad timing for him to be leaving, and he considered calling Morton but decided against it and headed back to the office. Not knowing what to do next, he opened up the doors that covered the whiteboard and began to lay out the companies.

FB and T had a corporate client owned by three brothers who were local. They had taken a

Company, or several companies public through the firm, and traded the stock through various offshore banks. It's probably how they ran their box.

But the funds seemed to have gone to banks outside of FB and T, and there was still Trent. Where did he fit into it all? It was looking more like Janet may be right and Trent was just a victim of circumstance, but his instincts were telling him otherwise, and it fit with what both Mike and Morton Feinstein had told him. But at the end of it all, it was just a bunch of diagrams on a white board that gave him few answers.

CHAPTER 15

It was late by the time Max got back to the office, and he knew he needed to get moving if he was going to make the flight. He quickly stuffed his files into the cases Kate had left for him, checked for his phone and keys and was almost at the elevator when he realized he had forgotten Morton's binder.

"Shit," he said as he sprinted back to the office and grabbed the binder. He kept it on top of one of the cases as he rode the elevator down.

Max was still holding the binder under one arm and was about to open the car door when he saw a reflection in the door glass. As he spun around he found himself face to face with the young man he had seen earlier that day in the coffee house. He was very large and appeared to be no stranger to the gym. His right hand was raised over his head, and then Max heard the unmistakable snap of the expandable baton as he came at him.

Max tried to pivot to his right, but his foot caught one of the cases. He braced himself against the car and used the binder for protection as the baton ricocheted off, catching him on his left arm. The impact knocked the binder from his hands, and he was now pinned back against the car. With little room to move, he dropped down and delivered a hard right to the man's midsection just as the shaft of the baton bounced off of the soft-top of his car.

Realizing he was off balance, Max moved in from the side and unleashed three punishing blows to his kidneys. He was about to drop him when he felt himself being grabbed from behind.

The second assailant had his arms wrapped around him in a powerful bear hug, and as he felt his feet leave the floor, Max drove his head backwards into the man's nose.

"Son-of-a-bitch," he cried, and as he loosened his grip Max felt his feet hit the floor just as the other one came back at him.

Max could see the anger in his eyes, and when he got within range he dropped down and drove his foot into the man's left knee with brutal force. He heard the snap as the femur split in two, and watched as he fell to the concrete screaming in pain.

One down, one to go. He turned his attention back to the one with the broken nose. He could see the confusion on his face as they stood staring at each other.

"Weren't expecting a fight, were you?" said Max as he calmly slid his right foot behind him.

"Self-defense classes at the Y ain't going to save your ass, hotshot," he growled as he wiped the blood from under his nose and then glanced at the back of his hand.

He made his move and Max hit him with a crushing front kick to the mid-section, but he never went down. Instead, he just kept coming at him with the force of a linebacker. Max tensed his stomach and took the full force of his shoulder. Max felt the crushing squeeze of his arms as the man lifted him up off of his feet and drove him backwards into the concrete column.

He had all of his 250 pounds hard against him, and Max

struggled to breathe as he felt the air being forced out of him. Going for his weak spot, he nailed him in the nose again but this time with his forehead. He felt the warm splatter of blood on his neck, and as his grip relaxed Max pulled free, grabbed a hold of his head and brought his knee up with all he had.

Max was breathing heavy and his chest ached as he watched him stagger back, and then couldn't believe it when he stopped and stood back upright.

"You sure you want to do this?"

"Fuck you," he grunted as he reached inside his bloodied jacket for his gun.

Max closed the distance, and gripped the man's wrist in his left hand while he took a hold of the pistol in his right. The attacker struggled to break free, but Max forced the gun back, snapping his index finger as he continued to twist the gun and force him down. Finally, he dropped to his knees and Max nailed him with a fierce left just above the temple.

There was a sickening thud as his head hit the concrete, and as he lay unconscious Max spun around and looked for the other attacker. He was gone. He could not have gotten far with a broken leg and Max was about to go after him when a security guard came running up beside him.

He was shouting something into his handheld radio and Max cursed when he heard the sirens. It was bad enough he had let his guard down and gotten attacked, but now he was going to have to answer some pretty tough questions and still attempt to get out of there in time to catch the flight.

"You ok, Mr. Duncan?"

"I'm fine, thanks, and you?" he said, recognizing the guard from earlier that day.

"Very funny, Sir, " replied the guard as he stood staring at the bloodied body on the concrete in front of them.

Seconds later it was total mayhem as two police cruisers and a paramedic unit arrived.

"A little overkill, don't you think," he said to the guard as a paramedic guided him over to the van and attempted to help him inside.

"I'm fine, really," he was saying to the medic as he looked up and saw the stunning blonde officer standing in front of him. "That may well be, but I need a few minutes of your time, Mr. Duncan."

"Well, I guess I can spare a few minutes," he replied smiling. This would take some fancy footwork if he was going to get out of there and still catch his plane he thoughts as he sat staring at the officer.

She really was a stunner, and for a brief second he considered asking her out. But then he quiclky dismissed it as he took a seat on the back of the van.

"Look, it was probably just some punks going through the cars and I just happened to get here a few minutes too soon, that's all," he chuckled as he tried to play the part. But he was beginning to feel the pain in his arm and back and hoped there was no serious damage.

"Listen, I appreciate the concern and certainly the help," he continued, but I have a plane to catch very soon and unless you need anything else, I really need to go."

"In case you haven't noticed, we have a seriously injured man here, and you are telling me he attacked you. So bear with me one more time so I can get this straight: you were walking up to your car when you noticed someone, a man, near the vehicle?"

"Yes, something like that."

"You say that he startled you, causing you to drop your cases and that's when he attacked you."

"Right so far," he replied, admiring her striking features.

"When he attacked you, you struggled and that's when you tripped and fell over your cases?"

"That's correct, officer, and that's when I heard his head hit the concrete. It really was an awful sound," he said with feigned concern. "I really hope he'll be ok."

"And the other guy…?" she asked, realizing everything he had told her was pure bullshit.

"I'm really not sure. As I say, it's all kind of a blur."

But even in the dim lighting of the underground, he could see somewhere back in those deep blue eyes that she just wasn't buying it.

"Listen, I don't know what you're up to, but you must have one hell of a lucky charm shoved up your ass. Did you see the size of this guy?" she said, pointing to the man lying on the concrete.

She wasn't going to let it go, and he needed to move the conversation in another direction. "The needle exchange, nothing but a nightmare, and the idiots who thought it up should be driven down to Main Street and left there with the addicts they are trying to support."

"Pardon me?"

"The damn needle exchange. They give the junkies free needles and no dope. I mean, how ridiculous is that? They get clean needles and no dope, so they hit the cars and whatever else they can in order to get a score. That's probably who tried to break into my car, some damn junkies."

"Ok, whatever you say, hot shot," she replied, realizing there wasn't anything to be gained by holding him any longer.

"Here's my card, in case you think of anything else," she said as she stood and started walking away. Then she stopped and turned, and he saw a thin smile spread across her face, "or if you need to call me with a more plausible story."

"You can count on it," he said under his breath as he walked back to his car and opened up the trunk. He was picking up one of his cases when he gasped for breath as a sharp pain shot through his shoulder. But after a few seconds the pain subsided, and he climbed into the car and turned the key.

He clipped his seat belt into place as the powerful V12 roared to life—then he shoved it into gear and followed the cute blonde's police cruiser out of the garage.

"Junkies. I doubt that," he said with a laugh. "Even I wouldn't buy that one."

Phil came bounding down the hallway as he put his cases down, and then followed him into the bedroom and jumped up as he fell back onto the bed. He lay quiet for a few minutes as Phil pushed his nose under his hand and waited for him to rub his head.

"It was quite a day, my friend," he said as he slowly pulled himself up. He went and got a glass of ice and poured a few inches of scotch into a tumbler.

"Medicinal," he said, as he stripped off his clothes and went and climbed into the hot tub. It didn't take long for the scotch, and gentle massaging of the jets to relieve the aching in his shoulder, and as he lay back he could feel the stress slowly melting away.

The game had escalated, and any doubts he had about Trent's death being somehow connected were long gone. But the Billion Dollar question still remained: how were they connected? And after a few minutes he turned off the jets, dried his hands, picked up the phone and punched in Kate's cell number. She answered on the second ring.

"Hope I'm not bothering you."

"Not at all. I'm just making some dinner and was thinking about watching a movie," replied Kate as she sat bundled up on her sofa.

"Sounds like a good plan."

"So what can I do for you, I thought you were on your way to Nassau."

"I am, but I got delayed at the office and just got home. Anyway, I can't go into anything in detail but something came up and I just wanted to check in and make sure everything is alright."

"And?"

"I've decided to take Phil and I need you to find out what customs officers are on duty when we land and send them his vet papers. I emailed them to you a little while ago."

"Great, I'm stuck here in the rain while you and your damn dog jet off to the Bahamas, but don't worry, I'll get it done before I crash for the night. And you, Mister, had better get your butt to the airport."

"I'm on my way," he said as he hopped up out of the tub and made a run for the shower.

Millionaire, the flight based operation in Richmond was located just off the main airport and was a first class facility. His driver helped him load his bags onto the trolley, and he followed him into the building with Phil at his side.

"Max, what the --- what's old man Feinstein going to say when he finds out you brought your dog along," asked Ken Chaplin as he approached them.

"I really don't care. He never gave me time to arrange for someone to take care of him, and we don't do kennels."

"Now, who do we have coming with us?"

"John Farrington and Jim Williamson, along with two compliance officers and one of their controllers. I guess that makes seven in total. Speak of the devil, here they come now," he said when he saw them coming through the door with a loaded baggage cart.

"Healthy boys," said Max as they came toward them.

"Max, meet Bjorn Swenson and Sven Larsen; they are from our Switzerland office," said Ken as he introduced them.

"You brothers?" asked Max as they shook hands.

"No sir," replied Sven, the bigger of the two." But we were on the Swiss Olympic shooting team, and then came to work together for FB and T."

"Call me Max," he replied.

Just then as he saw the pilot and co-pilot approaching, "Mr. Duncan, I'm Captain Stebbings, and this is our co-pilot, Mr. Davison."

"Pleased to meet you," replied Max as they shook hands.

Stebbings was broad shouldered with a weathered face, and looked to be in his late fifties or early sixties. Had to be ex-military. Davison, on the other hand, was much younger, but had a serious look about him.

"Well, if we're all here, we should get everyone on board, said Stebbings. And then he looked down and saw Phil, "Do you have papers for the dog?" he asked.

"Vet certificate and importation permit will be at customs when we land."

"Then let's roll," he said as he turned and disappeared into the pilots' lounge.

CHAPTER 16

Max had been on plenty of jets before, but he couldn't hold back a twitch of envy as he climbed on board. The interior was done in a cream white leather, and seats were finished in a light tan color with cream piping to match. The bar and woodwork were all light mahogany with a polished finish and it smelled like a new Bentley.

"Yowza! Now this I could get used to," said Ken as he slipped by him and dropped his case beside one of the lazy-boy style seats.

"I have to agree, it's a pretty slick ride," Max replied, but as he sat down in the seat beside him the sharp pain in his side caused him to catch his breath.

"You ok?" asked Ken.

"I'm fine," he lied. "I was out for a run and took a bit of header on the sea wall, no big deal."

The pain was not getting any better, and he hoped there were no cracked ribs.

"Good evening, gents," said the captain as he stood facing them in the cockpit door.

"Make yourselves comfortable and welcome aboard. Flying

time to Nassau will be about six hours and thirty seven minutes, and it should be a pretty smooth flight all the way." He disappeared into the cockpit.

Seconds later Max heard a low whine, and then felt the vibration of the Honeywell turbine engines as they came to life. They sat for a moment, and then slowly began to move as they taxied out and took their place at the ramp to the runway.

"If everyone would make sure they are buckled up, we will get this bird in the air," said the captain over the intercom. Less than a minute later they made a ninety degree turn to the left and then came to a stop. Max heard the thrust of the engines as they propelled them down the runway and as the g-force pressed him back into his seat as the plane took flight.

They were climbing at over three thousand feet per minute, and it was an experience he never got tired of. But as he looked over, he could see the color had drained from Ken's face as he sat pressed back in his chair. He was clearly not enjoying the ride anywhere near as much as Max was.

"A little nervous, sport?" he asked with a grin as he tried to give him some comfort.

"What can I say? I hate flying. Even in this luxury," he replied as he gripped the sides of his chair.

"Well, you can relax. This is one of the safest planes in the air."

"And we have three engines. So even if we lose one on take-off we can still turn around and fly back home safely."

"What do you mean, lose an engine," Ken cried nervously as he sat staring straight ahead.

"Lighten up," said Max, I'm only kidding. "So, as they say; sit back, relax and enjoy the ride."

"Thanks, I'll try."

As Jeanine, the attendant, came walking back Max caught a whiff of something good coming from the galley. It had been over ten hours since he had last eaten and he was ready for a good meal.

"What's on the menu?" he asked as his stomach began to rumble.

"Pacific Coast Sockeye Salmon, with asparagus and dill sauce with capers. And we have an excellent selection of wine," she replied. "May I start you off with the Caymus 2010?"

"Sounds good to me, but you better bring him a double scotch too," he replied as he looked over at Ken and grinned.

"On the rocks," said Ken as he looked back at Max and gave him a thumbs up.

Phil, the veteran flyer, was already sound asleep and had started to snore as Ken looked at him with admiration, "Flying doesn't seem to bother him much."

"No, we have racked up our share of miles; it's old hat to him now."

"You're a pilot?" Ken asked, obviously impressed.

"My dad was. It would have been my first choice but he wanted me to be a lawyer instead. And so, here I am."

Jeanine brought everyone their drinks, and while the FB&T group got into some deep discussion over the consolidation, Max enjoyed his conversation with Ken about life in general. After a few more drinks, Ken managed to relax and proved to have quite a sense of humor.

By the time they had finished their outstanding meal, Max had killed the entire bottle of wine. With the pain now gone, he fell sound asleep before he'd even reclined his chair.

The rest, however, had moved on to after dinner drinks of

Port and Cognacs. Unlike Max, they had not experienced this kind of luxury before, and were taking advantage of every minute as they cruised along at 45,000 feet.

Max had been sound asleep when he felt himself being jolted awake by turbulence. As he looked forward he saw the outline of buildings through the open cockpit door. He could see the radar screen glowing a bright pink, warning them of the impending danger they were flying into. And then the sky turned black, and he felt the plane vibrate beneath him as they flew straight into the storm.

The cross winds were tossing them from side to side, and then a powerful updraft shot the plane vertical and he felt his body pressed back into his seat as they continued to rise. And then all of a sudden they stopped for a brief second, and then the seatbelt dug into his waist as the plane began to free fall back down.

The pilot was clearly out of his mind. He ripped at the buckle on his seatbelt in an attempt to break free.

They were in deep trouble, but there wasn't anything he could do but watch as the pilot tried desperately to gain control of the plane. He could see the muscles in his arms bulge, and beads of sweat pour off of his forehead as he strained against the yoke to regain control.

"You have to abort," Max shouted, but the pilot ignored him as they continued to be tossed around by the full force of the storm. He heard cries of anguish as passengers began uttering prayers, and then the smell of vomit as people began to get sick.

"Screw this," he shouted as he continued to try and free himself from the seatbelt.

But then the turbulence stopped, and they broke through the clouds and ascended into clear blue sky. It was as if God's hand had come down from above and freed them from the grasp of the deadly storm.

"This guy has to be nuts," said Max as he looked over at Ken. But he was no longer there. Where the hell could he be? But then, he looked out the window and saw the water below.

That's weird—they were skimming over the Gulf Stream just off the coast of Florida. He could see the waves churning below, and then he heard the Pratt & Whitney engines scream in protest as the pilot pressed them to the maximum. But they were still dropping, and he knew there was nothing he could do as he saw the foam being ripped from the top of the waves in front of them.

Hitting the water at that speed was no different than hitting concrete, and as they made impact he could hear the metal being ripped from the fuselage as they plowed through the waves. When the plane finally came to a stop, he felt the rush of water as it began filling up around him. And then all of a sudden he saw his father's face. He was pulling him from his seat.

"Max, are you ok ---- Max, can you hear me?"

He felt his heart hammering against his chest, and his shirt was soaked right through as he sat bolt upright. He opened his eyes to see Ken standing beside him where his father had just been, "You ok, Max? Man alive you must have had one hell of a nightmare,"

"I'm fine," he replied slowly, and realizing it was all just a bad dream he felt a wave of embarrassment wash over him.

His shoulder and ribs were throbbing, and as he looked out the window he could see they were just passing over Grand Bahama. He had been out for at least four hours.

He got up, went to the lavatory, and splashed cold water onto his face. Then he stood staring into the mirror as snippets of the nightmare came flooding back. It was his father's last flight. They had ruled it pilot error, and although they managed to find most of the wreckage, the bodies were never recovered.

Although his body was aching, Max's head was clearing and he felt more alive than he had in a very long time. Be it the solid four hours sleep, or the living of a nightmare, it didn't matter. He knew what he needed to do.

There was a mug with fresh coffee and plate of pastries sitting on the table when he returned, and as he sat down he heard Captain's voice come on the overhead speakers. "Welcome to Nassau, we will be landing in about seventeen minutes, so if you could finish up your breakfast Jeanine will clear everything away and prepare us for landing."

The heat waves shimmered up from the runway as they rolled to a stop in front of the FBO at exactly two minutes after seven, just as the captain had promised. There was a knock on the cabin door as the copilot appeared from the cockpit. He opened the cabin door and was greeted by one of the local ground crew.

CHAPTER 17

Nassau, The Bahamas

Max could see the look on Ken's face as he viewed the steam coming out of the air-conditioning vents. "Relax, it's not smoke; it's just the humidity," he said as he led Phil off of the plane and over to the patch of grass in front of customs.

He watched while Phil sniffed the area for recent activity. He switched on his Iphone as he waited for him to do his business. Seconds later he felt the phone vibrate as he began receiving messages, along with a text from Kate.

He smiled as he read her text. She must have been up plenty early to pull this one off. He had been skeptical whether she could get it done on such short notice, but she had come through with flying colors. Fortunately, the agent on duty at the customs office at the FBO was Jerome Pratt, who happened to be a friend of his.

Max followed everyone into the pre-clearance area where their passports were inspected, Customs forms were collected and the usual questions were tossed out with little to no interest in the answers. They were processed and cleared to go within minutes.

Max was headed toward the group when Jerome came out of the side office with a big grin on his face and his hand extended, "Mister Max, how very good to see you. Welcome back."

"Jerome, great to see you, my friend," he replied as they gave each other the three way Bahamian handshake. And as he came around the counter and gave Max a hug, they heard Phil let out a low growl.

"I see you have the furry barracuda with you," he said as he stared down at him. It was a nickname Phil had earned from the Bahamians for his fierce loyalty to Max. Whenever anyone came close to him, Phil would slip in between them and snarl a warning that they were off limits, which suited Max just fine.

"Biggity as ever," replied Max.

"I received the certificates just a few minutes ago, so all is well. I just need you to sign here," said Jerome as he set the paper in front of him.

"Thanks, man, I appreciate it," said Max as he slipped him a U.S. one hundred dollar bill.

The runway staff had their bags loaded on two trolleys and followed them out the back to where the others were waiting under the shade of a small pergola. Max walked around and checked the front of the building and found the limousine parked off to the side just as the driver came walking out the front door.

"You here for the FB and T crowd?" asked Max as he approached the man.

"Yes sir, if you want to join your friends I will pull around and get everyone loaded."

Max tipped the porters forty dollars, and once everyone was inside he told the driver to take them to North Point. The bank had reserved rooms at the boutique hotel, which was right on the water in the Love Beach area and close to their office.

"Ken, why don't you give these guys a little history of our fine Island?" said Max as they drove out past the hangers and onto the road opposite the runway.

"Holy shit. Did you see all those jets?" said Sven as he stared back at the parking area.

"Yep, used to be citations and Lear Jets. Now it's Global Express, GIV's, Challengers and of course, Falcon 900s," replied Max.

"Must be a couple of hundred million dollars worth of aircraft sitting there."

"A lot more than that. Some of those babies could set you back up to fifty million. And a lot of the owners have a yacht sitting somewhere nearby that's at least one hundred and fifty feet long."

"I've even seen them over three hundred feet," said Ken jumping in.

"And these are our clients," said John as he sat staring out the window.

"Some of them are for sure," said Ken as he rolled down his window

"Are there many Canadians down here?" asked Jim.

"Yes, Canadians have played a major role here for some time. The Royal Bank of Canada and also the Bank of Nova Scotia have been here for over one hundred years."

"And the nouveau rich go as far back as Sir Harry Oakes, who made his fortune in Canada and moved here in the 1930s."

"Long since dead, I assume," said John.

"As a door nail. He was murdered in his home in 1943. But the family still has huge land holdings, or at least they did until some of the locals managed to steal it away from them."

"Who did it?" asked Mike.

"What, steal the land?" replied Ken.

"No, the murder."

"Oh, there's been plenty of speculation and books written, but it was never solved. Justice is not always swift, if at all, here in the Bahamas."

"Includes the drug trade," prompted Max.

"Ah yes, the drugs," smiled Ken. By the 1970s, drug running was rampant and if you ever saw the movie, Blow, the part about them running drugs from an island here was true. Carlos Lehder, the head of the Columbian cartel, built a runway on Norman's Cay in the Exumas, and it was his main distribution point up until the 1980s when the DEA shut him down. Back then it was big money, but the amount of wealth that's moving in here now is unprecedented."

"And, no doubt that's why FB and T is so anxious to get established here," said Bjorn.

"So where does the big money live?" asked John.

"There is a gated community at the western end of the island built by E.P. Taylor, another Canadian and a good friend of Oakes. It was started in the 1950s and there has to be over twenty billionaires now living there."

"What's their main source of wealth," asked Sven, who up until now had very little to say.

"Well, that is where I have a problem."

"And don't get me wrong, the vast majority of the residents here are legitimate business people who have made it on their own. And there are others that have generational money who still control some of the largest corporations in the world."

"But unfortunately, there are some who are not what you would consider to be pillars of our community," said Ken.

"But make no mistake; these can be dangerous waters to be swimming in."

"I'm afraid he's correct in his assessment," added Max. "Some of the real money belongs to corporate raiders, embezzlers, arms dealers...."

"What he means to say is, it's a short but powerful list," said Jim, cutting him off.

He knew that they had some rather sketchy clients, but he needed them to focus on the fact that it was not their place to judge.

And just then the crystal clear blue waters of the Atlantic Ocean came into view as they passed through a cut in the limestone rocks and headed toward the water.

"Wow, nice digs," said Sven. His face lit up as the brightly colored resort came into view.

The founder of the resort was a known record producer who had built a recording studio on the property back in 1977, and then added the resort much later. The list of artists who recorded there were impressive, and included ACDC, Emerson, Lake and Palmer, the Rolling Stones, Dire Straits, and most recently Shakira. The hotel was now part of his brand, and had become well known by the jet set crowd.

Arrangements had been made for an early check-in so they had time to go and change, enjoy a swim and freshen up before heading into the office. Max and Ken stayed in the limousine and had the driver drop them at their homes in the gated community of Sandyport.

"We'll be back for ten-thirty," Ken said as Max and Phil climbed out of the car.

Max unlocked the door to his condo, and as he stepped inside and dropped his bags he could feel the stress draining from his body.

He found Phil's bowl and filled it with water, and then went to the fridge and pulled out a beer. He went and opened up all the doors.

The altercation in the Parkade had finally caught up to him, and he needed some down time as he went out onto the patio, lay back in his chair and stared out across the water. But it wasn't long before Phil was sitting beside him, and nudging him with his nose.

"Time for a walk," he said as he got up and went and found the leash.

It was only eighty-two degrees, but the humidity still ran the heat index up over ninety and within minutes the sweat was pouring off him. They walked down the bridge, and after twenty minutes of playing on the beach he decided they had better head home.

He had just put his key in the door when he heard his cell phone ring, and as he ran to pick it up Phil shot past him.

His ribs objected strenuously as he drew in the humid air sharply. "Damn it," he said as he answered the phone.

"Max, my god. Are you ok?" shouted Kate.

"Kate? Yes, of course I'm ok, I was just shouting because we came from the beach and Phil is running around inside all covered in salt water."

"Oh," she replied dismissively. "I'm calling about the robbery. It sounded awful."

"Oh, that. It was an *attempted* robbery. Turns out they were not too good at it. Just some junkies jacking cars looking for dope money. Two minutes later and I would never have seen them ---- hold on, there's someone here," he said as he headed to the door.

Lillis, his maid, was standing outside with a big grin. She pushed her way in and gave him a light hug. Phil heard her and came rushing out of the bedroom barking, sliding on the tile, tail wagging.

"It's so good to see you. Miss Kate called and told me you would be here so I rushed over to make sure you are ok. You need anything?"

"Actually, I am talking to her now, and no I'm fine. But thanks for coming," he replied as he walked out onto the patio.

He could hear Kate on the phone, "Max, are you there, what's all that noise?"

"Sorry, it was just Phil saying hello to Lillis. Thanks for calling her, by the way."

"No problem, you sure you're ok?"

"Positive. Customs was a breeze, you're a hero and I owe you one."

He could feel her warmth, even through the phone, and all of a sudden he felt a hollowness he hadn't felt in a very long time.

"No problem. Anytime," she replied softly.

"Listen, I have to sign off, it's going to be a busy day. But I'll check in with you later," he said.

He went back inside and closed the doors. Then he went, switched on the air conditioning and headed to his room to take a shower.

"I'm on my way, Lillis, be back later," he said as he came into the living room. Phil was sitting beside her but seeing him dressed he never paid any attention. He knew the clothes meant he was leaving.

CHAPTER 18

The limo pulled up to the heavy steel gate behind the building and stopped as an armed guard came out of the security booth and spoke to the driver. After a brief conversation, he motioned for the gate to be opened and they drove behind the first of two large office buildings.

One belonged to an offshore shipping company that owned and operated a large fleet of tankers, and shared the space with a private bank. The other was owned by FB&T, who occupied the entire building with the exception of one floor, which they had just leased to Darington, Moskowitz and Calder.

The buildings were state of the art, and not the stereotypical colonial style buildings the Bahamas is noted for. They were ultra modern concrete and glass, and the FB&T building was a virtual fortress built to withstand a category five hurricane and had more security than the White House.

Once inside they came to another steel gate that secured the underground parking, and Max could see cameras at several locations with a clear view of the entire area. And when they stopped just inside the gate they were met by yet another security guard.

They all got out and followed Ken as he went up to a keypad mounted just to the side of an impressive set of glass doors. He punched in several numbers, and then placed his palm on a scanner and waited until they heard the sound of the electronic locking bolts release and the door swung open.

"Jesus," said Bjorn, "this has to be more secure than Fort frigging Knox."

"Absolutely correct," said Ken as they walked inside and got into the elevator.

"They have twenty-four hour armed security, all ex-military or DEA or some damn thing. Cameras everywhere, palm and fingerprint identity for access, you name it. The building is also supposed to be blast proof," he replied.

"Oh, and did I mention the helipad on the roof?"

It was Max's first time to visit the building, and as he listened to Ken explain the security systems it really began to hit home what kind of clientele they were dealing with. Clearly Morton Feinstein had more than just a suspicion that his move may be more than a little risky. And now he could not help wondering if Mike's firm had a bigger stake in this than he had let on.

The elevator stopped on the 4th floor, and as they got off they found themselves in a large reception area with expensive Italian furnishings arranged around a significant sculpture sitting on a solid granite base. And Max could see there were several paintings by some of the masters on every wall.

From there they followed Ken as he mounted the large marble and glass circular stairway to the top floor where the boardroom was located.

"Hell of a sight," said Jim as they entered the room and saw the unobstructed 180 degree view of the ocean floor through the ceiling bulletproof glass.

The furnishings however, were a deep contrast to what they had seen in the reception area. This was an area designed for work. Which was a good thing because that was what they had come here for.

"Access is strictly limited to senior management and very high net worth clients," Ken explained as he watched them staring at the view in front of them.

"The room is lead-lined for security against eavesdropping, but you will still get cell service through some gizmo they have installed on each floor.

"Works for me," said Max as he walked over and stood in front of the window. He had seen the building many times from the outside, and now seeing it first hand on the inside gave him a whole new perspective of how the less than one percent of one percent of the population lived.

"May as well get used to it," said Ken. "We might be spending a lot of time here."

There were served fresh coffee and pastries on a table near the entry, and once everyone got what they wanted Ken called the meeting to order.

Normally Jim or John would have chaired the meeting, but this was Ken's turf and they were looking to him to get things kicked off. The meeting lasted for three hours, and as far as Max could tell they hadn't covered any new ground; everything had already been discussed in the previous meetings with Morton.

By the time they finally broke for lunch, Max was starving and ready for a cold beer and suggested rather than eating in, they walk over to the little Daiquiri stand just down the beach for conch salad. There being no opposition, they all headed for the elevator.

Max noticed the humidity had dropped a little as they stepped outside, but it was still oppressive compared to the cool weather they had left behind in Vancouver. And as they walked along the road in single file two girls approached them on a little rental scooter and hit a pothole, causing the driver to nearly lose control.

Ken jumped to the side and as the bike bounced back onto the pavement the passenger's tank top fell down exposing her breasts, but she was hanging on too tight to do anything about it and just laughed as they sped past.

"God, I love this country," he said, laughing as he watched them disappear around the corner.

"Yes, I can see this will be a tough assignment for you," John replied as they reached the bar and took a seat on the stools in the shade of the thatch roof.

"Bring us all conch salads, and the coldest Kaliks you got," said Max as he climbed onto a wooden stool.

"And a club soda for our friend here," said Ken, pointing to John.

"You want them spicy, my brudder," asked the man behind the counter in a thick Bahamian accent. He was dressed in a pair of swim shorts and had an old T-shirt on displaying the logo of some private yacht across the entire front.

"One hot for me, and the rest not," said Max. "Make that two," said Ken.

"Ya, mon," he replied with a broad smile as he began chopping up the conch, green pepper, onion, and tomato on a large white cutting board and then mixed it all together in a large pile.

He added a few chopped up bird pepper, poured on a healthy dose of salt and then squeezed several fresh limes over top.

After mixing them all together he portioned out the first four into styrofoam bowls, and then added more peppers to the remaining pile, mixed them together and passed out the bowls with plastic spoons and fresh beers.

Bjorn nearly spit his out after the first swallow and was doubled over coughing, "Holy shit," he screamed as he downed half the bottle of beer.

"That's mild," he croaked, as tears began rolling down his cheeks.

Everyone, including the chef was howling as they watched him drain the rest of his beer.

"On the house," said the chef as he handed Bjorn another beer.

They finished their lunch and Max paid the bill and soon they were back in the office. There were small towels set out in the men's room and Ken went and grabbed a handful and passed them out as they got seated.

"Interesting lunch, and even more interesting country," said John as he took the towel and dried the sweat from his face.

Max was about to comment when he felt his phone vibrate, and saw he had a text from Janet. "Excuse me a minute," he said as he got up and walked over to the bar area.

He felt his stomach churn as he read the text, and then quickly headed out of the room without a word.

She was on her private line, "Max, Jesus Christ, have you heard? They just got information on the guys who came after you in the parking garage."

"What are you talking about? It was just some guys trying to break into my car. End of story," he replied, but he could tell by the initial text that she knew he was lying.

"No. Listen, that's just it. One of the guys that attacked you is still in the hospital. I don't know what you did to him, but they say his face is all broken up and he may have some serious nerve damage."

"Let it go, Janet. It was a simple case of being in the wrong place at the wrong time," he said.

"No. It's not. Listen to me, the one in the hospital is a two-time loser and this one could put him away for twenty-five to life so he rolled on his partner.

"What partner?"

"Look Max, I don't know what is going on, but you know damn well there were two of them," she said angrily.

And then he heard the tremble in her voice, "You told me earlier to be careful and I thought you were just being you. Am I in trouble here?"

He thought about it for a moment and considered the situation carefully before he finally responded, "Maybe Janet, I don't know. But all things being equal, yes, you need to watch your back."

"Oh, that's just fucking great," she said quietly.

He could feel the conch salad begin to burn as he thought about the two goons who attacked him. And although he tried to convince himself otherwise, he feared she may be in danger and knew he would have to move quickly before anyone got hurt.

"Did you find out anything more about Brian?"

"Yes," she said as he heard the excitement creep back into her voice. "I looked into the underwritings we filed over the past three years and you were right--Brian's clean."

"Brenton, on the other hand, has been involved in several and they all have the same pattern. Large amounts of shares are issued to the listed insiders and...."

"No big surprise there," he said, cutting her off.

"I agree, but let me finish. After every one of the companies was listed, the trading volumes were huge, and almost all the trades were done through the same brokerage accounts."

"Let me guess, the brokers were in Nevada, Arizona and Vancouver," he said. "It's called crossing the stock."

"Oh," she said. "Well, in any case, once it hits a certain level there are large trades completed through offshore holding companies and all these trades are done through a Nevada-based broker dealer. And then the buying dries up and wham, it tanks."

"What kind of numbers we talking here?"

"In total, or just the past couple of deals?" she asked pensively.

"In total."

There was a long silence, as if she were doing the calculation, "All total, it has to be close to a billion."

"Are you sure about this? Because if you are, I want you to stop digging any further. Let it go—at least for the time being. Whatever is going on here is far bigger than just a bunch of guys manipulating some stocks."

"I have one more thing I need to look into, and then I'll drop it."

"No, Janet, you drop it now," he said firmly but realized she had already ended the call.

CHAPTER 19

"Useless fucking morons." Amit was ranting as he paced around the room, "What were you thinking anyway? No wait, I forgot. You don't fucking think," he shouted as he threw his Monte Blanc pen across the room.

Amit was in his early thirties, well-educated and rich. And women of all ages were naturally attracted to his fine features and soft olive complexion. But he had a dark side to him, and it was a side that made him a dangerous person.

"I'm sorry, Amit, I had no idea it was going to get so out of hand," replied Harmel, the youngest of three brothers. At that moment he was doing everything he could to avoid the wrath of his older brother's tirade.

But Amit kept at him. "You're sorry," he shouted as he threw his can of Coke. Harmel ducked, and it flew past his head, smashing against the bookcase and sending a spray of brown foam across the wall behind him.

"Like when they went to visit the lawyer; that worked out real well for us, didn't it? They were supposed to talk to him, not beat him to death. And now it's only a matter of time before the cops start to put this all together."

"What do you want me to do, just tell me what to do?" he pleaded as Amit turned his back and picked up the phone. "Don't worry, I am going to clean up this mess once and for all," he hissed.

Harmel, froze with fear, wondering if he was part of the mess his brother was referring to. His stomach was churning, and as he stared at the Coke stains, it reminded him of the blood spatter he had seen earlier.

"It's Amit, they screwed up. Yes, again—you can believe it," he said as he turned and glared at Harmel.

"Don't worry," replied the voice on the other end. "We have him on ice, and trust me he's not going anywhere."

"What about the lawyer?"

"Unfortunately, he made the flight to the Bahamas. But don't worry, I have it covered. And by the way, you were right. This guy ain't no goddam lawyer," said Amit as he hung up the phone.

"Bitch, you better pray we get this straightened out," he snapped at Harmel. "Now go and get the car and meet me out front."

He waited until he had left before picking up the phone and making one more call. Letting the lawyer go could be a major setback, and he needed to get things back on track.

The Beluga colored Bentley came to an abrupt stop in front of the new four-story building. It was just one of many that had popped up in the area since the city council voted unanimously to change the zoning. Now, what was once an industrial wasteland of derelict buildings and vacant lots was home to high tech companies, galleries and the likes of Amit and his illicit operations.

He had purchased the entire top floor, and moved from their modest downtown offices less than three months earlier. They had no signage on the buildings register out front, and their doors were devoid of any corporate identity. It was as if they didn't exist and that was how he wanted it.

Harmel jumped out and slipped into the passenger seat as Amit got behind the wheel and slammed the 582 horsepower engine into gear. He cranked up the music and paid no attention to Harmel, who sat staring out the window in silence as they wove their way in and out of traffic down Hastings Street.

They were in the seedy part of town. It was an area where the drug addicts and mentally afflicted now occupied several blocks of what was once a very affluent street. But he showed no sympathy for those who had somehow fallen through society's cracks, nor did he care that it was the very neighborhood he had grown up in.

His father had immigrated to Canada as a young man, and was soon driving a dump truck for a distant relative. But after many years of grueling work he eventually managed to buy his own truck. And he now operated a small gravel and trucking business from their modest east side home.

They were good hard-working people who had scrimped and saved to ensure their children had the best schooling and were afforded the opportunities they never had. But to Amit, he was just a guy who never made an effort to succeed past anything more than truck driving. And instead, had settled for a life of mediocrity.

He came to an intersection and ignored the red light as he made an illegal turn and then sped through the side streets of the old warehouse district. Harmel felt an emptiness as he looked out at the once vibrant and thriving neighborhood that they had played in. And then he felt his stomach tense as they came to an abrupt halt in front of an abandoned building he knew all too well.

Amit killed the engine and then turned to his brother with a look of disgust, "You might want to stay in the car, bitch."

"Don't worry, I can handle it," replied Harmel, as he tried to muster up his courage.

"Do I look worried?" said Amit sarcastically as they walked around the side of the dilapidated structure and then ducked in a side door that hung precariously off of one hinge.

Harmel noticed the time clock that still clung to the wall as they found their way through the empty office, and thought of the people who had once worked there.

"Nothing but a bunch of Loogans punching the clock for the man," snapped Amit when he noticed him staring at the clock. May as well have been driving a truck," he said with a bitter laugh.

The light was dim as they navigated their way past the ancient milling machines and drill presses that now stood silent; the only sound now was the broken glass crunching beneath their feet.

Amit stopped for a second beside a giant machine that towered over them, and as his eyes adjusted he finally spotted Joel in the back corner along with Tommy, the piece of garbage they had come to see. He was seated on a box with his hands tied behind his back, and as they got closer it was evident his left leg was unnaturally bent to one side at the knee.

"Looks painful," said Amit.

Tommy's right eye was swollen shut, and his words were thick and slurred as he tried to respond, "Amit, is that you?"

"Right here," he said as he stepped around to face him.

"So, tell me what happened. Tell me how you got your pussy ass kicked by some pencil neck lawyer."

"Listen, we did exactly as you said. But this guy, he wasn't what we expected."

Amit was just warming up. "Joel, do you believe this shit?"

He was afraid now, and struggled as he tried to explain, "Look, this guy took down Mike like he was nothing. I never seen anything like it, it happened so fast he never had a chance."

"Did you talk?"

"No, I was outta there as soon as I saw what he did to Mike. I mean, he broke my fucking leg for Christ sakes."

"Tommy, you know better than to leave someone behind," he said in a cold and measured voice. "Tell me, where is your friend now?"

"I'm not sure, but I think he's still in the hospital. He won't say nothing, Amit."

"It's 'anything,' Tommy, you mean he won't say anything," he replied as he looked over at Joel. "Now let's get you cleaned up and get the hell out of here."

"Thanks, man, you know I…" but his words were cut short as Amit drew a katar from the sheath tucked into the back of his waistband and thrust it into the side of his neck, slicing the carotid artery as it penetrated deep into his body.

Tommy's head snapped to the side, and his body jerked backwards as he tried to speak. But his mouth worked soundlessly as blood spurted from the edge of the knife with each beat of his dying heart. Harmel could see the shock and fear in his eyes as he and Joel stood helplessly as the man slowly died in front of them.

But Amit showed no remorse as he kicked the chair from under him, sending the body sprawling to the floor.

And then they heard an awful sucking sound as Amit pulled

the razor sharp blade from Tommy's neck and then wiped it on his jacket.

"Get rid of this piece of shit," he said as he put it back in its sheath.

He never noticed the blood spray on his sleeve as he headed for the door, leaving Joel and Harmel behind to deal with the body.

"Jesus Christ, this is going to get ugly," Joel whispered as they watched him disappear into the darkness.

Tommy hadn't been easy, and he was glad it was Amit and not him that had taken care of him. But he knew it was up to him to take care of Mike as they placed the body in the trunk and climbed into the car.

"Where do we take him?" asked Harmel, still shaken by the scene that had unfolded before him.

"To the docks," Joel said with a hint of sadness in his voice. "In a few days he'll be buried under seventy thousand tons of sulphur and headed for a factory in China."

But deep down he was wishing it was Amit he had in the trunk and not the friend he had known his whole life.

CHAPTER 20

Every nerve in his body was on fire, and he likened himself to a lion coming off a fresh kill on his way back to his den for some time with his lioness. He plugged in a Remo Fernandes CD. As the voice came booming through the Naim sound system, he hit the gas and spun the car around. It was time to party.

Twenty minutes later he pulled into a spot marked Reserved, and didn't bother to lock the car as he jumped out and headed into a ground floor unit of the four-story condominium building. He owned several condos in the building that he had leased out, but he kept this particular unit as his private playpen.

He walked in without knocking, and there lying on the king sized bed in the middle of the living room were two naked brunettes covered in baby oil.

"Hello girls, did you miss me?" he said as he closed the door behind him.

"Of course we did," laughed Cindy, the taller of the two. And then she got up and held her arms out as she sauntered toward him, but stopped as he came toward her, "You stupid bitch, I don't want oil all over my clothes," he shouted as he forced her back onto the bed.

"Great, he's in one of his moods again," she whispered to her companion, Pam, as she watched him undress and climb onto the bed between them. Pam lay quietly and watched as he laid out three lines on the mirror he had pulled off of the side table. And then they all did a line before he fell back onto the bed and let Cindy take him into her mouth. Pam climbed on top of him and straddled his chest.

And then he heard his cell phone ring. It was the tone he had programmed for the last person on earth he wanted to hear from, and the only one he could not ignore. He hesitated for a moment, and then finally rolled over and picked up the phone.

"Can I call you back?" he said breathing heavily.

"No. Get dressed, we need to talk," replied the caller.

"Give me an hour, I have some things I need to take care of," he said as he stared up at Pam.

"Make time, we have a problem that won't wait. I'll be at your office in twenty minutes," barked the caller as he hung up.

"Asshole," he said as he headed into the bathroom and took a quick shower. He came out a few minutes later, and as he got dressed he flipped five $100 bills onto the bed "Hold that thought," he said to Cindy and then walked out never bothering to close the door.

"Asshole," she said. And as she lay back on the bed the two burst into uncontrollable laughter.

"No point in wasting a good buzz," said Cindy as she rolled over and kissed Pam deeply on the lips.

Amit started the car, and was about to back out when his frustration took hold and he began pounding on the steering wheel.

He needed to get control of the situation. But he also needed to get his life back once and for all. It was his ideas, and his hard work that had gotten them to where they were today. He was sick and tired of taking shit and was ready to put a stop to it.

"What are you so worked up about?" he said as he jerked open his office door and stood staring at James who was seated by the bar. But his cocaine induced courage quickly vanished as his visitor slowly turned and glared back at him. Clearly he had heard about the lawyers and was looking for answers.

It would not be answers he wanted to hear. Amit walked over to the bar and grabbed a bottle of Gray Goose. He took a handful of ice from the dispenser and dropped it into the glass, then poured in a few inches of Vodka before taking a seat.

James was one of the few people in the world that scared him, and for good reason.

"You remember when we had to send Harmel to the Bahamas and move all your cash out of Bermuda and the Cayman's?"

"Of course I do," he replied with a nervous laugh. "Someone had to take one for the team, but he pissed and moaned the whole time he was down there."

It had happened just over two years earlier, when he was running one of their pump and dump scams out of an office in a dumpy strip mall in Phoenix. Everything had been going according to plan when, by a pure stroke of luck, they had been tipped off that the SEC was onto them. They had folded up shop in one day, and split just before their offices were raided by Federal marshals.

But after a few months, the investigators had tracked them down and soon after there were multiple charges laid against them.

The case had been weak, as most of the business had been run through nominee accounts and they couldn't tie any of them directly back to the scam. But Amit knew it was only a matter of time, and hired a team of high priced lawyers to defend them while they sent Harmel to the Bahamas to wait it out while the dust settled.

"You're missing the point," said James in a low and calculating voice.

"What point?" replied Amit far too aggressively. "The SEC did their thing and they found dick shit, so what? We paid a half a million dollar fine and Harmel can't trade for five years. Nice trade for the seventy-five mill we made, don't you think," he said as he held up his glass.

But James was now on his feet, "Yes, I do think, Amit. It's a novel concept. You should try it some time. The point is, you fucking moron, someone has been snooping around."

"And?" he replied as he got up and was reaching for more ice. James snapped his arm out, knocked the glass from his hand, and sent it crashing to the floor.

"Listen to me, you fucking lunatic, someone is following your trail--which means they are following our trail. And in case you have forgotten, we made our trades through the accounts I set up, not you."

Realizing he was on thin ice, Amit sat back and turned silent as the severity of the situation slowly began to sink in. When he finally spoke his face was sullen, "Any idea who it is?"

"Good to see you're finally getting the picture," said James. "All we know so far is that a legal secretary in a local law firm has been making the calls." His face turned a crimson red. "Oh, and in case I forgot to mention, it's our firm."

"What do you mean, our firm?" said Amit.

"Jesus Christ, are you really that dense? The law firm that handled our underwiritngs."

And then before he could stop himself the words came blurting out, "Me. I wasn't the one who wanted to go after the lawyer in the first place."

Amit never saw it coming, but felt the sharp sting on his cheek as James backhanded him, knocking him backwards across the bar. And then almost on instinct, he felt himself reaching for the dagger but then drew his hand back, knowing it was not a fight he would win. Not yet, anyway.

"We've come too far, or more importantly I have come too far to have you screw this up."

There was no question a fortune was at stake, and he was in deep shit and needed to come up with some answers. But how was the firm involved? All their business had been wrapped up and concluded long ago.

"And what did you mean when you said lawyers?" said James as he stood seething over him. "Mr. Duncan was supposed to have been alone."

"He was," groaned Amit.

"Jesus, don't tell me Trent Jordan was your doing too."

"It's not what you think, he was banging one of my cousins. So we paid him a visit. You know ---- just to explain the facts of life to him. How was I supposed to know some secretary was going to start looking into our business? And besides, it was an accident. He fell and hit his head on the bathroom floor and died; there was nothing we could do."

"Jesus Christ, Amit, do you have any idea what you've done? You have jeopardized the entire operation, and for nothing!"

"It may be nothing to you, but not to us," he scowled as he snatched up a new glass and went for the Vodka bottle. "I admit you scare the shit out of me, but we are talking about family here. Something you obviously know nothing about," he said defiantly.

"Good to see you finally found your balls," said James. "Now, I need to buy us some time, and you need to deal with this woman. She's taking instruction from someone, and we need to find out who that someone is."

"I understand you perfectly; I will make it right," he replied.

"Good. We need to have a serious conversation with her-- make her understand it's in her best interest to stop snooping around. Am I making myself clear?"

"Crystal," said Amit through clenched teeth, and as he reached for the bottle James reached over and took it from him.

"Good, then I assume there will be no more screw ups," he said as he set the bottle back down on the table and walked out.

CHAPTER 21

When Max came back into the boardroom he had all but lost interest in listening to anymore boring bullshit about the FB and T clients. But he needed to sit it out, and maybe he might find something that could shed some light on what they were dealing with.

"How are you making out with the clients' files?" he asked with little enthusiasm.

"Actually, we were waiting on you," said Ken as he picked up a remote control and hit a series of buttons. Silently two wood grained wall panels slid open revealing a seventy-inch flat screen TV while at the same time the lights automatically dimmed and the window shades closed.

"This is something else," exclaimed Bjorn as the room became dark.

"Welcome to the inner sanctum," said Ken. "Meet Sergei Ivor, a Czech gangster and one of our largest and most colorful clients. By all accounts, he was the original self-proclaimed entrepreneur who took advantage of the privatization of state property in the Czech Republic."

"Terrific," said Max quietly as he studied the information on the screen. "This guy looks like a real piece of work."

"He sure is. He made a fortune off the backs of the poor people who he duped out of hundreds of millions of dollars in just the past few years."

"But how were they able to legally gain control of these State-owned assets," asked Sven.

"Very simple. In the Czech state, the assets were supposed to be handed over to citizens through a system of vouchers, which they could then use to buy shares in the companies. Boy genius here managed to hook up with a corporate raider in New York who helped him set up a series of funds. They raised a shit load of cash and then travelled around the country buying up the vouchers.

Once they had control of the companies they immediately stripped them of their assets and funneled the money here. The people were screwed and these guys were long gone."

"So where is the boy genius now," asked Jim.

"He was in the process of doing the same thing in Azerbaijan when the shit hit the fan and his empire began to crumble. They were flying his jet from here to Azerbaijan with about ten million in cash per trip and stashing it in a building he had bought in Baku.

They had bought almost four hundred million US invested in vouchers and had them stashed in his building when the government all of a sudden changed their minds on the privatization. And in the blink of an eye the vouchers were instantly worthless. His American backers sued, the FBI got involved, and that's where we came in."

"Technically they had not broken any laws, but he knew it

was falling apart and that's when he came to us. We set up a complicated set of trusts and since then, all the assets were rolled into them: homes, islands, yachts, the jet and a lot of cash are all safely stashed away."

"Puts my life in perspective," said Jim as he looked in awe at the numbers on the screen. "How much cash we talking about?"

"Over three hundred and fifty million. And I'm pretty sure he has more but we can't be certain."

"It's all very interesting, and at the same time concerning to me that Morton would be representing this kind of client," said Max. "But aside from him being a shady character, I don't see what he has to do with our being here. His assets are already safely tucked away, are they not?"

"You are correct," replied Ken. "I was just using him as an example. The majority of their assets are already held in offshore holding companies and trusts that are set up here in the Bahamas. It's the individual accounts and privately held companies outside of here that pose the challenge, and where we need to tread carefully."

"But don't the same know-your-client guidelines apply to cover our ass and comply with anti-money laundering activities for both individuals and companies," asked Bjorn.

"It's not the KYC rules we are concerned about, it's the logistics of moving all of these people, their companies and their assets from multiple jurisdictions to here. The Bahamas still has lax rules and we can wiggle around the compliance in most cases, but if we can't then the client will have no choice but to stick with their existing structures."

"Let me give you an example of one of our clients whose holdings are primarily outside of the Bahamas. He will be one of the first we'll be working with," said Ken as he hit the remote.

Max could feel his jaw drop when he saw his friend's face appear on the big screen.

"His name is Gino Capozzi, and he's the sole proprietor of a company called Global Agencies. And although his business models may be morally questionable, they are technically not illegal."

"In other words, no one has been able to shut him down, at least not to date?" said Max, not wanting to believe that his old friend could be somehow involved.

"Correct you are, they are constantly being sued and depending on the outcome they pack up shop and head to a new location, or more specifically a different country. He keeps a large team of defense attorneys busy year round with the ongoing lawsuits which include mail fraud, tax evasion, copyright infringement, wrongful dismissal suits, you name it," said John.

"So he keeps you busy, but I have to wonder why old man Feinstein would have taken on clients such as the Czech in the first place," said Max.

"It was an oversight; he was the main client of the company he had just purchased here in Nassau. Aside from him, most of these guys did not walk in and plunk down a large amount of cash or securities in one shot. It was built up over time. Now that Mr. Feinstein is aware of the situation, he is trying to deal with it as diplomatically as possible."

Max was thinking back to his conversation with Mike about the so-called small trust that FB and T had purchased in Nassau. Mike had told him they held assets of only about fifty million. Clearly he was either mistaken or had not been truthful. Either way it would be a point of discussion as soon as he got clear of the meeting.

"So why are we focused on these particular clients?" asked Sven.

"Good point," said Max, "I'm actually more confused now than ever."

"Well, in the case of our man, Gino, he has a potentially precedent-setting case against his companies by the United Kingdom, United States and Ireland," said Ken. "He has had four lawyers working around the clock on it for almost a year, and the Supreme Court will hand down its ruling any day now."

"So in other words they could be out of business," said John as he leaned back in his chair with his fingers locked and his arms stretched above him.

"Let's just say we are not expecting a favorable outcome."

"That may be so, but I've read his files and as far as I'm concerned he's clean compared to the boys on Wall Street," said Max as he tried to subtly defend his friend.

"Technically Max is right, there is no question he's been pushing the envelope. But it's not about that. The revenue boys are pissed because he's taking advantage of their tax loopholes, and I say too goddamn bad. Because when it comes right down to it, they don't give a shit about right or wrong, they just want their taxes."

At that point, Max felt as though they were going in circles and decided to call it a day.

"I don't know about the rest of you, but I could use a swim and a siesta. How about we wrap it up and we can meet back at the bar at North Point at seven? You all take the Limo and I'll get a ride back with Ken."

"So what are you really doing here?" Ken shouted over the road noise as they drove along the water in his Jeep Wrangler.

But Max never heard him, he was watching a scooter coming up behind them in the side view mirror and as it got closer he realized it was the same girls they had seen earlier.

"Seems you must have made an impression," he shouted as he pointed to the rearview mirror. And as Ken turned his attention to the mirror, Max turned and saw a black SUV coming toward them. And as they got closer, it began drifting over into their lane.

Ken was still focused on the girls behind them and never saw them coming, but then he swung his head around when he heard Max shouting at him. The SUV was now completely in their lane and heading straight for them, and as he cranked the wheel they were hit with flying glass as the side mirror of the SUV smashed against the roll bar.

Not realizing the consequence, Ken slammed on the brakes, and as they left the pavement the driver's side wheel dug into the sand and Max felt them begin to roll. They were pelted with empty beer bottles and junk food containers as the jeep flipped into the air, and then he felt his head hit the sand as they came to a rest on the roll bar.

They were hanging upside down with the wheels still spinning as Max released his seatbelt and climbed out of the side. He saw the scooter lying on its side about fifty yards behind them, and the girls were sitting in the sand just to the side of the road.

Then he saw the SUV stopped in the middle of the road with the passenger door open. He needed his gun, but his pack had been thrown from the jeep and was lying out of sight beneath a sea grape bush. He heard Ken screaming in the background and turned to see him pulling himself out of the jeep. When he turned back the SUV was gone.

"Goddamn tourists, learn how to fucking drive," he heard Ken shout as he came up beside him.

There was blood coming from his forehead, but from the way he was shouting Max was pretty sure he would be ok.

"Cool it, amigo, they're gone," said Max as started walking toward the girls.

Ken walked back to the jeep, and was surveying the damage when he felt his legs about to give out. He began to feel dizzy, and was standing holding on to the running board when Max came back with the girls.

"You better hold on, sport, and let me take a look at this hole in your head," he said as he guided him over to a log and sat him down.

"Let me take a look," said the prettier of the two girls as she shook off a towel that had been thrown from the jeep. Max handed her a bottle of water, and she wet the towel and began wiping his face.

"Nothing a simple bandage and shot of rum won't take care of," said Max as they all huddled around Ken.

What they lacked in medical skills, they certainly made up for in looks. Max stood up to inspect the jeep. Aside from being inconveniently upside down, it appeared to have suffered little damage.

It was clear the people in the SUV were out to get them, but was it coincidence that the two girls just happened to come along at the same time. Or was he just being paranoid? Either way, he needed to keep his guard up as there was little doubt in his mind that they would be back.

"I'm sure it was just an accident, even I get confused sometimes when I land here and start driving," Max lied.

"Now, let's roll this baby back onto its wheels and get the hell out of here before we have to start answering questions to some cop."

After a few minutes of searching the lot across the street, Max found an old pole they could use to leverage the vehicle over, and after the third try it was back on its wheels. Max finally found his pack, and was picking up the contents of the jeep and throwing them into the back while Ken was busy exchanging numbers with the girls.

He had to put the jeep into four-wheel drive to get them off of the beach, and as they made the drive home he could feel his arm begin to throb. And soon his side began to ache again as they bounced along the road on the way back to his condo.

"You ok to drive?" he asked Ken, as they came to a stop out front.

"Absolutely," he replied, "I'm going to head home and change and then I'll walk back over. I hope you don't mind, but I invited the girls to meet us at the Parrot Pub."

"Why am I not surprised?" said Max as he turned and headed for the stairs.

Max kicked off his shoes, took a Kalik Gold from the fridge, and poured it into an insulated mug. Then he went and climbed into the oversized hammock on the balcony. He drained half the beer as he sent a text to Kate, and asked her to have his friend, Ron, run the plate on the SUV. He set the phone down, finished his beer, and was sound asleep less than five minutes later with Phil snoring alongside him.

It had been a long week.

CHAPTER 22

Gino was sitting in his office with Sal when Frank walked in, his massive frame casting a shadow in the doorway as he passed through.

"Hi fellas," he boomed as he walked over to greet Gino.

"Any update on our boy," asked Sal, as he got up and motioned for him to take a seat.

"He promised to have us straight by Friday," he said as he took a seat.

"For his sake, he better have. The guy's a deadbeat and I want this taken care of, are we clear?" said Gino as Frank fidgeted with the custom-made cowboy hat Gino had bought for him on one of his trips to Colorado.

"There have been some developments with our lending operation that you need to be aware of, Frank," said Sal.

Gino could see the strain on Frank's face, "Relax, big man, nothing for you to worry about. Sal and I have discussed it and I am shit canning the lending, it's not only become a waste of time, But it's becoming too risky."

"Jeez Gino, you sure? I mean, I thought we've been making

money and--well, am I out of a job?" He sat staring down at his boots. Frank wasn't afraid of Gino, but he had a lot of respect for him and it sometimes made him nervous.

"Hell no, Frank. On the contrary, we want to move you into our offices here. I want you to replace Otto."

"Really," he replied as his face lit up with a big grin. But then the smile slowly disappeared, "I heard he had been let go."

"It happens," said Gino. "And hell, why not bring your gal, Gisella, with you? We'll find a place for her too. It would be a real waste not keeping her around."

Frank was smiling like a teenager going on a first date, "I mean, is she a looker or what?"

"Business, Frank, keep your mind on the business," said Sal as he gave Gino the "are-you-sure-you-know-what-you're-doing look.

"You need to clear out the office, and I mean sanitize it. And then call this guy," said Gino, handing him a business card.

"Joey Santos?"

"Yes. He's not the brightest bulb in the box, but he will take care of leasing out the office and from here on we just collect rent. Ok?"

"Hold on a minute," said Sal, as he started laughing. "Did you say Joey?"

"Yes, you got a problem with him?"

"I thought we talked about cutting some of the deadwood loose, Gino."

"Listen, he may be simple but he serves the purpose," said Gino with finality, and he's not smart enough to cause any trouble. Give him the listing."

"Frank, you know what has to be done so get to it. Take the

rest of the week to get things organized, and then have Gisella help get you set up in Ottos' old office," said Gino.

"And Frank, take care of this deadbeat and close the book on him," said Sal.

"You got it, cash is in the bank." But Gino noticed a slight hesitation in his voice, and he knew they were going to have trouble with this one.

"You know he'd take a bullet for you," said Sal as he watched him leave.

"Speaking of which, there's something we need to discuss. You recall way back when we were running the boiler room and had the little run-in with the cops?"

"Did I say something funny?" asked Gino as Sal starting laughing so hard he began to choke, "You mean when we did the bait and switch with the bag of cash. I felt like Redford in the Sting."

"Well, we were a lot younger then," replied Gino with a sad smile.

The incident he was referring to happened several years earlier when they were running a boiler room and pumping junior mining stocks on the Vancouver Stock Exchange. It was a time when the market was virtually unregulated, but then a local watchdog had taken it upon himself to expose the exchange for what it was. The Securities and Exchange Commission had little choice but to bring in a regulatory body and start investigating some of the more obvious companies.

When they had finally gathered enough evidence on them, the police raided Gino's office on the 3rd floor of an old building in Gastown. Two detectives had burst into the front office just as Sal made a run for it out the back. And he was standing at the bottom of the outside fire escape just as Gino snatched a bag off his desk and fired it out the window.

Sal caught it on the fly and was sprinting down the alley by the time the police had found Gino's office. The bag contained nearly $100,000 in cash and a small amount of coke, but Sal had made a clean getaway. Their lawyers managed to beat the charges, but the writing was on the wall and they closed down the boiler room not long after.

"Despite it all, those were good times," Sal said chuckling as he went and poured himself a beer. "Pool?"

"Sure, I'll rack."

"Bring me one too," said Gino as he pulled the balls out of the pockets.

Sal handed him his beer; "You break."

"Little ones," said Gino as the two ball fell into the corner pocket.

"Ok, so what's up with the walk down memory lane?" he asked as he chalked his cue.

"Four ball, corner pocket," he replied. "Do you remember the Indians we ran across some time ago?"

"Nice shot. Yes, I remember them. I also remember when our 'backers' had a run-in with them. Why?"

"Well, I think they were the ones that popped Aldo. Matter of fact, I'm sure of it."

"Really," replied Sal as he stood with his cue resting on top of his right foot. "don't tell me you are planning on doing something about it after all this time?"

"No. They wanted to take out our backers and Aldo may have gotten in the middle, but that's not our problem."

Sal was guarded and not in any mood for a trip down memory

lane, "Nice leave, asshole. So what about them, why you bringing it up now?"

"Amit, the older one came around a few weeks ago and asked if I would be interested in selling. Said I should consider it, no specific threats but you get the picture."

"Jesus, Gino, you're supposed to tell me when these kinds of things happen," said Sal.

"You can't underestimate these guys. So, what did you tell him?"

"What do you think? I told him to fuck off."

"No doubt. How did he take it?"

"How do you think he took it?"

"I don't like it, Gino. Why are they interested in our business? I thought they were busy fleecing widows and orphans out of their life savings."

"They are, or at least they were. But the word is the SEC regulators are on their back and making it impossible for them to operate. So they have been branching out and have just opened up an Internet gaming business in Costa Rica. Smart move actually, I'll give them that."

"From what I hear gaming requires a shit load of capital," replied Sal.

"Correct you are, which is what concerns me," said Gino as he tossed his cue onto the table.

"I think that's who Alphonso was going to sell our mailing list to, and our ears on the street tell me their last stock play did not go well. So if they are cash strapped, it would mean trouble for the gaming."

Sal's jaw was working overtime, and Gino could see the muscles in his cheek pulsing before he finally spoke, "They were in the Bahamas a while ago; remember? One of them had moved there while the dust settled on the stock they'd run--maybe the one you heard about."

"Yes, but they made a much larger score since then," said Gino as he took a decanter from the bar and poured two large glasses of scotch.

"Christ, Gino, what have you gotten us into this time?" said Sal as he went and sat down. He had learned to read Gino a long time ago, and instinct told him he was not going to like what he was about to hear.

"Well, I may have inadvertently redirected some of their profits into one of our offshore accounts."

"And just how much are we talking about," asked Sal as he rolled the tumbler between his palms.

"Just over four hundred, and change," Gino said as he sat back and took a drink.

"Excuse me, did you just say four hundred million?"

"And change."

"Fuck me," he said as he burst out laughing. "I don't know if I should laugh or cry. How the hell did we---sorry, I mean you, accumulate that much cash? And please tell me they have not traced it back to us?"

"I think they may have. A broker friend in Denver tipped me about one of the stocks they were running and so I took a position in it just before it took off. I mean it went intergalactic."

"Had to be one hell of a position," said Sal. "And so while you were dumping the stock, they would have had to suck it up."

"And now you think they are after what they would think was their cash."

"Yes, I do. But what I don't know is how," he said as he got up and walked back over to the pool table.

"One, they can't possibly know where the money is," he said as he pocketed a ball at random.

And two, even if they did I don't see how they could get access to it."

Sal finished his drink, and was sitting with his hands clasped tightly together. His fingers were red from the pressure as he finally released his grip and pushed his hair back with both hands. He sat with his head back and eyes closed.

When he finally spoke, his voice was cold, "We need to start taking precautions."

"Already have," said Gino as he pocketed another ball.

"Shit", said Sal as he spat the words out, "I thought we were past all this, Gino. I'm getting too fucking old to be back fighting in the gutter, I have grandkids for Christ sakes."

"It's not something I went looking for either, but we have friends that I may be able to reach out to. In the meantime, let me see what I can find out, and you do the same. But right now, I have someone I need to speak with."

CHAPTER 23

Max was drenched in sweat when he finally woke up, and a quick look at his watch told him he'd been out for just over two hours. His head was aching from dehydration, and he felt wasted as he lay back and thought about the accident and how lucky they had been. And again the two girls--was it a coincidence that they just happened to show up at the right time?

He doubted it very much, but decided to let it go. At least for the time being.

"Coincidence it is," he said as he gently prodded Phil off of the hammock. He stood for a moment, and as he rotated his shoulder it felt better, the heat had obviously loosened it up and the pain was easing.

He had just finished taking a shower and getting dressed when the limo driver knocked at the door. Max followed him outside, and as he and Phil climbed inside, he noticed the only one missing was Mike.

"Ken was just explaining the injury to his head," said John as they cruised down the narrow road toward town. "Sounds like you guys were damn lucky."

"Happens here more often than you think," said Ken as he gently touched the bandage on his forehead. "Goddamn tourists are always on the wrong side of the road."

"Well, we are glad you're alright," said Bjorn as he sat back and took it all in.

"Must be a hell of a change for you guys," replied Max.

"You could say that," said Sven. "So where we headed to?"

"Well, Ken in his infinite wisdom invited the two young girls you saw on the scooter today to join us on Paradise Island at a little marina bar under the bridge. They have great music, excellent chicken wings and cold beer."

"And young girls--what more could you ask for," laughed Ken as he held up his beer in a toast.

Max dug one from the cooler and used the seatbelt to pop off the top.

"To the girls," he said.

The car came to a stop and he felt his chest begin to vibrate as he lowered his window. He heard the loud and familiar sound of Junkanoo music, an odd mix of drums and whistles, and then cow bells.

"What is it, a music festival?" asked Jim.

"Junkanoo."

"Junk and who?" asked John.

"It's a parade they have every Christmas Eve and New Year's Eve," Max replied. "They practice all year for just those two days, and it's what the Bahamians live for. Ken, help me out here."

"Junkanoo is, as Max says, the biggest deal ever, and the parades are always a passionate debate with the locals as to how they came about. But I can tell you, after centuries of practice, it's a cultural extravaganza and one of the most entertaining street carnivals you will see. It's like Carnival in Rio."

"So what do they do, exactly?" asked John.

"They spend all year making incredible costumes in broken down old buildings called Junkanoo Shacks, and they keep tight security for fear of anyone seeing the costumes before the parade. The dance and music is inspired by a different theme each time, preparations for the Boxing Day, New Year's Day and summertime Junkanoo literally take months and bring together men and women from all different walks of life.

"Sounds awesome," replied Sven as he began rocking his body to the beat of the drums.

"It is. Some of the costumes are as big as moving trucks and weigh hundreds of pounds. Each competing group is called a tribe, and there could be as many as a thousand people in each. If they put a tenth of the amount of energy into their work as they do the festival this country would be number one."

The music had brought Max out of his funk, and he was feeling a lot better when they finally began to move again and the music faded behind them. Fortunately, the streets were empty and they arrived at the tollbooth at the foot of the Paradise Island Bridge less than ten minutes later. The driver paid the one-dollar toll, and then wound his way through the roundabout and down under the bridge to the pub.

As they got closer Max could see the lights of the yachts as they highlighted their massive superstructures. As their car came to a stop near the water, Ken hopped out and almost sprinted toward the boardwalk around the marina.

"Hot date," cried Bjorn as they all hurried to catch up to him.

The marina slips were nearly full, and Max could see some of the yachts had their underwater transom lights on, creating a surreal picture as the fish and sea life were drawn to the light.

"Holy shit," said John as his face lit up. "Is that a shark?"

"It's a nurse shark," said Ken. "And far more personable than some of the ones you'll meet here on the land." He laughed.

"Don't laugh, you can go and do a shark dive with one of the local companies on Sunday if you want to get up front and personal," he replied.

"No thanks, I'll stick to the beach if you don't mind. Are there many shark attacks here?"

"Some," said Max.

"One of my old clients, actually the builder from Vancouver that I bought my condo from. They had a guy working for them down here that got hit by a bull shark. Nearly lost his legs."

"Crap, I think I'll stick to the beach for sure."

"I don't know about you guys, but the food smells good and I am out of beer," said Sven as he held his bottle upside down.

"Amen, nothing like the smell of old grease and French fries to get your appetite flowing," replied Ken as he led them toward the last unoccupied picnic table on the harbor side of the bar.

The temperature had finally dropped a few degrees, and Max was enjoying the food and his beer and listening to John Fogerty's voice as it rang out from a cheap set of bar speakers when he noticed the small boat heading for the dock below them. He could see the young man at the helm was fighting to keep control as the strong current pushed him dangerously close to the rocks.

And then one engine clipped a rock and he heard the roar of the propeller as it kicked violently up out of the water. The noise drew everyone's attention, but Max was already up and sprinting toward the boat as Phil sat watching his every move. Max cleared the short wall, and landed on the dock as he got the attention of the young girl on board.

"Throw me a line," he yelled at her as he heard the other engine stall out.

She managed a near perfect throw, and Max quickly tossed two quick wraps on the piling and got his hands free just as the line went taut, bringing the boat to a dead stop. The young man grabbed a hold of her as the current swung them hard up against the side of the dock sending them both back hard against the helm seat.

"You guys ok?" shouted Max as he stared down at them.

"Yeah, the current caught me and I just lost control," he shouted back.

"Kind of figured that," He stared at the girl as she climbed up onto the bow, her half T-shirt riding up on her breasts exposing a firm and flat midriff.

"The current can be a bitch; you need a hand to tie off or are you ok?"

"We're good, but thanks, man, you saved our ass," he called back.

And one worth saving, he thought. As he turned to head back to the table he felt someone staring down at them from the yacht in the slip across from them. He seemed to be focused on the girl as she bent over to pick up her bag, but as he moved into the light Max recognized him from the SUV.

He felt his heart begin to race as he ducked for cover in the shadows of the little dock house. He was pretty sure the man had not seen him, but he stayed out of the line of sight and decided he needed to get them out of there before they were spotted.

"Nice work, Max, did you get her number?" Ken asked, laughing as he mimed her curves above the table.

"Aside from me being old enough to be her daddy, no, I did not. But feel free, I think they're still at the dock," said Max as he waved the waiter over.

"Sorry gents, but time to head home. We have a full day tomorrow and Ken needs to change that bandage," he said as handed the waitress $300.

"Come on," Ken pleaded. "My dates haven't shown up yet."

"And if they are not here by now, they won't be," said John as he got up and started to leave.

CHAPTER 24

Janet awoke to a flash of lightning, and seconds later felt the room shake as the thunder rolled ahead of the storm. She was exhausted and needed to sleep, but she was on edge with thoughts of her conversation with Max.

It was like she had a faulty electrical circuit somewhere deep in the back of her mind, and as the images popped in and out she could see Trent as he lay beside her. Then she was back in the coffee shop with Max. Her cat, Sampson, oblivious to her distress, lay curled up on the bed beside her, purring away in a sound sleep as the light show continued outside.

She never heard the back door glass break, or the men who had entered her room, now standing beside her bed as she lay curled up in a pile of pillows. It was not until they grabbed her arms and brutally forced her face down into the mattress that she became painfully aware of their presence.

She heard Sampson yowl, and then he sprang from the bed as one of them took a wild kick at him. She was wide-awake now and stricken with panic as she struggled to breathe. She fought back with all she had. Deep down she knew it would be futile. However she wasn't going without a fight.

She began to kick wildly, and she heard one of them cry out as her foot caught him square in the balls. And then she felt a searing pain as he drove his fist into the back of her head.

"What the hell are you doing?" she heard another one say. "We need her alive."

And then she felt herself being pulled backwards until she was bent over the end of the bed.

It was a woman's worst nightmare unfolding before her, and in her very bedroom. She thought of the self-defense classes: make mental notes. Don't stop fighting. Make as much noise as you can and maybe someone will hear you.

But then her heart sank and she felt as though she would be sick as she felt her G-string being ripped off.

"Great ass." And then she felt a terrible pain as he shoved himself into her.

She could smell his disgusting breath with every thrust as she fought hard, and then nothing as she slipped into unconsciousness.

She didn't know how long she had been out, but she woke to someone slapping her on the side of the face, "Time for a chat, little lady."

Still lying face down, she could hardly breathe as she listened to every word.

"If you scream, you will never see the light of day, do you understand me?"

She managed to nod, and as they let her go she rolled over and felt the rush of air burn deep into her lungs. There were three of them standing over her. They each had some kind of bandana over their faces, but it wouldn't have mattered as it was too dark to be able to recognize any clear features.

"So here's the deal," continued the spokesman of the group.

"My friends tell me you have been snooping into their business, and so we are here to deliver a message." He grabbed a handful of her hair and yanked her head to the side.

His words were cold and completely void of any emotion. "Are you listening, pretty lady?"

And then to his surprise, he heard her weak and raspy voice, "I hear you, asshole."

And then her cheek exploded as his hand came down hard against the side of her face.

"We can stay here all night if we have to," he said bitterly. "And you will learn the pain of respect if you do not tell me what I need to know."

"Go fuck yourself," she shouted, and then felt herself blacking out again as he wrapped his hands tightly around her neck.

At that same moment, across town at Vancouver General Hospital, an orderly was wandering down the corridor. He stopped in front of the room with an empty chair sitting beside the door.

Checking to make sure there was no one else around, he slipped inside and closed the door behind him. The patient was asleep and had an IV line hanging from the bar overhead with a clear tube trailing down to the needle in his arm. The orderly found the access port to the line, pulled a syringe from his side pocket and injected a clear substance into the port.

Moments later he was back out on the street, stuffing his lab coat into a waste bin as he stared back at the entrance to the emergency room outside the hospital.

"It's done," he said.

"Complications?"

"None. Easy peasy Japaneesy, house was a snap to get into," he said and then he began to laugh, "and so was she."

But James had no feelings about what he said one way or the other. His narcissistic personality reflected little ability to care.

"Ok, I will take care of the other situation, but it's time we cleaned house. No more screw ups, and no more loose ends."

"Don't worry, she won't be poking around anymore; you can count on it."

"There better not be, or it will be your ass next time."

CHAPTER 25

Max checked his watch, it was seven in the morning Vancouver time so he excused himself from the meeting and walked out of the boardroom. They had already been at it for over three hours, but his mind was on Janet and he needed to give her another call. He was about to hang up after the fourth ring when he heard a woman's voice come on the line.

"This is Sergeant Kim Leung with the Vancouver Police department, with whom am I speaking?"

Max felt his heart skip a beat, and he was at a loss for words. He just stood there holding the phone. And then he snapped out of it when he heard the voice again, "This is Sergeant Kim Leung with the Vancouver" ———

"I'm sorry, sergeant, this is Max Duncan. Janet is my friend, has something happened to her?"

"I'm afraid so," she said. And then there was a pause, "May I ask where you are calling from?"

"I'm calling from the Bahamas," he replied impatiently. "Now can you please tell me what is going on?"

"I'm very sorry to tell you this, sir. But your friend was attacked in her home last night."

"What do you mean attacked? Is she ok or not? At least give me something," he asked.

"I'm not supposed to disclose information," she replied apologetically. And then her voice softened, "but I can tell you the paramedics say it's not life threatening. As to what exactly happened, it looks like maybe a home invasion gone bad, but I'm not so sure."

"Thank you for your honesty, sergeant. God knows it's in short supply."

The sound of the sirens grew louder, and then faded away again as she fell in and out of consciousness; the sedatives gave a short reprieve from the horrific ordeal she would soon have to live with, and then relive again and again.

The ambulance stopped in front of the doors to the emergency ward, and she was jarred awake by the abrupt snap of the stretcher as the legs dropped down and the wheels hit the pavement. The lights were passing by overhead and she could hear the sound of the automatic doors opening, then the voices as she let out an ear-piercing scream.

She had to get away, why was it so bright? Her thoughts were disjointed. Nothing was connecting as she felt herself moving again, ever so quickly now as the voices grew louder.

She felt the pain again and ached all over. Her head felt as though it would split in two as the memory of the vile attack flooded back, and she began to cry. Her body shook uncontrollably as she felt them on her, inside her. She heard a scream, and then nothing.

"Keep her sedated and let's get her into X-Ray," the doctor said. "I want a full assessment and no one gets in to see her before I have reviewed her charts. You know the routine, bag everything and once I give the nod we'll let the detectives come in and interview her."

Kate was in the temp office that Mike had set up for them when she heard the phone ringing in her purse, and then a cold chill gripped her as she answered. It was the one Max had given her for emergencies only, and the first time since that it had rung.

"Max, is that you?"

"Yes, Kate, are you in the office or at home?"

"Office."

"Ok, go to the boardroom floor and go out onto the patio, I'll call you back in five," he said, and then the line went dead.

The rain had stopped, and there was even a promise of some sun as she stood by the balcony and waited impatiently, staring at the phone. He had never called her on what he referred to as "the shoe phone" before.

She jumped as it began to vibrate and then fumbled as she tried to answer it, "Max, what is it? What's wrong?"

He sounded tired, and she could feel his voice was full of emotion as he spoke, "Have you heard about Janet?"

"No, why. What happened to Janet?"

"She was beaten up last night. Someone broke into her home."

There was silence on the end of the line and when she finally spoke, her voice quivered, "was she ——-raped?"

"I don't know the details, Kate, but sadly I believe she was. She's on her way to Vancouver General, and it would be good if you could check in on her as soon as possible."

His voice was calm, but she could feel his anger as it boiled just below the surface.

"Listen, Kate, things may ---- no, they will get a lot worse," he said. "So I need you to listen to me carefully, and do exactly as I say. Do you hear me?"

"Yes, yes I do," she said as the fear welled up inside of her. She had a million questions, but for now she would have to wait.

"Good. As soon as we hang up I want you to call a friend of mine. His name is Ron. Program his number into your phone and keep it on you at all times."

"Oh shit, Max, these men. The ones who hurt Janet; are they coming after me?"

"No," he replied quickly. But then decided not to make the same mistake twice.

"Actually, to be honest, I don't know. But we are not taking any chances. Now call Ron, he is going to come and get you and take you to your condo. He will stay with you while you go and get your things."

"What do you mean get my things?" she asked cautiously.

"Listen, there is no time to explain. You just have to trust me. Take what you need to last you at least a couple of weeks and go with him to my place. You will be staying in the guest room beside Beatrice and you can work from there. And do not leave unless you absolutely have to. If you do, call Ron, and he will accompany you."

"Jesus, Max, you're really scaring the shit out of me," she said as she ran her hand through her hair and let it fall across her forehead.

"Good. It's called situation recognition, and I'm afraid it's best that you be aware of what is happening so you don't let your guard down. Now, when you get to my place I need you to make a call for me, there is someone I need to find. Use the Iphone that's in the bottom left hand drawer of my desk. The access code is P-H-I-L."

They said goodbye, and then she went back to the office and

and began packing up her things as she dialed the number Max had given her.

Her nerves were frayed, and she struggled to keep her emotions in check as she waited for an answer, "You must be Kate," said the deep and calming voice on the other end of the line.

"Be downstairs in ten minutes, and don't come outside until you see me in the lobby."

"How will I know you?"

"I'm hard to miss, my dear. I'm six foot seven, two hundred and seventy five pounds and exceedingly handsome," he said, laughing. "I will be wearing a black suit and tie, short dark cropped hair and I'll have a red rose in my left hand."

As nervous as she was, she couldn't help but laugh. It was textbook Max to set something like this up. And when she got off the elevator she saw the giant of a man standing in the lobby, the red rose barely visible in the fist of his massive hand.

She felt as if a weight had been lifted as he moved toward her and then handed her the rose as he took the oversized briefcase from her hand. She felt as though she was in a movie as she watched him scan the area, and then he took her by the elbow and led her out through the revolving doors.

He walked her to the Phaeton that was parked in front, and as he helped her inside and then closed the door she felt as though she had slid into a cocoon. Everything fell silent. There was some jazz playing in the speakers behind her head, and she all of a sudden felt safe again as she watched in awe as her newly appointed bodyguard expertly maneuvered them in and out of traffic.

"Max gave me the address," he said in answer to the puzzled look on her face. She realized they had just pulled up in front of her apartment.

They took the elevator to her floor, and then he waited outside her door while she collected her things. To his surprise, she emerged less than ten minutes later with only a small suitcase and overnight bag. Impressive. Not only drop dead gorgeous but she could pack light enough for a trip on a Harley. He had to hand it to him, Max knew his women.

They arrived in the underground parking of Max's building less than fifteen minutes later, and were standing at the elevator as Ron punched the code into the keypad. She was exhausted and stood quietly as they ascended to the top floor.

When the door opened, he helped her set her bags inside and then stood smiling as he towered over her. "You can call me anytime, day or night," he said as he looked down at her.

"Thank you, Ron. I really appreciate it," she said staring back up at him.

"And thank you for being such a good friend to Max."

"I appreciate the compliment, but it is I who am grateful for Max's friendship," he said as he turned and disappeared back into the elevator.

She stood for a moment, overwhelmed and not quite sure what to do next when Beatrice appeared.

"Hello Miss Kate, Max called and told me you were on your way and to prepare the guest room nearest me," she said in a soothing motherly voice as she picked up her overnight bag and led her to the bedroom.

Although she had been to the condo many times, she had never been into the bedrooms before, and was surprised by the quality of furnishings and the detail in which the room had been put together.

"Is everything ok, darling?"

"Yes – yes, I'm sorry. I'm just a little tired. Did Max have a decorator put this room together? It seems pretty amazing for a rental apartment, don't you think?"

"Rental?" Beatrice said with a laugh.

"I'm sorry but no, Mister Max owns this home, Miss Kate. Surely you must have known, you do work for him, no?"

Her equilibrium was now completely on vacation as she looked for a place to sit down and clear her thoughts, "Max owns this penthouse?" No, she thought, dismissing what she had just heard--surely she must he mistaken.

Beatrice, now realizing her mistake simply ignored the question, "Why don't you take a hot shower and relax, and then let's sit and have a nice dinner. I have fresh empanadas and salad all ready for you."

CHAPTER 26

Max walked back into the boardroom and stood for a moment as he stared out at the ocean. The purity and beauty of the beautiful turquoise waters was a deep contrast to the ugliness that he felt as he turned and looked at everyone seated around the table.

"I have some bad news," he said, feeling a lump of emotion blocking his throat. "A very dear friend of mine, and a valued employee of Darrington, Moskowitz and Calder was beaten and raped in her home last night.

'Jesus, Max," said John. "I'm very sorry to hear that."

"This whole thing is getting way out of control," said Ken as he slouched back in his chair.

"Although I echo John's sincere concerns for your friend, I don't see how this has anything to do with us," replied Jim.

"It has everything to do with us," replied Ken as his voice began to rise. "I mean, come on, Trent Jordan, Howell, what happened to us yesterday. And now this? How could it not be connected?"

"I'm afraid he's right," said Max.

He had little doubt things were about to get ugly, and he needed to get control of the situation before it got totally out of hand. And then he had an odd feeling as he looked over at Jim. It wasn't what he had said, but how he said it that gave him an uneasy feeling. Was this guy to be trusted? And given he was one of Morton's most senior people, it made him even more uneasy.

"I need to make some calls," said Max. "You all carry on without me."

Kate had just gotten out of the shower, and was wrapping her hair in a towel when she heard the phone ring and quickly sprinted into the bedroom to answer the phone.

"Is everything ok?" Max asked when he heard her rapid breathing.

"Yes, sorry I was in the shower and had to run for the phone," She glanced down and saw the water dripping onto the floor.

He was still feeling the effects of the news about Janet, but couldn't help but smile as he thought about her standing naked in his home, "Everything go ok with Ron?"

"Yes, he's a very nice man. And very big," she said as she stepped back into the bathroom and onto the bath mat.

"That he is. Did you get the info I asked you for?"

"Oh my god, no Max, I'm so sorry?" she exclaimed. "I was enjoying the fabulous shower and I guess I lost track of time."

She sensed the agitation in his voice, and could tell he was not in the mood for conversation, but even still she had a hundred questions she wanted answers to. And especially about the comment Beatrice had made about the penthouse, but again she knew she would have to wait.

"I will do it immediately," she said as she hung up. She grabbed the housecoat that had been laid out on the bed and slipped it on before heading to his office.

Did Max really own this penthouse? she wondered as she walked down the hall, checking out the artworks along the way. She had never really paid attention to them before, but now she was looking at them in a whole different light. And they looked expensive. She was going to have to do some research and find out more about her Max. She switched on the light and took a seat at his desk.

She was looking around the room when she noticed the decanters on the bar across the room and thought what the hell, "It's been a long day," she murmured as she went and poured herself a glass of scotch.

She took a healthy drink and then sat back in the chair and closed her eyes as the waves of emotion began washing over her. She could see his face, his muscled forearms, and that awkward smile as he walked toward her. She could no longer tell what was real, and was about to say something when she was startled by a knock at the door, "Miss Kate, are you ready for some dinner?"

"Shit," she said aloud as she abruptly sat up, spilling her scotch on the bathrobe.

"Yes, Beatrice, I just have to make a call and then I'll be right there."

I am such an idiot, she thought, as she picked up the phone and dialed the number. Moments later she heard a man's voice on the other end of the line. At first he was unreceptive, but after she answered a few personal questions about Max he gave her the information she was looking for, and then hung up before she had a chance to thank him.

She texted Max the information from the Iphone, and then placed it back in the drawer as she picked up the glass and downed the last of the scotch.

"Just one of the boys," she said aloud as she thought about pouring another. Then her stomach grumbled at the smell of fresh empanadas coming from the kitchen.

"Those smell incredible," she said as she took a seat at the eating bar in the kitchen and took two of the steaming patties and placed them on her plate.

"Would you like some lentil soup?" Beatrice asked as she placed a chilled glass of Chilean Chardonnay in front of her.

"My god no, but thanks. There is already enough food here to feed an entire family," she said as she took the glass of wine.

After reading her text, Max spent the next twenty minutes on the phone making the necessary travel arrangements, and after a short debate he decided to make one more call.

Mike's voice was tired and he seemed on edge when he finally picked up, "Hello Max, I was expecting to have heard from you sooner. I'm sure by now you would have heard about Janet."

"I did," Max replied. "I don't know what the hell you have gotten us into, but I sure as Christ intend to find out. As for Janet, well, we will deal with it," he said coldly.

"I understand you are upset, but please don't do anything rash," replied Mike, knowing it was just wasted words.

"I gotta say Mike, for a smart guy you sure seem to have missed the ball on this one."

"It's easy to say after the fact, but no one could have foreseen this coming. So can we drop the blame game and just try and deal with it? Tell me about the Bahamas."

"Too much to discuss on the phone. I am coming back to

Vancouver, tonight if possible. Can you authorize the use of the old man's jet,"

"I take it that this is not good news," said Mike as he leaned back in his chair and loosened his tie.

"Do whatever you have to, I'll cover you. When do you think you will be here?"

"Should be by tomorrow night, but I have a stop to make. I'll be in touch."

Mike heard the line go dead, and as he hung up he worried about what Max had found so important that he had to fly back so quickly. Whatever it was, he knew he would find out soon enough.

Max called the chief pilot next and asked him how quickly they could be in the air. He called back fifteen minutes later and they agreed to make it for six o'clock, which would give him enough time to go home and shower, collect some things and then head back to Millionaire FBO.

It was finally starting to come together. But when he walked back into the boardroom and announced he would be gone for a few days, Jim showed little sign of concern, which made him even more on edge.

"Ken, this is your turf, so watch their backs. And let's get this damn consolidation over with so we can all go home," said Max as he picked up his pack.

"We got it handled," said John. "Go and take care of your friend, we'll be here when you get back."

The driver pulled up in front of his condo, and Max told him to be back by 5:40. It was going to be a long night. He took the stairs two at a time, and was looking for his key when he heard the deadbolt turn.

"You're back early," said Lillis as she opened the door and let him in.

"I know, but I have to go back to Vancouver tonight and I will be leaving Phil here with you. Can you stay with him for a few days?"

"Of course," she said without a care.

"You are an angel," he said.

"Take a cab home today and get whatever you need, there's plenty of money in the usual place."

The driver was on time and they arrived at Millionaire less than fifteen minutes later. He was relieved to see the pilots were already there as he walked over to greet them.

"I understand we are off to Vancouver, Mister Duncan?"

"That's correct. But with a slight change of plan, I need to make a stop in Cabo San Lucas."

Max could see by the expression on the man's face that this was a wrinkle he was not expecting.

"Is that a problem?" he asked

"No. No problem, I just need to re-file our flight plan." he said with a smile.

"But we will have to allow enough time for sleep as we will be over our hours."

"I realize that, and I'm sorry for the inconvenience but can you please try and get us out of here as soon as possible? If we are in the air by six thirty we should be on the ground by two," said Max as he looked at his watch.

"Or sooner if we push her a little," replied the captain with a wink. And then he turned and headed into the pilot's room to re-file their flight plan.

Air traffic was light, and it was only 6:18 when they taxied onto the runaway and came to a stop.

"Ready for take-off, Mister Duncan?" said the captain. Max heard the engines spooling up and then felt himself being forced back in his seat as the plane roared down the runway. They were climbing fast, and he could hear the engines' soft whine as they banked hard to the south and circled around as they set a direct course to San Jose del Cabo.

He had been careful to keep his trip a secret, and had made his own arrangements for the Presidential Suite at The Ridge at Playa Grande. It was not only a four star hotel, but the suite had a perfect view of one particular marina he needed to get to.

The flight was uneventful, and after a meal of yellow tail snapper with peas and rice, and the better part of a bottle of Pinot Noir he lay back and was soon sound asleep as they flew due east across the Gulf of Mexico.

He slept soundly and without nightmares. But the night would prove to be anything but peaceful.

CHAPTER 27

It was 4:30 in the morning and at first the guard never heard the jeep as it pulled to a stop in front of the security gate.

But when he did finally raise his head he saw the self drive plates, and assumed they were guests as he raised the bar and then laid his head back down on the desk.

The driver took the first left and drove to the far end of the parking lot, then backed the jeep into a dark corner far away from the security booth. He killed the engine, and he and his passenger got out without a word.

Phil's ears perked up when he heard the noise outside the door, and then he jumped from the bed and shot out of the bedroom. Lillis was still asleep and never heard the deadbolt on the front door retract as the man on the other side expertly picked the lock and twisted it open.

But Phil was crouched down, muscles tense and his upper lip rolled back as the shadowy figure slowly pushed the door inwards. As he slipped his leg inside, Phil sank his teeth deep into the man's calf. Lillis shot up in bed when she heard him cry out, and as she ran from the bedroom she saw Phil, shaking his head from side to side as his teeth ripped deep at the muscle until they hit bone.

The intruder was trapped, and as he desperately tried to push the door open Phil stayed hard pressed up against it and was not letting go. Confused and unaware of the danger that stood just outside the door, Lillis switched on the light and then began screaming when she saw Phil hanging onto the man's leg.

There was blood spatter across the door, and she watched in horror as Phil continued to rip at the intruders. Not realizing the danger she rushed toward him, and as she yelled for him to stop, she saw the leg disappear from the door and she slammed it closed and set the deadbolt.

"My goodness," she said as she stood staring down at Phil. Then she went into the kitchen and sat down in a chair and began to shake. Her heart was pounding and her hands trembled as she picked up the phone and tried to dial the number for Security.

Phil, having done his job, came and lay down at her side. As she sat waiting for them to answer she could see the bloody paw prints he had left on the tile floor.

Meanwhile, the would be attacker had managed to limp back to his jeep, and as he climbed inside the passenger seat the driver gunned the engine and headed for the exit. The security officer on duty had just woke up when he saw the headlights coming toward the booth, and then saw the gate arm slam against the building as the jeep flew past.

The passenger was hunched forward in his seat, and groaning in pain as he held his leg. There was a deep gash in his calf, and he could see the blood pouring down onto his foot.

"Fucking stupid asshole, he was supposed to be gone. They said the place was going to be empty," he cried.

"We need to get you to a clinic," said the driver as he looked down at the pool of blood on the floor.

"No way, we can't risk it. Just get me back to the boat," he groaned as he reclined the seat and put his leg up on the dash.

Meanwhile, Max could see the lights of San Jose del Cabo off in the distance, and as they made their approach the runway lights came into view. With nearly 360 days of sunshine per year, the weather here was near perfect and visibility was excellent for flying.

Minutes later they were rolling to a stop in front of the small terminal, and were climbing off the plane just as a customs officer came to greet them. They followed her into the small customs area, were cleared without delay, and were soon sitting in the back of the cab on their way to the hotel.

He had slept well, and was wide-awake looking out at the night sky and studying the stars when he felt his phone vibrate. It was too early for anyone to be calling from Nassau, and too late in Vancouver. He felt his stomach tighten as he pulled the phone from his pocket and looked at the screen.

There was a missed call from Lillis, and then he felt his grip tighten on his phone and a wave of anger wash over as he read the text from his home security system; someone was in his condo in Vancouver.

Lillis answered after the first ring, "Oh, Mister Max, I am so sorry to bother you but it was terrible, there is blood everywhere and Phil, well he was so brave, he just -----," she was rambling and not making any sense.

"Ok, take a breath and slow down; start from the beginning. Phil, is he ok?"

"Yes, he's fine but that man, the one who broke in, he's not in too good shape," she replied with a nervous chuckle. As Max listened to her recount the story, he realized that none of them would be safe until he brought an end to it.

Whoever had tried to get into his home must have known that he had left town, but he had no idea what they could possibly have been after. Thank god he had left Phil with her, God knows what would have happened if he wasn't there.

She told him that their security had come by and made an incident report, but thankfully she had not called the police yet and he warned her against doing so. The last thing he needed was the local police to get involved.

"I'm very sorry for all this, Lillis, but try and get some sleep," he said and then ended the call.

The view was just as he remembered it. He flipped open his laptop and then went and stood on the balcony looking out over the marina. He took a cold Pacifico from the outside bar and gave it another full five minutes as he waited impatiently for the Internet to do its thing.

But when he finally got connected he was able to access his system and the remote cameras he had set up in the exterior and main rooms of all his properties. Everything seemed on the quiet at the penthouse, but as he sat studying the second camera feed he dialed Ron's number.

Among other properties, Max also owned a condo seven floors below his penthouse. He had decided to use it for his official address to avoid solicitors, and people seeking donations. It was also a convenient place to bring casual dates. But tonight his cameras had captured some unwanted visitors turning the place upside down.

Ron answered after the third ring, and Max gave him a quick rundown on what had happened.

"Whoever broke into the condo was a pro, and it's only a matter of time before they figure out where I live. So check it out and I'll call you once I'm back."

"And if they still happen to be in the apartment," asked Ron with a gruff snort.

"Consider it a bonus."

It had been a coordinated attack on both his residences, and he was pretty certain where the information on his whereabouts had come from. The only ones who knew he was heading back to Vancouver were the team in Nassau and the flight crew, and he had already ruled out the latter. As he undressed and climbed into bed he could feel the pressure pushing hard against his temples.

He felt as though his head had barely hit the pillow, but as he slowly opened his eyes and stared at the ceiling he saw the soft rays of early daybreak filtering into his room. Realizing he had overslept, he jumped out of bed and headed for the outdoor shower.

The sun would soon be up, and he knew the man he had come to see would be heading out to sea ahead of the charter boats and he needed to get moving.

Unlike Nassau, the air was dry and a pleasant seventy-two degrees as he headed down the hill toward the marina. As he walked past the local vendors opening up their stands they gave him warm smiles. It wouldn't be long before the tourists would be descending upon them as the margarita blenders began cranking out the cash.

Thankfully the gate to the marina was open, and after walking for almost five minutes he found himself staring at a sign indicating he was on B Dock, and had to turn around and head back toward the entrance before finding Dock C. Typical for Mexico.

He began making his way out to slip 29, where the $6.5 million dollar, eighty-five foot custom built Jarrett Bay Sport Fish was docked.

Max loved boats, and reminded himself it was time he started reviewing his options again as he stood for a moment, admiring the yacht in front of him. It truly was a magnificent craft with beautiful lines, and an impressive tuna tower that stood nearly forty feet above the water, casting a long shadow down the dock.

"One of these days," he said as he walked up to the stern of "Reel Time." He was just about to knock on the side of the hull when he fell into the shadow of a figure towering over him from the deck above.

"Morning, counselor," boomed the voice from above.

"Permission to come aboard," replied Max. And although he couldn't make out the face as squinted into the sun, the shape of the man was unmistakable.

"Shoes stay on the aft," said Frank as he opened the transom door and welcomed their visitor on board. Max kicked off his shoes and followed him into the main salon, where he could hear the telltale sounds of a cook hard at work in the galley below. He could almost taste the fried bacon and chorizo sausages, and could feel his stomach do flip flops as he looked around the salon.

He was just about to take a seat when he heard the distinct and familiar voice coming from somewhere forward, "We do have phones down here, you know."

Max just laughed. "Thanks, but I thought this was a trip better done in person."

"It's good to see you, Max," said Gino as he emerged from below, sporting a tattered Bob Dylan T-shirt and khaki shorts.

"Join me for breakfast," he said as he watched Max's nostrils working overtime.

"Absolutely." They shook hands, and then Gino put his arm around him and gave him a big hug.

"Follow me," he said, and then turned and spoke in rapid Spanish to someone in the galley as he motioned toward the side door.

Max followed him out of the salon and up a staircase onto the bridge. Once on top he was impressed with the incredible selection of fishing gear and high-tech electronics.

"It's quieter up here, and it will give us some privacy to discuss whatever it is that is all so important that you could not discuss it over the phone," he said as he took a seat near the helm.

"I appreciate that," said Max as he stood staring at nearly a dozen rods and reels. "Quite the collection of gear you have here, and the boat's not too shabby either."

"Just took delivery a few months ago," Gino said proudly as he gave him a run down on some of the equipment. "Have a seat," he said, as a very attractive young woman appeared with a tray of food and set it down on the table in front of them. Gino thanked her in Spanish as she filled their glasses with fresh orange juice, and then watched her as she disappeared below without a word.

"A cutie, isn't she," he said. But as he turned back to face him, his expression was all business.

"So, tell me. What's on your mind? Must be something pretty important for you to have to track me all the way down here, or did you just develop a sudden urge to go deep sea fishing?"

Max took one of the plates and set it in down in front of

him before answering, "I have a problem," he said as he poured a generous amount of hot sauce onto his huevos rancheros.

"Go on."

"I think it has something to do with KLG."

If he didn't have Gino's attention before, he certainly had it now. "That deal was done and dusted a long time ago, Max," he said abruptly.

"And, as I recall it worked out pretty damn well for you, did it not?"

"Kinda worked out well for us both don't you think?" said Max as he sat back with his arms spread wide.

"Look, it's not that I don't appreciate the visit. But a walk down memory lane is not exactly what I had on my agenda for this morning. And whatever I did or did not make on that particular venture is none of your business."

Max was taken aback by his response, and chose to ignore it as he continued, "I realize that, and I did not mean to infer anything by it. But it seems the directors have surfaced again, and are causing some trouble for a new client of Michael's."

"Sorry to hear that, but what's it got to do with me?"

"Come on, Gino, this is me you're talking to," said Max as he pushed his plate back. "I need to know what these guys have been up to and what I've gotten myself into."

"What makes you think I would know what they were up to," he said. But Max could tell by the look on his face he had come to the right place.

"Look, with all due respect I know you well enough to know you would have kept tabs on the likes of these guys. So, cut the bullshit will you, please?"

It seemed Gino had enough breakfast as well. He sat back

and stared at the entrance to the harbor, "Fair enough," he said.

"I guess I suspected you might show up sooner or later. So, tell me about Mike's client."

"Feinstein Bank and Trust, or better known as FB and T."

"Oh, I see," replied Gino.

He never fully disclosed to Max the reasoning behind bringing him the KLG case in the first place, but now it would be almost impossible for him not to find out. And once that door was opened, god knows where it would end.

"These guys, the ones you are asking about. They're bad news, Max. And I mean seriously bad news. So you want my advice, tell Mike to find another client," said Gino, staring hard into Max's eyes.

But Gino knew him all too well. And he knew he needed answers and he wasn't about to leave until he got what he had come for.

"Not an option Gino, so can we go to door number two?"

"Your choice, counselor. But don't say I didn't warn you." He went quiet for a few minutes and just as Max's patience was about to run out, he spoke again.

"Tell me about your involvement with FB and T."

"I take it you have heard of them," said Max, as he realized Gino was not only familiar with FB and T, but likely knew more about what was going on than he did. And so for the next fifteen minutes Max described in detail what had happened since Mike had called him, and about what had happened to Janet. He chose to leave out the incident with Trent Jordan, at least for the time being.

When he finished, Gino got up and opened one of the small

lockers in the dash of the salon and took out two cigars, "Join me," he said as he handed one to him.

Max was not a smoker. But he did enjoy the odd cigar, and under the circumstance he accepted as Gino cut the tip off a fat Monte Cristo and handed it to him. He repeated the process, and then picked up a handsome gold lighter that had the same sailfish emblem engraved on it as Max had seen on the mirror over the bar.

Satisfied the stogie was properly lit, he sat back and exhaled a long plume of smoke. As he began rolling the cigar between his thumb and forefinger Max noticed the distinctive band on his wrist, "Been to Nassau lately?"

"As a matter of fact I was there just two weeks ago, had dinner at Gray Cliff and bought some of their cigars. And before you insult me with your next question, the answer is no. I am not involved with those clowns."

"Look Gino, help me, don't help me--It's your prerogative. But we go too far back for you to just sit here and play me."

"I'm not playing you, Max. And believe it or not, I am looking out for you." He stood and walked to the back of the salon and rolled the handle on the reel of one of the big game fish rods.

"It's just not that simple, you show up here, expect me to just enlighten you on a deal that you and I both know was not exactly kosher. And all without consequence?"

Max knew he was probably right. And although he'd always suspected Gino had been involved in some way, he had never known for sure until just now. But for whatever reason, he trusted him and needed his help.

"You're right, and maybe I am just as culpable as you are. But the fact is, I need to know everything you can tell me about these guys."

CHAPTER 28

Max sat staring at his friend, and for a brief moment he saw the old, and much younger Gino standing there playing with his rod and reel as though he had no care in the world. But the deep lines in his face, and receding hairline painted a much different picture now.

"Ok, Max, but you know the story; be careful what you ask for. Because once I answer your questions, you are going to be left with some very difficult choices to make."

"And your point is…?" Max rolled a large piece of ash off the end of his cigar and into the ashtray. "People make difficult choices every day."

"Fine. I believe one of the lawyers you referred to earlier is into us for some large dollars, and I am sad to say our chances of collecting from him now are slim to none."

"And how is that?"

"Dead men not only don't tell tales, but they don't pay their debts either," said Gino. And then he hesitated for only a second, "and no, I did not kill him."

"Well, I am glad to hear it," Max replied with some relief, "but

I would really appreciate it if you could get to the point and tell me how he's connected to the Singh brothers." He poured fresh coffee from the stainless thermos.

"When I told you the brothers are bad news, I wasn't being exactly truthful. They are seriously bad fucking news. The oldest brother, Raj, came to see me a while ago and offered to buy one of my businesses."

"But you weren't selling?"

"Nope, told him to fuck off. But I knew it wouldn't end there."

"And I assume it didn't."

"No, it did not."

Max could almost feel the contempt in Gino's voice as he continued, "Raj is a two bit, penny ante stock hustler who has managed to make a small fortune on dime stocks. Including our little venture. But he's a lunatic, and a dangerous one at that."

"Christ," replied Max as he thought about Janet.

"Well, you don't want to underestimate these guys. They are not only tough, but they are reckless. And that, my friend, is a deadly combination."

"I get it," said Max, "But whoever is behind this is sophisticated in the inner workings of offshore banking, and has to have some serious connections. He, or they, are not just some street level hustlers."

"God does not always just favor the weak; this guy has been able to be in the right place at the right time more times than I can count, and sometimes it's better to be lucky than smart. So, whatever your suspicions are about these guys, trust your instincts."

"Ok, so how do you come into play in all of this?"

"Well, that's where our paths cross for the second time. Our lotto business is on its way out, and we are in the final stages of getting our Internet gaming business up and running."

Max thought about it for a moment and then it hit him. "It makes perfect sense; you already have the client base to build from, and the organization is in place. All you have to do is switch gears."

"Exactly, but as chance would have it, they are doing the same thing. They set up shop in Costa Rica, and were well on their way to going live when they hit a snag."

"What kind of snag?" asked Max as he felt his pulse begin to quicken.

"Well, they recently had some problems with the SEC, and they lost a large chunk of their cash. It's thrown a wrench into the plans."

"I'm sorry, Gino, I get that they may want your business for obvious reasons, but why would they be taking such a personal interest?"

"I'm afraid this is where it gets ugly." Gino reached over and picked up the boat phone and punched the call button, "Is the jet here or did they take it back to LA," he said into the receiver. "Alright, tell Captain Wieberg we will not be fishing today." He hung up the phone.

"Well, looks like the jet has already left so Frank and I will be riding back to Vancouver with you," he said as he blew a dark blue smoke ring in Max's direction.

"I'm sorry," replied Max, now totally confused.

"Let's take a walk," said Gino as he got up and headed down to the lower deck.

Max lagged for a moment, and stared across at the yacht

beside them as he watched the two deckhands coiling up the lines that were laid out on the bow. Maybe Gino was right, maybe he should just cut and run. He felt his fists tighten. But then what about Mike? Max heard Gino call from below, "You coming, counselor?"

Max was feeling conflicted as they wandered down the dock, "So where does the lawyer that owes you the money fall into all of this?" he asked as they stopped beside a yacht that he estimated to be at least 150 feet long.

"Ah, this is where it really gets interesting. I had my suspicions before, but now you have confirmed it. The late Mr. Calder owed me over a million. I wasn't sure of the connection before, but now I think the boys were planning on blackmailing his son into helping them in their plan to take the bank."

Max stopped dead in his tracks, and found himself staring at Gino's back before he finally stopped and turned to face him.

"I'm sorry, did you just say Calder?" He stood staring in disbelief.

"One and the same, and they were using the old man as leverage."

And then it was like the first time solving a Rubik's cube; all the pieces just began falling into place.

"They never knew he owed you money," Max exclaimed as he stared over at him. "It was just pure coincidence that you found out about the connection."

"Not as dumb as you look," said Gino, "with the old man gone, so goes their leverage."

"But that makes no sense," said Max. "Trent Jordan was the one assigned to the file and now he is dead. Calder's son was only just assigned to take his place."

And then he saw Gino's body stiffen as he stopped in front of him, and just stood staring into the hull of the yacht beside them, "This, I did not know," he said.

"Jesus Christ, Gino, this gets more complicated by the minute."

"And why didn't you tell me about Trent when you were giving me your little dissertation?"

"I never told you about Trent because I thought it might prejudice your thinking," he said, now irritated with himself for having held back the information.

"Alright, let's forget about it for the moment," he said as he began walking. "This is really unbelievable, but I am almost certain whatever happened to Trent was not their doing. And if the old man died, it was probably a jammer from all the stress. But whatever the hell happened, there goes their plan," he said as he took a deep breath of salt air.

"But they must have at least one person on the inside of the bank, and maybe the firm," replied Max.

"Probably, but without the old man they will have lost their leverage. And if their plans are falling apart, they will be acting irrationally. Which explains what you have been telling me," he said as though he had just come to some revelation.

"But if I am right about old man Jordan, and I hope I'm not, I will not only be out a shitload of money but they will be looking for options."

Max slowed and then grabbed Gino by the elbow and waited until he stopped, "So, it's your money they're after," he said.. "It all makes sense now. It was you who cleaned them out on the stock deal, wasn't it."

"I know you may not fully believe this, but we are truly playing for the same team," replied Gino staring directly into Max's eyes.

"Well, at least it answers my earlier question about why they were taking it so personal," said Max.

"Look, the how or why does not matter. What matters is it's my money they're going to steal, and we have to figure out how they are going to do it and stop them before it happens."

"Wait a minute," shouted Max. "What do you mean when you say they are going to steal your money?"

"You mean you haven't figured this out yet?" said Gino as they stopped in front of the Cantina at the end of the dock.

"Take a seat," he said as he pulled up a wooden stool and took a seat at the bar.

"So, are you going to enlighten me or what?" said Max impatiently as he sat down beside him.

"I'm not sure," replied Gino as he ordered two Pacifico beers.

"Ok, and bear with me here, let's say it is your cash they're after, or at least we're after. It makes sense? They not only have a good idea how much is there, but also a pretty good idea of where it is."

Gino was suddenly listening very intently.

"What if it first started out as a plan for them to get into your company to gain access to the money? When that didn't work they figured a way to somehow steal it when FB and T moved your assets to the Bahamas."

"I think you're not as dumb as you make yourself out to be," replied Gino as he sat picking at the label on his beer.

Max ignored the off-handed compliment for the second time. "I've read all the files and studied the consolidation, if they are bold enough to go after your cash, then why not all of it?"

Max could see the perspiration begin to form on Gino's face, and it wasn't just the heat that had him sweating.

"Christ, Max, do you have any idea of the implications if you are right about this? But I'll tell you this, it would certainly have been a big enough carrot to turn old man Calder."

And then his voice took on almost a fatherly tone, "But tell me, where's the upside in all of this for you? It seems like a lose, lose, if you ask me."

And that's when Max told him about his father.

"I'm sorry to hear that, Max, I guess the stakes are high for all of us now." Gino let out a dry laugh, "You know the real beauty of it all; they just might get away with it. I mean, think about it, who are these clients going to go to in order to get their money back. It's the perfect crime if there ever was one.""

"Trust me on this one, they are not going to get away with it," said Max as he bent a beer cap in between his thumb and forefinger.

"Well, I think I may just believe you," replied Gino as he drained his beer. And it was as though Max could see the stress beginning to leave his body as he leaned back and stretched out his legs in front of him. "Look Max, there is no secret to my past. To say I sailed close to the wind would be an understatement, and I have done some things that I am not all that proud of. But you have to believe me when I tell you I never dreamed any of it would come back on you."

"I don't hold any of it against you, Gino, you did what you had to do."

"Thanks. I appreciate it. And I appreciate your friendship."

"We're good, Gino, and although I didn't exactly get all the answers I was looking for, I at least now have a pretty good idea what I'm up against."

"The pilots are good to go in another two hours, so we should get ready to head to the airport," he said as he tossed a ten dollar bill onto the bar.

They walked in silence back to Gino's boat, and as Max continued on to the hotel he could not help but think about Janet. He decided to stop in at one of the small vendor stands and buy a few pieces of the silver jewelry Mexico was known for.

He collected his purchase and was about to leave when he was drawn back by the aroma of fresh fish tacos. He got two to go and then went straight back to his room, took a long shower, and packed up the few items he'd brought with him. He had almost forgotten about the tacos, and tucked into them with vigor while he sent an email to Mike to let him know he would be in his office by 6:00 p.m. at the latest. He thought about calling Kate, but then decided against it as he stuffed his laptop into his pack and went to check out.

The sky was grey, and a light rain streaked across the window as they descended down over the valley on their final approach into Vancouver. They had barely taxied to a stop when two ground crew members rushed out with umbrellas and quickly walked them over to customs.

"Well, this is where we part ways," said Gino as he gripped Max's hand. He pulled him in close, "You call me if you need back up, you hear me?" he said in a low growl.

Max just nodded, and looked over at Frank, "Take care of him," he said as he picked up his pack and headed outside to the limousine that was waiting for him.

CHAPTER 29

Max was generally a very pragmatic person, but he was having great difficulty keeping his emotions in check. He genuinely liked Morton, and although the chickens may have come home to roost he was still going to do everything he could to help him. As for Gino, he was pissed that he had done what he did to the Singh brothers but what's done is done.

Max handed the driver a fifty dollar tip, and then hopped out of the back seat and sprinted for the building in the light rain.

He was surprised to see Mike nursing a glass of scotch, and from the look of the dark circles under his eyes he hadn't gotten much sleep in the last few days.

"Dare I say welcome back?" he said. He got up from the sofa and offered a weak smile as Max walked into his office.

"We've made some progress," replied Max as they shook hands, and then he crossed over to the bar and poured himself a coffee from the silver carafe.

"How's Janet faring? I called the hospital but they wouldn't give me much information."

Mike was slow to answer, and Max felt that she could be the source of the darkness under his eyes.

"She's doing as well as can be expected, at least physically anyway. My assistant was able to get in to see her. No broken bones, but some pretty bad bruises and two cracked ribs."

Max's shoulders dropped as he let out a long sigh, "And the other?"

"I'm afraid so, she was raped by at least one, maybe more. They have DNA but it was inconclusive," he said as he emptied his glass.

"And it sickens me to think that what happened to this poor girl comes as a direct result of me and my goddamn firm," he said, spitting the words out.

"You and me both," said Max as he stood and stared at the painting behind Mike's desk and thought how ironic it was. It was a classic: "Passing the Ace Under the Table Dog Poker picture.

"Listen Mike, you can't beat yourself up over this. You couldn't have known how this was going to turn out. And besides, I think what I am about to tell you should ease your conscience a bit."

"Well, I hope you're right," he replied.

"I think I have this figured out, but it will take a while to give it to you in detail. Can we go someplace quiet and have a bite? I'll give you the whole story."

"Absolutely." Mike picked up the phone and called Hy's Steakhouse. It was a long time institution in Vancouver that had tables offering privacy and it was just a few blocks away.

Max sampled the Clos Apalta and nodded to the waiter. Then he waited until their glasses were filled and the waiter had left. "It's not good," he said.

"Then why did you accept it," said Mike as he lifted his glass and sniffed the deep red nectar. "Smells good to me."

"Not the wine," Max replied laughing.

"Right, I guess I'm just wound a little too tight right now. Sorry, please continue."

Max could see a lightness coming over Mike as he listened intently to a recitation of the events that had taken place since he had left Vancouver. And by the time he was done, Mike had not only cleaned his plate but was actually smiling when he ordered a second bottle of wine.

"You're sure about this," he said quietly as the waiter poured their wine.

"No question. If I'm right, these guys could be planning what would be one of the biggest heists of all time."

"They must have people inside the bank here and in Nassau," he said thoughtfully.

Max could see a glimmer of his old mentor begin to shine through as he began to come to grips with what he now knew. And the more they discussed it, the more certain he became that the Singh's were going to take a run at the bank.

"Alright Max, said Mike as he carefully folded his napkin and threw it onto the table, "based on what you have told me, I think it's time I do the right thing and call in the authorities."

"And tell them what? That we have a bunch of clients that are sheltering money offshore, and we think some criminal clients whom we have represented are going to steal their ill gotten booty?"

"That would go over real well, wouldn't it?" Max could tell by the look on his face he was genuinely embarrassed, "Shit, I must be losing it."

"It's a conundrum, no doubt about it. And I'm afraid that at this juncture, we're the only hope Morton's got," said Max as Mike sat staring at his wine glass.

"If we are going to do this, and I am still not one hundred percent on board. But if we are going to do this, then I need to know every single fact," he said as he rolled the glass back and forth between his thumb and forefinger.

For the first time, Max saw that old look of confidence solidly etched in his friend's face.

"Fair enough, Mike. I know what the firm means to you, and I wanted to be certain before I told you this. I'm sure they have someone inside your firm helping them, and it's why Janet was attacked. She had been looking into some of the old IPO's for me before I left, and obviously stirred the wasp's nest."

"Jesus. They sent her a message to back off because of me."

"No Mike, we've already gone over that," replied Max as he called the waiter over and ordered two espressos.

"So let's agree here and now that the culpability rests squarely on the shoulders of the Singh's, and whoever else is helping them."

Their coffees arrived, and although Max could see a load had been lifted, there was still a heaviness in the air.

"You know, Max, I got up this morning and was standing there, you know ----just standing looking into the mirror. And not only was I mesmerized with what I saw, it was like I didn't recognize the person staring back at me."

"I mean I knew it was me, but what I saw was this tired old man that I barely recognized."

"Listen Mike, you can't" ---- but Mike cut him off.

"No, let me finish," he said, "that was this morning. But now I feel that I have things back into perspective, and thank you for that. I also realize that I have been naive in my whole approach to this situation." And then his voice took on an edge that Max had not heard in some time, "It's time to take off the gloves," he said as he waved the waiter over and handed him his American Express.

"There may be implications."

"You let me worry about that," said Mike.

They walked to the door together, and then Max walked off down the sidewalk as Mike handed the doorman his valet ticket. Once Max was out of sight, Mike pulled his cell phone from his pocket and waited for the line to connect.

"Harry, it's Mike. We need to talk, you still at the office?"

The rain had let up and so Max decided to walk a while and clear his head. Before long he found himself standing in front of the emergency room entrance of the hospital. He wanted desperately to see his friend, but at the same time was afraid of what he might see.

He was feeling the weight of it all, like a lead blanket draped over him and wondered how he would get through it when he heard Thomas's voice,

And so, he took a deep breath, walked through the main entry, and headed to up to the 4th floor.

The pungent odor of disinfectant and decay made his nostrils flare as walked down the hall to the nursing station. After a brief exchange he signed in—then followed the nurse to Janet's room.

They stopped just outside the door, and he felt the softness of the nurse's fingers as she lightly touched his hand, "It'll be fine," she said. Then she turned and walked back down the hallway.

Janet was sitting propped up in her bed watching TV and did not notice him come in. At first she did not recognize him, and as he got closer he saw her recoil slightly as she grasped her hospital nightgown and pulled it tight around her neck. But when she saw it was him, the tears began to flow.

"Shush," he said softly as he sat on the edge of her bed. Then he felt his heart tearing into pieces as she sat up, put her arms around him and began sobbing uncontrollably. He gave her a few minutes and then tried to lay her back down but her fingers dug into him as she held on tight.

He felt helpless as he sat, not knowing what to do next. But then she finally let go of him. Her breathing was still coming in fits as she wiped her face and looked up at him, "Oh Max, it was so terrible, I ---,"

"It's ok, you're safe now," he said as he got up and gently put his finger to her lips.

He spotted a chair and as he pulled it over and sat down, she began to ramble, "I should have listened to you, I was so stupid, what was I thinking?"

The light was low, but he could see some bruising around her eyes, and one cheek was badly swollen. Those wounds would heal; it was the damage she had suffered on the inside that was breaking his heart.

"It could have been a lot worse, but you're a tough kid and we will get through this," he said with a wink.

She had a hold of his hand and squeezed it tight as a faint smile pried its way onto her face. "I want you to come and stay at my place for a while, at least until this all blows over. And I'm not taking no for an answer."

"Oh Max, what will the neighbors think?" she said as she let out a weak laugh. Then she flinched as she pressed her hand to her side.

At least she still had her sense of humor, and at that moment he saw a strength in her he had never seen before. "Screw em!" she said

"I will send someone to collect you as soon as the establishment says you're fit to travel."

"Send them first thing tomorrow," she said as the smile slowly left her face. "I've had enough of this place already, and there's nothing they can do for me that I can't do myself."

"Tomorrow it is," he said as he leaned down and gave her a light kiss on the forehead.

Janet felt drained as she watched him leave, and she knew she had a long road to recovery. But she would take it one day at a time. She lay back down and drifted off into a night of fitful sleep.

The vision of Janet in her hospital bed weighed heavy on Max's mind as he pulled up the zipper on his windbreaker and began to formulate his plan as he walked toward home. Thanks to Gino, he knew now who the enemy was.

It was time to take the fight to them. Thomas's words resonated inside his head once again, "If you know the enemy and know yourself, you need not fear the result of a hundred battles. If you know yourself but not the enemy, for every victory gained you will also suffer a defeat. If you know neither the enemy nor yourself, you will succumb in every battle."

CHAPTER 30

Although he felt his plan coming together, the long walk home had done little to lighten his mood. Unable to wash the memory of Janet lying in her hospital bed, he went into the kitchen and pulled two Boddingtons and a chilled mug from the fridge and then went to his bedroom and got undressed.

He popped the top of one of the beers and poured it into the mug as he settled into one of the lounge seats of the hot tub. Then he hit the button and waited for the jets to come on. He was angry, and knew that it was better to embrace it than to try and hold it down. He lay back and took a long drink of his beer as he continued to formulate his plan.

He managed a few hours of restless sleep, and by 5:00 a.m. he finally gave up and went and had a workout in the gym. By 6:30 he was dressed and ready to leave.

"Morning, Bea," he said with a smile as he saw her come shuffling into the kitchen.

"Good morning," she said. "Dare I ask what you are doing back here? And where's Phil?" She was beginning one of her interrogations.

"Don't get your apron in a knot; I just had to come back and take care of a few things." He handed her the note for Kate. "She'll know what to do."

"Fine, be that way," she replied as she poured coffee into an insulated mug.

It was a beautiful clear morning, and he could see the sun coming up over Mount Baker in his rearview mirror as he crossed the Lion's Gate Bridge and headed toward the freeway entrance. It was a perfect day for the drive. He merged onto the Sea to Sky Highway, and took it up to eighty miles an hour as he switched on a Golden Earring CD.

He had the top down and the heated seats on as he listened to their hit song, Radar Love blasting from the speakers. The highway had been rebuilt for the 2010 Winter Olympics, but was still well known for its treacherous curves and vertical embankments that had claimed countless lives over the years.

It was a special drive for him, and after about half an hour he was finally starting to relax as he cruised along listening to the music.

He wasn't paying attention to his speed, and was doing almost one hundred miles an hour when he noticed the sign ahead and had to work the brakes as he felt the force of gravity push him toward the passenger seat.

His heart began to race as he heard the tires low squeal as he came out of the curve, and was focused on the road ahead as the large SUV began to close in on him. Still unaware of the vehicle behind, he saw the straight-away ahead, and was about to open it up when the vehicle flew past him.

He took his foot off the gas, and then all of a sudden he heard the screeching of the tires and watched as smoke billowed from underneath the vehicle as it came to an abrupt stop in front of him.

He knew in an instant there was not enough time to stop, and against logic he turned the wheel, hit the gas and heard his V12 roar as he blew past them with just inches to spare. He checked his rearview mirror and let up on the gas, but was still doing over 120 miles an hour when he spotted a vacant parking lot ahead on the right.

He glanced at the speedometer and knew it would be close, and as he gently applied the brakes and aimed for the exit he felt the car go airborne as he left the highway. It seemed as though his stomach was halfway into his throat when he dropped back down and slid to a stop facing the highway.

He took a quick survey of the area, and then hit the gas and headed to the far end of the lot where the trees would provide shelter from the road and give him a safe vantage point from which to watch the exit. He had just swung the car back around and come to a stop when the HEMI Jeep Wrangler came into sight, and for a moment he thought they had missed him as they flew past the exit.

But then he saw the front of the vehicle go nose down as they slid to a stop almost directly across from him. Smoke poured from the tires as the driver reversed and the vehicle swung around and headed back toward the exit.

Despite the fifty degree temperature, Max felt the sweat begin to run off his forehead as he lay in wait. His anger was near boiling as he stayed focused on the entrance. Then he saw the SUV as it slid sideways into the parking lot and came to an abrupt stop about a football field length away.

The smell of burnt brake lining filled the air as they sat facing each other, each seemingly waiting for the other to make the first move. With the distance and tinted windows Max could not tell how many were in the vehicle, but he hoped they were all accounted for as he stared them down.

And then, as if taunting him, the SUV jumped forward a few feet and stopped.

"In the Art of War, there is no room for doubt. Remember your teachings: You have to believe in yourself. You know what you have to do, Max. Do it without doubt."

Max felt the muscles in his jaw flex, and as plumes of blue smoke swirled from the rear tires he grasped the wheel tightly and aimed the car directly at them.

The driver hesitated for a second, but then took up the challenge and began closing the distance as they accelerated toward each other in the ultimate game of chicken. There was less than a hundred feet between and Max thought for an instant they would collide, but then the SUV swerved to the left at the last second.

Max hit the brakes and spun the car round as the Jeep went into a fishtail. Then the front wheel hit a pothole and it flipped into the air. Max heard the grinding of metal and the sound of breaking glass as the Jeep cartwheeled off of the front corner and then crashed down onto its roof.

He hit the brakes and came to a stop less than twenty feet away, threw his door open, and grabbed the baton from beside his seat as he leaped out and ran toward them.

The front wheels were still spinning and the smell of gasoline permeated the air as he cautiously approached from the side. And as he slowly circled around he heard noises coming from within the wreckage. Then he spotted someone climbing out of the broken rear window.

"You're a dead man, you son-of-a-bitch," the man screamed as he pulled himself up, but as he struggled to gain his balance Max took a full swing with the baton. He heard the shaft snap into place, and drove it down with all his strength, hitting him just above the left ear with a loud crack. He was dead before he hit the ground.

It was quick, and probably far less painless than what Janet had endured, and if he had more time he would have drawn it out.

"Not today," he said to the lifeless body as he moved toward the front of the Jeep. The front side door glass had been blown out, and he could see the passenger was still strapped in and there was blood flowing from a deep gash in the side of his head. He saw smoke coming from the engine, and as he came around the driver's side, both doors opened and two men began climbing out.

The one at the front was closest, and was barely standing when Max moved in and swept his feet out from underneath him, sending him sprawling back against the vehicle and onto the ground. The other one appeared to be disoriented as he held onto the side of the vehicle. As Max moved toward him the other one reached inside his jacket and pulled out a gun.

Max saw the muzzle flash, and as he dove to the side he felt a burning sensation on his right arm as the bullet ricocheted off the bumper. The second shot went wide as Max dove to the ground, then rolled to the side, driving his heel into the base of the man's nose. Seeing the gun fall to the ground, and the blood splatter out from beneath Max's foot seemed to shake the other to his senses.

"Guess that just leaves you and me," said Max as he stood facing him.

"Fuck you, asshole," he growled as he pulled a knife from behind his back and came at him. Max could tell he was dangerous by the way he moved, and just managed to sidestep his advance as the knife caught him on the chest. He knew he'd been cut, and as he eyed the baton lying on the ground his attacker fell into a crouch, swinging the knife toward him in a deadly arc.

But this time he was ready, and as the attacker made a second swipe at him, Max dropped down low and drove his right fist up hard into his left side, breaking two of his ribs and knocking him backwards.

Max saw him spit out a wad of blood, and could see he was still dangerous as the knife hung menacingly from his right hand. The man only needed a few seconds to regroup, but he wouldn't get the chance as Max moved in and drove his right foot down hard on his left knee. He heard a loud crack as the joint snapped, and then stepped back as the victim hit the ground howling in pain. Max felt the cut on his chest, and saw the blood on his hand as he walked over and put his right foot on the man's wrist and removed the knife.

"Sounds painful," he said as he glared down at him.

He was struggling to take in air as the rib fragments dug into his side, but he still had a look of defiance as Max spoke to him in a cold and even voice, "Did you hurt my friend?"

"Go to hell," he groaned.

"Did you hurt my friend?" he said again as he leaned down and put more weight on his foot, grinding the man's wrist into the pavement.

"You have no idea who you are fucking with, asshole," he screamed as his head twisted in pain, "We're going to be coming for you. You and that skank bitch of yours will wish you had never been born."

"Actually, I do know who I'm dealing with," Max replied calmly as he took his foot off of his wrist. And for a brief second, he could see the man actually believed he was backing off. But then he saw his eyes go wide as he stepped back, and teed off on the side of his head with the force of a punter going for a field goal.

He was breathing hard as he stood back and surveyed the carnage, and for a moment he felt a twinge of conscience as he saw the smoke had now turned to flames.

"You made your choice," he said as he dragged the limp body closer to the vehicle.

It was early, and although he had not seen any traffic he hoped no one had seen the SUV on its side. He sprinted to his car and climbed in and pulled the small towel from the cubby behind his seat and stuffed it inside his shirt.

He had just gotten back onto the highway when he heard the explosion, and watched the flames climbing into the sky in the rearview mirror as the parking lot faded out of sight. Four down, he thought to himself, as he settled back into the seat. He then began chastising himself for having allowed himself to get cut.

His heart rate had dropped back to normal, but the implications of what had just happened were beginning to sink in. It was a game changer, and there was no going back. But so be it. He felt his phone vibrate on the passenger seat.

He had a missed call.

Ron answered after the second ring, "Any news on the break in?" Max asked as he opened his shirt and glanced again at the wound.

"Professional for sure, sloppy but professional," he said.

"Damage?"

"Usual, they tossed the place but nothing to speak of. I'm sure the maid can put it back together in no time. I never bothered to take prints, all it would do is make a mess," he said with a chuckle.

"Thanks, Ron, can you run a plate for me?" he said as he gave him the number of the SUV.

"I'll be back in town by early afternoon, so see what you can do."

"Anything I need to know," he asked.

"I'll fill you in later. In the meantime, I need you to swing by the hospital and pick up Janet. Let her get whatever she needs from home and then take her back to my place."

"Starting to become a habit, this collecting of women," Ron replied with a chuckle.

CHAPTER 31

Less than an hour later he pulled into Pemberton, and then turned off the main street and headed down a side road until he came upon a nondescript, overgrown driveway. It had been almost a year since he had visited the old farm, and he felt a lump begin to form in his throat as he started down the long and winding drive.

The pollen began to tickle his nose as it whirled around inside the car and he could feel the tall grass as it brushed gently against the side of the car before coming to a stop in front of the old house. He cut the engine and sat quietly for a moment as he envisioned his mother, riding up to the house on her buckskin mare with a big smile on her face as she waved down at them.

He and his father had moved out shortly after she died, and he had been coming up on a regular basis to make sure it was cared for. But with the sudden loss of his father, he had stopped coming. His mother had loved this place, and it would have broken her heart to see it in such disrepair. A sudden wave of guilt washed over him.

He shook it off because for now he had work to do. He

climbed out of the car. He was alone, but he looked around out of habit and then walked around the side of the house. Making his way to the small barn at the back, he finally stopped in front of a small door off to the side.

He fished a key from his pocket and opened the padlock, and then slid back the bolt and slipped inside. He stood for a moment and let his eyes adjust to the near darkness as he slowly looked around. Memories and emotion collided together all at once as he reflected on his years spent here as a child. Then he smiled as he thought about the night he had lost his virginity to Janice in the loft above.

"How times change," he murmured as he walked over to the far corner, took the broom and swept away the straw, exposing a hatch door in the floor in the middle of the room. He knelt down and brushed away the last of it by hand, and then dialed the combination into the lock and hefted up the steel door.

He had forgotten how heavy it was, and groaned under the weight as he rested it back onto the floor and peered into the darkness below. He reached in and fished around until he finally found the switch and turned on the lights. He could smell the mold and decay as he climbed down the stairs into the old cellar, and realized there must have been a leak as the floor was now wet and damp.

The previous owners had been part of the survivalist movement during the 1970's, and had built it as a bomb shelter in preparation of a nuclear war. His family had only ever used it as a root cellar, but later on he found it useful as a place to store his weapons and other such valuables he needed to keep safe.

He took an old fishing spear off the shelf, and brushed away the cobwebs as he walked over to where he had stored the black waterproof duffel. It was his "Go Bag", and was what he had come for. He pulled back the zipper and opened it, and after carefully checking the contents he closed it back up again.

He felt a sharp pain in his chest as he dropped the door back in place, and had to take a deep breath as he reset the lock. There was nothing he could do about it now. He spread the straw around, and then closed the door behind him and retraced his steps back to the car.

He had been careful to make sure the bag would not only fit into the tiny trunk of his car, but also into the concealed compartment in his plane. And although the size limited what he could fit into it, he had what he needed.

He made good time on the way back to Vancouver, and was passing the parking area when he noticed the two marked police cars, an unmarked sedan and an ambulance all parked beside the SUV. The fire had been extinguished, but there was yellow crime scene taped draped around the area, so it was obvious they had figured out it was more than just an accident.

The idea of the ambulance sitting there somehow struck him funny, and he began to laugh at the thought of them pulling out one of the charred bodies and checking for a pulse. But his mood soon began to swing as he thought of Gino's ominous warning, "Cross that threshold and everything changes."

It was late afternoon and the sun was already beginning to set when he wheeled the car into the underground and pulled to a stop in one of his private stalls by the elevator. His spots were secured from the rest of the parking, and he waited until the garage door closed behind him before taking the bag from the trunk and climbing into the elevator.

He headed straight to the gym, where he secured the bag, and then headed into his bedroom to check on his wound and get out of his bloodied clothes. The cut wasn't very deep, and after cleaning it with hydrogen peroxide he applied several steri-strips, put on a waterproof bandage and hopped into the shower.

He was feeling amazingly well for what he had been through, and after about ten minutes of letting the water wash away the day, he threw on a pair of sweats, and went looking for Kate. He finally found her sitting on one of the Persian rugs in his living room with a dozen thick file folders arranged neatly around her as she sat reading.

"You got my message, I see," he said with a broad grin.

"I did," she replied happily as she got up and gave him a hug, then quickly stepped back as her cheeks slumped, "Any word on Janet?"

"As a matter of fact, I went to see her last night. She actually looked pretty good. And was in pretty good spirits too."

"In fact, she should have been here by now," he said as he went and sat down cross-legged beside the files.

"There's more than you think," she said when she saw him looking at her notes.

"I figured as much," he replied as he thumbed through one of the folders.

"You think it's a good thing? I think it's kind of depressing."

"Not at all, my dear," he replied as he did his best Chinese impression. "Remember Sun Tzu ---'Opportunities multiply as they are seized,' and we are going to seize some serious opportunities here."

"Am I missing something?"

"Our guests have arrived," he shouted as he sprinted out of the room.

Max grabbed for the door, and then they all stopped when they heard Kate burst into tears. "Oh my god, you poor thing," she cried as she wrapped Janet into her arms.

"Easy girl, I'm the injured one here," said Janet as she looked over at Max.

"Umm, excuse me ladies, but could we take this out of the hall," said Ron, as he stood patiently holding two large suitcases.

Max led them to the bedroom that Janet would be staying in, and once Ron set her bags down they left them to get settled and headed out onto the terrace. Max went to the fridge under the bar and got out two beers while Ron went and took a seat.

"You wouldn't just happen to have taken a trip to Pemberton today, would you?" asked Ron as Max stood lighting one of the overhead heaters.

"Actually I did," he replied as a wry grin spread across his face. "Why?"

"Well, gee now counselor, why do you suppose?" he said as he leaned back in his chair and threw his massive arms out to the side. "I ---," but he stopped mid-sentence as he watched the girls come through the doorway.

Max passed them each a blanket as he looked over at Ron, "C'mon give me a hand to bring some drinks to these fine ladies."

"Ladies, I am at your service," Ron said as he stood.

"Pinot Gris," said Janet.

"I'll have one of those Boddington beers," said Kate as she wrapped the blanket in close around her.

"Coming right up," With a snort, Max headed to the bar.

Max poured the beer, and then left to check on Beatrice and found her in the kitchen preparing a feast of baked Chilean corn pies, empanadas and broiled chicken. But he didn't get far before she stopped him, "You take care of those precious young ladies out there, and leave this to me." "Yes, mother," he replied respectfully.

"And bring them back inside; it's far too cold out there for them on a night like tonight." And be in the dining room in twenty minutes," he heard her say as he stopped and turned back around.

He went over and gave her a kiss on the cheek. "I don't know what I'd do without you."

"You'd be lost, now out!" she said as she waved him off.

He had noticed Janet was moving around quite well, and she looked ten times better than she had just a few hours earlier. It made him feel good to see the tears of laughter rolling down her cheeks as Ron recounted some of the stories of when he was an RCMP officer. He was in the middle of a story Max had heard many times before, when he noticed the time and quickly jumped up and announced it was supper time.

The dining room quickly fell quiet as they dove into their meal, and it wasn't until they had wiped the last from their plates that Max began rapping his knife alongside this wine glass.

It had been an emotional struggle for him over dinner, but he needed to share the truth with his friends about what had happened. And to some degree, the plan he had mapped out since his run-in on the highway earlier that day.

"So are you telling us that what happened to Janet is all because of the job we are doing for Michael?" asked Kate as she tossed her napkin down onto her plate. Max was about to answer but Janet cut him off before he had a chance.

"You can't blame any of this on Max, Kate. I knew, or should have known, what I was getting myself into," she said slowly as she pushed a few beans around her plate with her knife.

"Max warned me to drop it, but I just couldn't let it go."

"Oh, I see. So the end justifies the means, is that it?"

"Ladies, if I may interject," said Ron. He had been leaning on the back legs of his chair, and it fell forward with a loud thud as a serious look came over his face. "There is no one to blame, other than those who did this terrible thing. And it is now up to us to set it right," he said.

"And I am happy to say, Max has already begun the process. You could even call it, the road to redemption," he said and then broke out laughing.

"I'm sorry, but just what's so funny," said Kate as she reached over and squeezed Janet's hand.

Max felt his stomach tighten as he glared over at Ron, but he knew there was no stopping him now. And in any case, they were going to find out sooner or later.

The room was quiet as Ron gave them an animated version of what had happened on the highway earlier that day, and by the time he had finished Max was expecting the worst. But then Janet slowly got up and walked around the table and stood beside him, and to his surprise she threw her arms around him and gave him a soft kiss on the cheek.

"My hero," was all she said and then slowly walked back to her chair and sat back down, "May justice be swift and sure," she said, raising her glass.

"An eye for an eye," agreed Kate.

"Kim Pei," shouted Ron, as they emptied their glasses.

The girls began to clear the table and Max and Ron headed into the game room to discuss his plans.

"Have a seat," he said, as he gestured to the bar and went and took two snifters from the shelf, pouring two generous shots of Hennessy.

"Salud," he said as he passed one to Ron.

The glass disappeared inside Ron's hand, and then his face went serious as he sat and stared across at Max. "Before we get started, I need you to come clean with me on a few things, my friend."

It was a conversation Max had been expecting for some time, "Okay, what's on your mind," big man."

"Well, for starters you can fill me in on what happened when you left the firm, and how in the hell you ended up being able to afford a place like this," he replied without taking his gaze off his friend.

"I wondered when this was going to come up," sighed Max as he got up and walked over to the window. Ron was his best friend, and he had a right to know. In fact, it had been bothering him that he had kept such a big part of his life a secret for so long.

"It's a long story," he said sheepishly as he stared at his reflection in the window. But he finally went and sat back down, and by the time he had finished his story it was the first time he had seen his friend speechless.

"I hope you can appreciate why I have not told you this before. I mean, it took me a long time to adjust to it all myself. And when I lost Dad, well --you know what happened after that."

Ron sat there staring back for a long while before he finally spoke, "Brother, I do understand. And you know how sorry I am about your father, but when this is all over you and I are going to talk."

A weight was lifted, and he could not believe how much lighter he felt as he sat looking back at his friend, "I'd prefer to have the discussion now," replied Max as he took the bottle and topped up their glasses. "I want you to come to work with me full time, starting right now. We can discuss your over billing rate later, meanwhile, we have work to do."

"Done," replied Ron as he thrust out his hand.

"Now, do you have a current passport," replied Max as he shook the big man's hand.

"Yes, I do, and where are we headed?" he asked grinning.

"Get your summer clothes together and bring along your grab bag. We are heading to Nassau first thing."

"What time you want me here?"

"Be here by six am, we will have breakfast in the air."

They shook hands again, and Ron was almost at the door before Max called him back.

"This may get ugly, and more people will likely get killed before it's over. So you can tell me no and I won't think any less of you."

Ron just looked back at him and snorted, "Brother, I'm in it all the way. You can give me all the details in the morning. Now, I'd like to be able to stay and help you with the ladies but that's a job you will have to tend to all on your own."

Max stood quietly and watched Beatrice directing traffic as Kate and Janet finished cleaning up the kitchen and putting away the last of the dishes. The activity in the kitchen made him feel like he had a family again. But all of a sudden, he found himself thinking about the near miss he had with Ken in Nassau and he worried that they were all ok.

He was still standing in the entry when Beatrice declared the kitchen a work free zone. Kate picked up the half full bottle of wine still sitting on the counter and was about to walk out when she noticed Max.

"Hello boss," she said with a smile and a slight slur in her voice. "Ladies," he replied with a broad grin.

"So what do we do now?" asked Janet as the smile he loved so much crept back into her face.

"Now, we go and sit and have a very quick chat about our upcoming trip," he said as he gestured for them to follow.

"Nassau," Janet said with a mixture of excitement and trepidation. "I don't know if I am able to."

"Of course you are. And besides, I need your help," he said with finality. "I can't possibly leave either of you here."

"Ok then, you're the boss," she replied as she looked over at Kate and winked her approval. He could see she had a glow on, and hoped that it wasn't the booze talking when Kate cut in.

"I'm not going anywhere until you finish explaining just exactly what is going on, and what we are getting ourselves into. And, I am not doing no red eye to the Bahamas," she said defiantly.

Max didn't have any more time to explain; he felt like he hadn't slept in days and needed to get to bed, "Well, first of all we are not flying commercial, we are on the FB and T private jet." And then he got up and headed for the door.

"And secondly," he said as he stopped and turned around. "At last count, I am still your boss and I don't need to explain anything. Be ready to leave here at six a.m. Pack whatever you have that will be comfortable for the warmer climes. We'll buy whatever else you need once we get there."

CHAPTER 32

Raj lay motionless on the bed, his head pounding as he tried to pry his tongue off the roof of his mouth. It was swollen and as dry as sandpaper as he tried to work up enough saliva to get it moving. It had been a marathon party session with his girls since they had left the nightclub, and as he struggled through the fog, snippets of the evening slowly began flashing through his mind.

He could feel his heart pumping deep in the back of his chest, and with every beat he felt as if his skull would split in two. His eyes burned, and as he pushed himself into a seated position he spotted the half empty bottle on the nightstand.

He had been spiraling out of control ever since the SEC had started closing in, and last night was the topper of all nights. He squinted through the slits in his eyes. He had to get up, but as he swung his feet over the edge of the bed the room began to spin and he had to lie back down.

He waited a few minutes, and then managed to stagger into the bathroom where he took three Advil from the cabinet, cupped his hand under the faucet, and swallowed them down.

He steadied himself under the head of the shower with his palms pressed against the wall, and waited for his head to clear as the steaming hot water beat down on the back of his neck.

He knew he was late, and began cursing as he slowly put on his pants and began buttoning his shirt. He needed to find his phone, but a quick search came up empty so he picked up the house phone and dialed his number. He heard the familiar ring echoing from under the bed, and got on his hands and knees and fished around until he finally found it.

After scrolling through the missed calls and a dozen text messages he called Harmel back, and stated that he would deal with whatever the crisis was later.

"Dude, where the fuck have you been?" said Harmel as Raj pulled the phone away from his ear and cringed.

"Stop shouting for Christ sakes," he replied as he got up and began pacing around the room. "What's the problem? You've called me a hundred times already."

"It's bad, Raj, I don't know who this lawyer asshole is, but whoever it is, it ain't good. You hear what I'm saying?"

"No, I don't," he shouted back in frustration. "And if you have a point, make it for christ sakes." He went and took a cold beer from the fridge and held it up against his forehead in an attempt to stop the throbbing.

"Amir, Dipen, Jay and Ramesh, they're all dead," said Harmel.

"What do you mean dead? They were supposed to be keeping an eye on the lawyer!"

"That's just it, they were following him to Whistler when Dipen called and said they had him cornered in a parking lot. The next thing I hear, the cops found his Jeep upside down, all burned up and they are all dead."

Raj hung up the phone and felt the room begin to close in around him as he broke out in a cold sweat. They had come too far. No, he had come too far for this to blow up now, and he knew he was on thin ice with James and had to get it back on track. Or was James just using him now, and then planning on terminating him like he had ordered him to do with the others?

He sat back on the bed and swiped the screen on his phone after the third ring, "I want you to get your boys together and go to Nassau," said the voice.

"I can't, I have a problem here that I need to take care of," replied Raj in a defiant tone.

"You listen to me asshole, and listen carefully. I am well aware of your problem. We lost four good men because of you, and now we have even bigger problems because you are incapable of following even the simplest of instructions."

Raj was on edge, and was about to cut him off as he listened to the miserable son of a bitch ramble on, but knew he would just have to bide his time until it was over. Raj had become rich during their short and often rocky relationship, but he saw it just the opposite. And the fact that he reminded him of it on a regular basis just pissed him off. As far as he was concerned, if it wasn't for him the arrogant prick wouldn't have been able to pull off any of the deals.

But their business would soon be coming to an end, and once he got his money he would take care of him once and for all.

"Fine, you're so fucking smart you tell me what happened," he replied, and then immediately regretted having lost his temper.

There was a long silence and when the voice came back, it

sent a shiver through his entire body, "Be careful Raj, you just lost two cousins today. I would hate to see anything happen to one of those lovely sisters of yours."

"You stay the fuck away from my family," he shouted into the phone. If anything happens ---" but he was cut off before he could finish.

"That's up to you now, isn't it? In a few days you will have more money than even you could ever piss away, so just drop the drama and do what you are told."

"Fine, you're right," replied Raj, choking on every word. "What do you need me to do?"

CHAPTER 33

Max could hear Ron's infectious laugh rolling down the hall as he headed toward the kitchen, and then stopped short as he took in the sight of his newly formed team.

"Little too long in the saddle, counselor?" Ron asked as they all turned and stared at him. "Come on in and join the party."

Janet and Kate sat nursing their coffees while Beatrice, despite his instructions to the contrary had put on quite a spread. "Looks like we're having breakfast here after all," he said, trying his best not to show his annoyance.

He had to admit, the food smelled amazing and the grumbling in his stomach told him it was probably a good idea as he scooped a pile of eggs and chorizo onto his plate. Everyone seemed to be in good spirits, and he was relieved to see Janet doing so well. She was moving about more easily, and the pain in her side was obviously a lot better. He watched her dig into her breakfast.

They finished eating and were about to clear the table when Beatrice put a stop to it and told them all to clear out of her kitchen. Max gave her a peck on the cheek as she shooed him out, but then a stern look came over her face as she stared up at him,

"You take care of that precious cargo of yours and come back quick, ok?"

"Affirmative," he said as he leaned down, gave her a hug, then headed for the door. Ron had loaded the luggage onto the cart Max kept in the storage room beside the elevator, and was pushing it down the hall when Max turned around and ran back inside. He emerged moments later with his go bag slung over his shoulder, and then hustled to catch up to Ron as he hefted the bag on top of the suitcases.

"Purely precautionary," he said, trying to make light of the situation. "Whatever," replied Ron as continued toward the elevator.

He was expecting some commentary from the girls but they seemed excited to be leaving the rain, and seemed to be accepting of whatever the trip had in store.

The traffic was light, and despite their delay due to the extravagant breakfast they arrived at the FBO only a few minutes behind schedule. The baggage handler unloaded the car and took the cart directly to the plane as Max went and found Captain Stebbings. He had just completed his weather check and was coming out of the pilots' lounge when he noticed Max and came over to greet them.

"How are we looking?" Max asked as they shook hands.

"We're good to go, and there are no other flights on deck so we can leave as soon as everyone is on board."

"How about the weather?" asked Max.

"We have some thunderstorms just off the coast of Florida, but we should be above them so I expect a smooth ride."

The only one of the group, aside from Max, that had ever flown privately was Ron. And that had been a long time ago when he had joined Max and his father on a trip to Los Angeles to drop off one of his bosses' light jets and pick up a King Air. So when they climbed on board the Falcon he had to smile as he watched the look on their faces.

The cabin attendant introduced himself as Kevin, and seemed competent as he helped the ladies take their seats and then directed Ron to one near the sofa that would provide him a little extra legroom.

Max was thinking about the situation in Nassau when he felt the engines come to life. He smiled as he looked across and saw the expression of pure exhilaration light up Janet's face. It was a sensation only a handful of people in the world would ever know, and it gave him a great sense of satisfaction that he could share it with those so close to him.

But the thought vanished as quickly as it had come as he began thinking about the storm they were about to fly into.

They were just twenty minutes into the flight and Captain Stebbings had leveled them off at 39,000 feet when Kevin got up and came back to offer breakfast.

"I don't know about the rest of you, but I am stuffed," sighed Kate. "I could go for a coffee and one of those light pastries."

Janet broke out laughing, and then patted her tummy, "Yep, me too. I'll take one of those light pastries as well."

There was still much Max needed to discuss with them, but he knew it was going to get crazy very soon and decided it would be better to let them rest and enjoy the ride. And with the coffee and cakes duly devoured, he reclined his chair and was sound asleep less than five minutes later.

He never noticed that their air speed had dropped, or that the plane's nose had dipped severely until he was jolted awake when he felt himself being thrown forward in his seat. At first he was confused and thought he was just having another nightmare. But he soon realized they were in real trouble when he saw Kevin slumped over in his seat with his head hard up against the fridge in the galley.

It was happening in real time, and, as he ripped up the clasp on his seat belt, the plane pitched steeper into its dive. He felt himself falling and quickly spread his legs apart and dropped to the floor as he struggled against the ever-increasing G-Force as the plane picked up speed.

He was fighting hard to maintain his balance as he moved toward the cockpit. Ron was in a rear facing seat and had not felt the plane pitch. As Max passed, he gave him a rough shove on his shoulder, "We got trouble," he shouted as he ripped open the cabin door.

Then his heart began to race when he saw both the pilot and co-pilot slumped against their seatbelts.

"No shit," replied Ron as he leaned hard against the bulkhead behind him.

The plane was now pitched at a dangerous angle, and he saw the ground approaching at a terrifying speed. This made it difficult for him to maneuver as he began working to free the pilot from his seat. A quick look at the altimeter told him they didn't have much time. He shot a glance backwards and saw Ron braced up against the doorjamb.

"Get him out of his seat, and now," he yelled as he unbuckled the captain's seat belt.

"You got it," said Ron as he leaned into the cockpit and grabbed a hold of Stebbing's jacket with his right hand. And in one swift motion, he hoisted him out of his seat and nearly knocked his head off as he dragged him out of the cockpit.

Max felt a sharp pain as he hit the side of the cockpit door, and it took him a moment to catch his breath as he dropped himself into the empty seat. He fought his instincts to just take a hold of the yoke and pull up as he scanned the instruments, but after a few seconds he had his bearings and took control of the plane.

Grateful once again for his pal's sheer strength and ability to remain calm when others would be losing their minds, he thought about how things might have turned out had he not been here. And although he had a decent amount of hours in similar planes, the Falcon was a unique bird that required a particular amount of finesse to fly. He knew a single wrong move could turn an already desperate situation into a sure disaster.

"Am I correct in assuming you can fly this thing?" asked Ron, as he maneuvered himself back into the cockpit.

"Two minutes and counting," said Max as he slowly advanced power and brought their airspeed back to an even 340 knots.

Seeing the look on Max's face Ron just grinned, "Hey, you don't have to tell me twice," he said as he began pulling the copilot out of his seat. "Give me a minute and I'll be back up here to join you," he said as he dragged him into the back.

Aside from having dropped to almost 15,000 feet, the plane seemed to be operating perfectly, but they were far from being out of danger. They had passed through layers of restricted airspace and needed to get in contact with the nearest air traffic control and back up to altitude.

Max put on the headset and instantly heard an agitated voice coming through, "Repeat, this is Portland air traffic control calling unidentified jet cruising at fifteen thousand feet, please identify."

"This is Falcon 900 C6FBT en route to NAS, Nassau Bahamas requesting permission to climb to four one thousand; over."

"C6FBT can you confirm status as we have you in unauthorized and heavy airspace,"

"Roger that, we hit a bad bit of turbulence and had to make a rapid descent; over."

"C6FBT you are cleared for four one thousand; please advise if you are still experiencing heavy turbulence."

"Negative, must have been a microburst. Sorry about that, Portland. Will level off at four one thousand, C6FBT out."

When he finished, Max turned off the communication microphone and then looked over at Ron as he maneuvered his huge frame into the rather confined space.

"All good?" he asked as he glanced around the cockpit.

"We're straight," said Max as he pushed his seat back and stretched his legs.

"What's the status in the rear?"

"The girls are a little shaken to say the least, but I gotta say they got some salt."

"Crew?"

"Sleeping like babies, Janet is taking care of them."

Max did a quick system check and then sat back for a moment as his heart rate returned to normal. He knew that they had been dealing with a formidable adversary, but this changed everything. Someone within their own camp was working against them, and he needed to find out who.

No one but Mike and the FBO staff knew their schedule, and although he couldn't fathom the possibility that Mike was involved, neither could he rule it out.

"Someone has been following our every move," he said to Ron as he pulled his headset off.

"Okay," he replied, staring straight ahead. "Who?"

"Not a fucking clue. No one knew our schedule except those of us on the plane--and Mike."

"And the staff at the airport?" said Ron, almost in defense of Mike.

"The FBO? No, they wouldn't have had enough time. I only confirmed with the captain an hour before flight time that we were leaving and how many would be on board. It has to be someone in the firm."

"How can you rule out the flight crew?" he asked. But then he blushed, "Never mind, I get it. They would not knowingly dose themselves. So who is it?"

"That's just it, I have no idea, but I feel we are coming down to the wire. I thought I had it all figured out, at least up until now." He threw his head back and ran his hands through his thick hair.

"And now…" Ron asked, trying to see where he was going with this.

"Now we are back to fucking square one."

"All warfare is based on deception. When we are able to attack, we must seem unable; when using our forces, we must appear inactive; when we are near, we must make the enemy think we are far away; when far away, we must make him believe we are near," said Ron.

Max could not help himself as he broke out laughing, to the point he began to choke, "Sun Tzu?" Are you kidding me," he said between fits of laughter.

"Hey, you're the grand master that's been preaching this crap to me for years now," he replied in a very serious tone. "Think about it, we need to set the trap, and now is the only time you can do it with impunity."

Max leaned forward, and stared back at Ron for a few seconds and then hit the autopilot, "I'll be back in a minute." He pushed himself out of the seat and then left the cockpit.

Once inside the cabin he saw Janet kneeling beside the captain; he was laid out on the floor and was still out cold. She had his head resting on a pillow and was wiping his face with a cloth. Kate was sitting beside the co-pilot who appeared to be semi-conscious, but his face was void of color.

"Everything ok back here?" he asked as he went to his pack and pulled out his satellite phone.

"Peachy," they said simultaneously, and then stared at each other as the reality of the situation finally hit home.

"Go," said Janet, "do what you have to do, we got this covered."

He had no idea from where their resolve was manifesting, but who was he to question it? He headed back into the cockpit and got himself settled behind the controls.

"You know, Ron, sometimes I underestimate you," he said as he pulled the Sat phone from the pouch and powered it up.

"You're right, we'll never be in a position like this again. And I'm thankful for that," Ron said.

Max dialed a number into the phone. "Deception, it shall be our ally at forty one thousand feet." He waited impatiently as he heard the delayed ring tone, and then static as a voice came on the other end of the line, "Mike, it's Max."

"Max, where are you? I thought you were flying to Nassau today?" he replied sounding confused.

"We are, but we had a little problem along the way," Max fired back. "Someone doped the crew, and had Beatrice not fed us all breakfast before we left, we'd be splattered halfway across Oregon by now."

"Jesus, Max, this is getting out of control. I wish to god I never heard of FB and fucking T, or Feinstein for that matter," he spat back into the phone.

Mike was clearly upset, and he heard genuine concern in his voice, but he had to be certain as he replied coldly, "Who else knew?"

"What?"

"Who else besides you knew?"

There was a deadness on the line from the delay of the satellite link, and after what seemed an eternity he heard Mike's voice, empty and hollow as he came back on, "You're wrong, Max. I understand how you must feel and respect that you cannot afford to trust anyone, but I'm not the enemy and I have no idea who is."

Max felt himself flush with shame. "I know, Mike, but you got to see it from our perspective. Not a lot of options up here and no room for mistakes," he replied.

"Jesus Max, whatever. Enough already, it's time to bail."

"Too late now; the die has been cast. If I'm right, we can fly into Governor's Harbour in Eleuthera undetected and take the ferry to Harbour Island. The girls will be safe there, and it will give Ron and me time to do what we have to in Nassau. In the meantime, I need to know when you are planning on pulling the trigger on the consolidation of the banks."

"We haven't. And if it helps, I can easily delay it."

"That's good news. Delay it until you hear otherwise from me," replied Max as he felt himself begin to breathe easier.

"You take care of yourself, and do what you have to do," said Mike. "I'll find the fucker that's been selling us out."

Max put his headset back on and began navigating his way through the appropriate channels to change their destination from Nassau International to Governors Harbour. After half an hour he had success, entered the new coordinates into the GPS and let the autopilot take them up to 45,000 feet where he knew it would be a smooth ride.

"Keep an eye on her, will you? I'm going to check on the crew," he said to Ron as he pushed himself back and got out of the seat.

"Right," chuckled Ron as he just sat staring at the instruments in front of him. "Just don't get too comfortable back there."

As he stepped back into the cabin, he was relieved to see both Captain Stebbings and the co-pilot sitting upright, but looking a lot worse for wear. Kate was standing in the galley making coffee and Janet was seated next to Stebbings holding a wet towel.

"Is everything ok up front?" she asked in a weary voice.

"It's not been your best week, has it," he replied as he went and sat across from her.

"No, it hasn't," she said as she looked up at him through bloodshot eyes. He could tell she had been crying but was putting on a brave face not to show it.

"Who's flying the plane?" croaked Captain Stebbings as he tried desperately to keep his eyes open.

"Not to worry, Captain, I have plenty of hours under my belt, and enough in one of these babies to get us to where we need to go." He placed his hand on the man's shoulder and gave it a firm squeeze.

"If you get your sea legs back, you come and join me," he said. And then nodded at Janet to join him as he headed back toward the cockpit.

"So what's the verdict," he asked once he got settled into his seat and she had closed the door behind her.

"I am sure it was in the food, and it's a good thing we never ate is all I can say," she said as she wrapped her arms around herself.

"I guess we owe Beatrice a bonus when we get back. Can you bring us some coffee, and Janet ----, pour yourself a scotch, would you?"

"Will do, boss, or umm, Captain," she mumbled as she left the cabin.

"So now what?" Ron asked as he stared out the window.

"Now, we wait and see how all this unfolds." He pulled a thick binder from the captain's flight bag and looked up the chart for the Governor's Harbour Airport.

CHAPTER 34

The crystal blue waters of the Exuma Sound came into view as they descended to 15,000 feet. The captain and co-pilot were still drowsy, and aside from skull-splitting headaches the effects of the drugs seemed to be wearing off. The flight attendant however, was still unconscious and they were unsure of his condition.

They continued their descent, and as they broke through the clouds the island came into view, A few minutes later Max had the runway in sight. The islands were notorious for strong crosswinds, but Max managed a smooth landing as he set the jet down onto the runway and deployed the reverse thrusters.

He used the full extent of the runway, and when they finally came to a stop he turned and taxied them back to the small but colorful customs and immigration building.

"Ron, can you go back and open the door so we can all set foot on good old terra firma?"

"Sounds good to me," he said as he pried himself out of the seat and exited the cockpit.

Max sat back and took a long deep breath as he checked the

instruments and did his best to make sure he ran it through the proper shut down procedures. But what he was more concerned about was the fact that someone from within the firm had sold them out. And he felt more vulnerable than ever; he knew they were now totally on their own.

After a few minutes the customs and immigration officer arrived, along with a local medic and climbed on board. With a little help, Captain Stebbings and the copilot managed to exit the plane on their own, but the attendant needed to be carried off and was placed in a wheel chair.

After a brief debate inside, it was decided that a king air medevac would take the three of them to Nassau to be checked out at the private hospital, and the rest would take a taxi over to the docks.

Ron and Max waited as a ground worker unloaded their luggage and placed it on a trolley while the girls helped the crew through customs. Max kept an eye on his duffel as they wheeled it up to the desk, and was relieved the officers didn't bother to check their bags as they stamped their passports and passed them through.

Once processed, they took the crew and went into the waiting area and got them seated while the medic did a more thorough check of his patients.

"Sounds like I owe you a debt of gratitude," said Captain Stebbings hoarsely as Max sat beside him.

"Actually, you owe it to my maid," he replied with a broad grin.

"Excuse me?"

Max could see he was still suffering from the effects of whatever drugs they had ingested and decided to let it go "Another time, Captain. Meantime, you get some rest. I have made arrangements for the plane to be secured and it will be here waiting for you once you recover."

"Godspeed, son," he said weakly as he made a futile attempt to shake his hand.

You got that right, Max thought, as he led everyone out of the building and over to one of the old taxi vans. Once their luggage was loaded they climbed into the back and headed for the docks only a few miles away. Everyone was exhausted, and little was said until they reached the water taxi, and after a fifteen minute ride across the water they landed on Harbour Island.

"My god, did we crash and land in heaven," Janet cried as she looked out over the pristine waters and then up at the quaint little buildings along the harbor.

"Close," replied Max as he and Ron hoisted their bags and sauntered down the dock toward the dirt road that ran along the harbor. Once on the road they walked over to an area reserved for golf carts and Max led them up to two carts named: "Don't mess with Texas."

"What's with the Texas deal?" asked Ron as he stood towering over the roof of the cart.

"A friend of mine from Texas has a home here that he said I can use anytime I want," explained Max as they loaded their bags onto the cart with the small cargo deck.

"Ron, you and the ladies ride in the four-seater, and I will lead in the working car," he said as he climbed into his cart.

They took a short bumpy five-minute ride along the rough dirt road to the top of a hill in the center of the island, and then entered a small winding drive that took them to a house with wrap-around verandahs and spectacular views of the beach and ocean.

"Hill House," said Kate as she looked at the hand-carved wooden sign beside the double French doors.

"Makes sense to me," chuckled Ron as he grabbed the bags and headed for the stairs. Max followed with the rest, and then pulled a key from his packsack and opened up the door, motioning for everyone to enter as he stepped inside.

Janet continued straight to the doors at the other end of the room, then stood motionless as she looked out over the Atlantic and then began softly sobbing. Kate dropped her bag, ran over and put her arms around her, and did the best she could to comfort her.

"It's so---so beautiful," Janet stuttered through her tears, I didn't think I'd even survive the attack."

"It gets better," replied Max with a little theatrics as he went and opened up the double doors, allowing the fresh salt breeze to blow through.

"I don't know about you all, but I think we deserve the rest of the day off," he said as he went into the kitchen and returned moments later with a bucket of ice cubes and some limes.

"Gin and tonics, and it's not a question," he said as he walked behind the bar and began mixing.

"Come on, ladies, it wasn't a question." He motioned for them to join him.

Kate took note that Max seemed to know his way around the place pretty well as he opened up a cupboard and filled a bowl with mixed nuts.

"I noticed a picture of Phil on the wall," said Kate as she pressed the glass up against her temple.

"I spent a lot of time here after my dad passed," said Max as he led her out onto the porch and into one of the hammocks.

"I don't know about you guys, but I could use a swim," said Ron as he stood staring down at the beach below.

"I think I'll join you," said Janet, as she looked over at Kate. "Coming?"

"I'll be there in a few minutes; I just want to sit and enjoy the view for a bit."

"Just follow the path to the beach, you can't get lost." Max looked over and smiled. "But watch out for the foot fuckers."

"The what-fuckers?" said Janet with a giggle.

"The grass here has little round thorns that can be very painful on bare feet. But don't worry, you'll know them when you see them. Just stay on the path."

"Okay, see you there," she replied with a renewed sense of vigor in her voice as she went to her bedroom and changed. Max got up and poured himself another drink and then came back and took a seat beside Kate, "Think I'll pass on the swim and just take a shower and hang out here."

"Suit yourself."

It had been a long day, hell--a long month, she thought, as she went back inside in search of a bottle of water. She was tired, but at the same time had not felt this alive in longer than she cared to remember. Maybe it was the near death experience on the plane, or just the events of the past few days that had her senses tingling. Whatever it was, she was experiencing feelings and sensations that needed attention.

Relieved that she was finally alone, she reached inside her blouse and with one quick flip of her thumb and forefinger opened the clasp of her bra and headed to her room. Throwing caution to the wind, she tossed it onto the bed and then stepped out of her shorts and headed toward the corner bedroom.

She was breathing rapidly, and felt a shortness of breath when she heard the sound of the shower coming from outside. She stopped for a moment, and considered a retreat as her heart drummed against her temples. Her mind was alive with a thousand reasons why she should turn around, "Not this time," she said as she padded through his bedroom and onto the porch.

As she stood staring at the water wash over his broad shoulders she flushed away any last lingering doubts and walked up behind him.

"Got room in here for one more," she whispered as she gently placed her hand on his thigh.

Feeling her touch, Max spun around, almost knocked her over, and seeing her standing there in front of him he froze. It wasn't like he hadn't thought about it, but good sense and judgment had always prevailed. Now, here she was and before he knew it, he pulled her in close and kissed her deeply as the water poured down over them.

"It's been long overdue," she said as she blinked away the water and smiled up at him.

"Clearly a mistake," he groaned as he lifted her into his arms and slid inside her in one effortless motion.

The smell of her perfume tasted bitter on his tongue as he kissed her neck; and he could feel her legs tense as she wrapped them tighter around him and they rocked back and forth. It felt good, but his mind was still firing off warning signals. All of a sudden he felt her body shudder.

He could feel the goosebumps on her arms, and as she arched her back and moaned, he felt himself let go and his entire body shook as they fell back onto the wooden seat.

She could hear her inner voice rattling around in her head

telling her it was all wrong, but she managed to shut it out for just a few more moments as she just sat there straddling him. As the seconds ticked by she felt herself basking in the warmth of the salt air as the blood pulsed through her overheated veins.

"I was never known for my great timing," she said as he brushed aside a long strand of hair that dripped down over her left eye.

"We'll figure it out," he replied as she pulled his face down into her breasts and rested her chin on his head.

What felt like an eternity lasted only a few precious moments before she gently pushed back, and then she felt him slip out as she stood and smiled down at him. He was sitting staring back up at her, searching for something to say when she gently touched her finger to his lips, "No illusions," she whispered.

And without another word, she turned around and let the shower wash over her. Then, as quickly as she had appeared she picked up a towel and left without turning around.

"And then she was gone," he said quietly as the smell of her still lingered around him. He stood naked and alone in the middle of his bedroom for a few minutes, contemplating what had just happened. Things were complicated enough already, and as much as he wanted it he knew this would be a one-time affair. He pulled on a pair of shorts and a T-shirt, and headed back to the living room.

Finding himself alone, he slid into one of the oversized hammocks and was soon dozing to an Adele tune coming from the portable Bose sound system when the sound of Ron's voice shattered the silence.

"Hell of a guy, your buddy from Texas," he said as he stood beside him and stared down at the beach below.

"Hey, I don't think any the less of you, even if you don't have a ten million dollar beach house to lend me," Max countered with a laugh.

"Whatever, I may have been born at night, Max, it just wasn't last night. So what's the skinny on this place anyways?"

"Well, in short, Harbour Island, or 'Briland' as the locals call it, was a sleepy little Island with one of the best beaches in the world. But then it got discovered, and a boatload of stupid wealth moved in and has kind of taken over…."

"Sounds like trouble to me," said Janet as she came out onto the deck. Her hair was wet and she had it pulled back into a pony tail. It seemed that the island had worked miracles in the healing process.

"There have been some problems for sure, but on balance it seems everyone has settled in and are getting along."

"In that case, I think I'll have a martini," replied Janet as she headed to the bar. "Anyone want to join me?"

"Absolutely," said Kate as she went and joined her.

"Shaken, not stirred," said Ron as he sidled up beside Kate. "Looks like we all have gotten over the day from hell and are on our way to a much needed party.

"Amen," said Janet as she passed them their martinis.

Max came over and joined them. "Salud, dinner is on me, and we are off the clock until noon tomorrow. So if you will allow me, I would like to treat you all to a spectacular meal at the Rock House."

"May you be in heaven a full half hour before the devil knows you're dead," said Kate as they hoisted their glasses in unison.

"Aye lass," said Ron as he drained his glass.

When Max finally managed to open one eye, he could see his

room was already filled with sunlight. He went and found his shorts and headed down to the beach. He had a slight headache from the night before, but after twenty minutes in the water he was feeling great--and hungry.

"You gotta blow out the carbon once in a while," he heard his father say as he walked back up the path to the house. And although he felt invigorated, his stomach was beginning to feel sour with the thought of the day ahead. They had their fun, but it now was time to go to work.

He headed to the outside shower, and fifteen minutes later wandered into the kitchen and let the aroma of fresh coffee and frying bacon draw the rest from their dens. He was on the second batch of bacon when they came drifting in, and he was happy to see Janet was the last one up.

Janet set the table on the verandah, and, once the food was delivered, they all took a seat and dug in.

"Smells awesome," said Kate as she stared out at the ocean, but she had barely touched her food.

"You should eat," said Max as he handed her the plate of bacon. But he could see she was someplace else, and as he followed her gaze out over the water he saw the sea breaking over the reef. He turned his attention back to the others.

"So, what's on the agenda?" asked Ron as he devoured an enormous helping of bacon and eggs, and washed it down with his second mug of coffee.

"The three of us are headed to Nassau, and Kate is going to set up post here and act as base camp between us and Vancouver," said Max.

"Hold on a minute," replied Kate. "I am---"but he cut her off.

"Listen, I wish I knew exactly what we were up against, but I don't. I do know we need someone here in case something happens and we need to call in reinforcements," said Max.

He turned to Kate. "Now, may I see you for a moment in private. I need to discuss a few matters with respect to Mike's office." He stood and headed toward the office at the back of the house. She was on edge, and began rambling as they entered the room but he held up his hand in protest.

"If something does happen, and we are unable to get back here, I want you to call this number," he said as he handed her a card.

"There is a plane sitting in West Palm Beach, and the pilot is first rate and one hundred percent trustworthy. You call him and he will be here within ninety minutes and will take you straight back to Vancouver.

"And what about you?" she said, as tears began to well up in the corners of her eyes.

"Listen, Kate, yesterday was special. And I'd be lying if I said I didn't have strong feelings for you."

"Me too," she said quietly as she sat down in one of the lumpy old armchairs beside a well worn mahogany desk.

"Timing has never been one of my strong suits, and I guess this is a classic example," he said as he sat down across from her. "But we are in too deep now, and there is no turning back even if I wanted to."

"I don't know that at all," she replied as she thrust her chin to the ceiling. "In fact, I don't know much at all about what the hell is going on, period. Surely there must be some other way of dealing with this."

Max never offered her a response, but the look in his eyes said enough. So with great resolve she slowly locked the door on her emotions, and tucked away the key.

"There's one more thing," he said as he took her hand. "If something should happen, I need you to go and see Mike and ask him to give you access to the safety deposit-box in the safe room in their office. Inside, you will find instructions on what to do."

He was ready for a fight, but was surprised when she sat up straight in her chair and looked right back at him, "Alright Max, you can count on me," she replied. But her efforts to hide the fear that she was feeling fell short.

"You are right, these are bad people. So you take them out, once and for all. And then get your ass back here, do you hear me?"

"Loud and clear," he said with a wink as he got up and headed for the door.

Ron was standing in the living room with the bags beside him, and smiled when he saw Max come back into the room.

"We ready?"

"As much as I'll ever be, my friend," he said. And as he looked around the room his eyes settled on Kate as she emerged from the office.

"You all take care now," she said as they followed Ron down the steps.

"May God look over you and protect you."

CHAPTER 35

"I think we may be in for a bit of a storm," said Max as a bolt of lightning flashed from a giant anvil cloud that now dominated the horizon. And then he heard the roar of thunder as the sharp fresh smell of ozone filled the air.

"Getting a bit breezy too," replied Ron as they bumped to a stop alongside the empty dock.

"It will pass," said Max as they loaded their bags into the water taxi. But he did not like the looks of the dark clouds that were forming around them, and knew they may be in for a bumpy ride.

They sat in silence as the boat skimmed along the water to the main Island, where they loaded their bags into the old Chevy taxi van and headed back to the airport.

"Hi honey, miss me, did you?" said a rather disheveled, barefooted woman in her early fifties as she headed toward them.

Max could not help but laugh when he saw the look on their faces, and had to take a moment before finally introducing them.

"Meet Kim, one of the best damn island pilots you will ever have the privilege of flying with," said Max as he introduced them.

"Pleased to meet you," said Kim.

And then she turned to Max, and he could see the look in her weathered face that something was on her mind. "Let's get your bags loaded and get out of here. We have a Nor'wester coming in, and I want to be in the air as soon as possible."

"Is it just passing or are we in for some weather?" asked Max as he climbed into the seat beside her.

"Strange for the time of year, but it's a front that is packing some strong winds and a lot of rain. So I would not plan on any fishing over the next few days."

"Roger that," said Max. A front could limit their ability to move if they had to, and that would not be a good thing. He listened to the propeller begin to turn over.

Thankfully, the flight wasn't as bumpy as he had expected. Kim wound the little Cessna in and out of the clouds with ease and had them parked at the executive FBO less than forty minutes later. Max had called for a private car, and they arrived at the FB&T building just past two in the afternoon.

Once they cleared security, they put their bags in the locked storage facility, and then headed back to the boardroom. Max had always been good at reading people, and from the looks of everyone seated at the table he could see they were relieved to have him back. All, that is, except for Jim.

On the surface he appeared to be at ease, but as Max got closer he could see the nervous twitch as he picked away at his right thumb with his forefinger. The cuticle was worn back and bleeding, which meant he had been at it for a while.

Max wondered if he was reading into Jim's nervousness.

"Everyone, I'd like you all to meet Janet," he said as he guided her to a seat. And this is my right hand, Ron."

"Now, first things first. Before we get started, he will be assisting Jim in collecting his things and will escort him to the two central intelligence department officials waiting downstairs."

Max could see by the look on Ron's face that he had caught him off guard, "Sorry, my bad, I should have told you I called them when we landed."

'No worries, I got this," he replied as he walked over toward Jim.

"The hell he is…," cried Jim as he jumped to his feet.

"Sit down and shut up," said Max in a cold and level tone. "I am in no mood to argue. You can either go straight up, or draped over the saddle. It's up to you."

Jim's face was glowing, and his mouth twisted into an ugly grin as he tried to hold his ground, "I don't know who the fuck you think you are, but when Mr. Feinstein hears about this it will be your ass in a sling, not mine."

And so the leopard had shown his spots. It was a stark contrast to the mild, soft spoken professional that Max had seen up until now. And he felt some vindication in knowing he had called this one right. Ron grabbed a hold of his elbow.

Realizing what was about to happen, he ripped his arm free and slammed the top down on his computer before Max had time to take it from him.

"What the hell is going on?" shouted John as he stood and watched in disbelief as Ron manhandled Jim out of his chair and began dragging him out of the boardroom.

"Minor setback," replied Max. "I had a feeling Jim was doing a little banking of his own on the side, so I asked Janet to join us today, in case we needed a little help with the computers."

"We are all very sorry to hear what happened to you," said John as he reached over and gently took her hand.

251

"I appreciate that, thank you," she replied as her cheeks went a little crimson. She couldn't help but wonder what people were thinking, if they knew what had really happened or just felt pity.

And then she decided the best way to not play the victim was to put her mind to work. "As I am the newcomer to this group, it would be helpful if you could explain to me exactly what it is that you need me to do. Max has filled me in with little bits here and there, but I am feeling at a little bit of a loss."

"You are not the only one, my dear," replied Ken as he gestured for everyone to take a seat and then turned his attention back to Max.

"Maybe you could enlighten all of us, and an explanation as to why you just dragged one of our most senior executives out by his collar would be a good place to start."

"Right, and I will, but you'll have to bear with me because it will take a little time for me to explain," said Max as Ron came walking back into the room.

"Two of your friends from CID took our buddy down to their office, so I don't think we will be hearing from him anytime soon," Ron said as he took a seat beside Janet.

"Good," said Max as he rolled his head from side to side like a boxer getting ready for a fight.

"When Michael Darrington brought me on board, I had no idea what I was getting myself into. And it never even really became apparent until just recently."

"How so?" asked Janet as she sat studying Jim's computer.

"The banks all know what is coming down with respect to the international regulation and governance of the private banking Industry, but their options are dwindling."

"Which allows them to give the illusion they are taking care of business, when in fact they are only prolonging the inevitable," said Ken.

"Correct you are. In fact, the U.S. has been actively closing accounts, especially Venezuelan nationals, almost without notice. So they are running the risk of huge complications in sorting out the cash and securities as they try and unwind these account closures."

"Nothing you have told me so far is anything new, so where does all the cloak and dagger come into play?" asked John.

"Well, as it turns out some of the clients that FB and T inherited when they bought the bank in the Bahamas had previous connections to both FB and T and our own beloved firm, Darrington, Moskowitz and Calder," said Max as he began to pace around the room.

"And here is where is gets really tricky, because although Morton was ahead of his time in his thinking, he has opened himself up to someone swooping in and taking off with the funds as they are transferred in."

"You can't be serious," said John, as if Max had lost his mind.

"I mean, come on, there are safeguards in place. It's just not possible," he said emphatically.

But then they all diverted their attention to Ken who was scribbling furiously on his note pad while simultaneously punching at the keys on his laptop.

"Over one hundred separate accounts and in excess of twelve billion. All in one day. And yes, it is possible," he shouted as he jumped to his feet.

"Christ, Max, whoever is behind this must have started planning it almost as soon as the old man hatched his plan. Which means they must have people working on the inside," he said.

"No way. I have worked beside the man for years," said John. "And you mean to sit there and tell us Jim has been in on this the whole time?"

"I don't know when he got involved," replied Max. "But you saw him today, he's as guilty as shit. And if I had to guess, he must have some how stumbled across what old man Calder was up to, and the temptation was just to great."

"Great. Just fucking great," said Ken as he stood up and left the room.

Ron was about to go out after him but Max nodded him off. "He'll be back."

"So what are we going to do?" asked Janet.

"I'm not really sure, but I believe once we, or should I say you, get us into his computer we should be able to find a way to stop them from diverting the transfers."

But he knew it wasn't going to be that simple. These were motivated individuals who had no problem eliminating anything or anyone in their way. And from what he could tell, there were a lot more of them than he had originally thought.

"FUBAR," said Ken as he walked back into the room and stood staring at Max, his expression the likes of a deer in headlights.

"You do realize that all these transactions are, or at least were scheduled to be, completed tomorrow morning," he said. "So I am not sure what kind of magic you have shoved up your sleeve, but it better be good."

"FUBAR?" said Janet.

"Fucked up beyond all recognition," said Max.

"So Ken, I appreciate the urgency but for now you could call security. I'd like to have a meeting with them and try and get a clear lay of the land." He got up and motioned for them to follow.

"You seem to be rather cool in all of this," John said quietly as he caught up with him.

"Quite the contrary, but there is no percentage in showing weakness when there is a job to do," he said as they came to a stop outside the security office.

After a brief conversation, he learned there were three guards stationed outside the building, one in the booth at the entrance to the underground parking and three more inside. The inside persons were on rotation between the main guard desk and floor patrol.

"And we have five floors including the parking to try and watch," said Max as they took to the stairs.

"Correct," said Ken as he began descending the stairs to the lower floor, and then stopped outside of a door with a sign on it that read "Janitorial."

"Well, what do we have here," said Max as Ken walked toward the back of the small room and opened up a cupboard door.

"Control central," replied Ken with a smile as he placed his hand on the palm scanner inside the cupboard and then stepped back and watched as the wall pivoted inward, revealing a large computer room.

The room had to be at least twenty by fifty, and had six computer terminals set in a circle atop one huge desk. The east and west walls were covered from one end to the other with floor to ceiling filing cabinets. But it was the north wall with the safety deposit boxes set behind a wall of heavy metal bars that really caught his attention.

"Virtually impenetrable" he heard Ken saying. "It's where we not only control the entire building, but where all the real work of the bank is performed. We can run the entire operation from here, control all access and egress, plus we have direct satellite links to all of our offices."

"Very impressive," said Max.

"So what are all the work stations we have seen through the rest of the building?" asked John.

"Fully functional and used for very basic accounting and day to day operations. But this is where it all happens."

"So walk us through the process of how the transfers will take place," said Max as he stood staring at one of the computer stations.

"Actually, if you don't mind let's wait until we get Janet down here so we don't have to go through the process twice," said Ken.

"Back in five," Ron said as he went to collect Janet.

"The process is surprisingly simple. Each bank outside of the Bahamas will be sent an initiation code tomorrow morning. Those banks in turn will then use an ABA or a SWIFT CODE number to route the funds through a correspondent bank directly to us," said Ken.

"Okay, so I'm confused," replied Ron. "If these transactions are essentially in a vacuum, how can anyone intercept them?"

"Because the funds have to flow through intermediary channels, and then someone here has to physically key in the account information for them to finally be parked," said Max.

"I'm impressed," said Ken. "Whoever is sitting at the terminal has to key in where the funds are to be credited. So, if you have the key codes to access the system you can, in fact, systematically redirect the funds to an account of your choosing."

"Provided you have the correct information," said Max.

"Yes. And given what you've told us, I would speculate that whoever is behind this has already set up a series of accounts so they can redirect the funds as they are transferred.

"They can't trace them?" asked Ron.

"Sure, the initial transfer may be easy. But these in turn, will be broken into several smaller amounts and parked in dozens, if not hundreds of different accounts."

John was looking like a fighter who had just gone ten rounds and was giving in to his inevitable defeat when he finally spoke up, "You really believe this is happening?"

"I do," said Max, and as he turned to Janet he could see by her posture that she had not made the progress he had hoped for.

"You telling me you are stumped?" he said as he came up behind her and rested his hands on her shoulders.

"Whoever set this up is a genius," she replied as she let out a faint moan and pressed lightly back against his hands. Max could feel the tension in her muscles as she twisted her neck from side to side, and wondered how much more of this she could endure.

"I got by his entry passcode no problem, but the files are somehow locked, and I have yet to figure out how to access them."

"Listen, why don't we just delay the transfers? Or hell, just cancel them entirely," said John.

"Can't do that," Ken said as he slumped down into a chair across from Janet. "We are dealing with dozens of banks in multiple countries, not to mention the time zones. It would be virtually impossible to track down who is initiating these on the other end."

"So what do we do if Janet can't get into his computer?"

"Jim wasn't the only one who had the codes," said Max.

And no sooner had he finished talking when he felt his phone begin to vibrate, and when he saw the number he jumped up and walked toward the safety deposit boxes and answered.

CHAPTER 36

The look on his face said it all.

"Talk to me," said Ron as he got up and headed toward him.

"My guys at CID," he replied. "Looks like someone broke into their office on Cable Beach, which is pretty goddamn hard to do."

"And what about Jim?" asked Ken.

"Looks like he and whoever got him out have done a Houdini."

"Shit," said Ron as his eyes narrowed. "Call me paranoid, but if they got to him, then they can get to any of us."

As he stared back at Max they both spoke at the same time, "Kate!"

"Goddamn it, how could I have been so stupid?" shouted Max as he picked up his cell and punched in the number of the house in Harbor Island.

"Good evening, Mr. Duncan. I was wondering when you would call."

And then he felt his body stiffen when he heard the voice on the other end of the line. He was furious at himself for allowing them to lose their advantage, and he knew he had to find a way to get it back. But after a moment he calmed down as he thought of Sun Tzu,

"If your enemy is secure at all points, be prepared for him. If he is in superior strength, evade him. If your opponent is temperamental, seek to irritate him. Pretend to be weak, that he may grow arrogant. If he is taking his ease, give him no rest. If his forces are united, separate them. If sovereign and subject are in accord, put division between them. Attack him where he is unprepared, appear where you are not expected ."

"Balls in your court," hissed Max as he felt his heart pounding into his throat.

"Well, I have to say, I really thought you would have checked in sooner," said the man as he toyed with him. "What were you thinking, leaving a pretty lady like this all alone on such a remote and romantic island and all?"

"Listen, you son-of-a-bitch, you hurt her in any way and there will be no place on this planet small enough for you to hide!"

But his threat did little more than illicit a mocking laugh. "Don't be so melodramatic, I'm told it's not your style."

Max could feel the phone begin to flex as his grip tightened, "Then get to the point," replied Max.

"My point is simple, I want you to stop fucking with us. You do that and you get your precious Kate back, we get our money and everyone—-how does it go again, sails off into the sunset," he replied tauntingly. "But if you don't, well, use your imagination. It will make our little visit to Janet seem like a kindergarten party."

"Fine, you win," said Max quietly in an attempt to buy some time. "It's your show now."

"See, that wasn't so hard to swallow now was it?"

"Go home, we will be in touch come morning," he said and then the phone went dead.

Max's first instinct was to go after them, and although he knew he shouldn't leave the bank, he knew he couldn't leave Kate to fend for herself.

"Ron, take everyone back upstairs and let them collect their things, and then meet me at the storage room," he said as he headed for the lockers.

Max dug through the bags they had left in the secured storage and then stopped for a moment, as he stared down at the Glock 17 he was holding. "Attack where he is unprepared," he said as he placed four spare magazines into the outer pouches of his packsack and then stuffed a snub nosed 38 along with his police baton inside and an assortment of throwing knives.

"Man, now those are impressive," said Ron when he pulled out two sawed off stainless steel shotguns.

"A DEA friend of mine gave them to me," he said as he pulled out a box of shells. "I think they may come in handy for the twins."

Ron chuckled to himself as he slipped on a shoulder holster and tucked the beretta into place, then loaded a box of spare cartridges into his pocket.

"John, this place is like a fortress and I think it would be best if you all stay here while Ron and I go and get Kate."

"As you said earlier, it's your show. And I can tell you one more thing, whatever we do from here on is well above my pay grade," he replied.

"I'm sure you are familiar with the likes of these," said Max as he handed the shotguns to Bjorn and Sven.

Not exactly a precision weapon, but it'll do the trick," said

Sven as he checked the weapon and then racked a shell into the chamber.

"Spare cartridges," said Max as he handed them the box of shells.

"I really have to say for the record, I don't like this," said John nervously as he sat, taking it all in.

"It's the safest place I can think of," replied Max. "Keep the door locked, and try and get some rest. Ron and I are going to take a little boat ride."

"Are you nuts?" replied Janet as she spun around in her chair with a look of panic. "In this weather?"

"Ah, I would have to agree with her, Max," said Ken. "In case you didn't notice, the waves were hitting the breakwater."

"No choice, they have Kate and we need to get her back before morning."

"Well, in that case. I guess I'm in," said Ken as he sat staring at the gun that was almost completely hidden by Ron's bicep.

Seeing the look on his face, Max reached into his packsack and pulled out the 38.

"You sure you want this?" he asked as he handed the gun to him.

"I would seriously regret dying if I at least did not make some attempt to protect myself," he replied as he took the weapon and stuffed it into his waistband. Besides, it just so happens I held a bit of a record at the gun range back home."

"Really," said John as his eyebrows went up and, for a moment, Max thought he might even smile.

"Yes, really. There was a time I thought I might like to go into law enforcement. So I joined a range. Turns out I was a pretty good shot, but decided it was not for me and became a bean counter instead."

"Alright then, keep the door locked, and don't open it for

anyone," said Max. He gave Janet a wink and turned and followed Ron and Ken out the door.

Ron slowed and let Ken get ahead of them as he took a hold of Max's elbow and held him back, "I don't think he will be of much help if all hell breaks loose," he said as he watched him head up the stairs.

"I don't know, he may surprise us," said Max.

Phil came running out of the bedroom and met Max at the door as he stepped inside the condo. Kneeling down and rubbing the dog's ears gave him a slight sense of relief. The inexplicable bond between man and his dog could do wonders for the soul. He heard Lillis calling from the kitchen, "I made you dinner, and packed some food for the trip," she said. "Now take a seat."

"No time, we have to get going," said Max as he took a cooler from the closet and placed the food inside.

"You sure we can't fly," said Ken, staring out the patio doors. "The jet seemed pretty damn capable to me."

"It' not the plane. It's just very unlikely that we could land in these winds. "They're just too strong," said Ron.

"And even if it wasn't, we can get in undetected by boat," said Max as he headed toward the door.

Phil was sitting beside Max in anticipation of what was to come as his tail swept slowly back and forth across the floor.

"He's not going with you," said Lillis as she watched them head for the door.

Max stopped and then hesitated, but never turned around as he felt Phil's head on his knee, "I'm afraid we are going to need all the help we can get."

CHAPTER 37

"I saw them delivering this baby a few months ago," said Ken as they climbed aboard the custom built thirty-eight foot Protector.

"State of the art, twelve hundred horse inboard diesels with Jet Drive," replied Max as he started the engines and waited for the instruments to initialize.

"You take the bow line, I'll deal with the stern and spring lines," he said as he stowed his pack down beside his seat.

The inlet to the canal was relatively protected, but it tended to silt up, limiting the water depth, which could be a problem getting out. But they were on a full moon and the tide was at its highest point for the month–they made it out with ease.

The sky was clear and the moon was now high enough to provide them with reasonable light, but the wind speed indicator showed a steady twenty knots and he knew the seas would be building. Given the weather, he expected they would be the only boat on the water but decided to leave the running lights off in case they were being watched.

If the winds held at twenty knots the passage through the

Devil's Backbone would be treacherous but manageable, and they should arrive before midnight.

"What can I do?" asked Ron as he settled into one of the seats.

"Keep an eye on the horizon and let me know if you see anything in our way," Max shouted as the winds buffeted the cuddy.

He knew the area waters well but they had a lot of sea to cover. And as they made their way farther out, he could feel the wind gusting stronger as it whistled across the deck.

"Better strap in," he called as they rounded the reef to the north of the island and he pressed the throttles, taking them up to thirty-five knots.

The seas were now over three feet, and as the bow cut through each wave it sent a frothy sheet of spray over top of them as they headed into the storm. It wasn't long before they could hear the waves breaking on the reef off Rose Island, and as they turned north Max took the boat up to forty-five knots.

"You familiar with the sailor's mantra," he shouted as he stared out at the horizon.

"I'm afraid not," said Ken, tightening his seat belt.

"Simple; black and brown we run aground, white we might, and blue will see us through," he said as the boat rose suddenly and then shuddered as they landed back down the other side of a large wave.

"Sounds great, but just how in the hell am I supposed to tell the difference in the dark, let alone in the seas?" he replied as he strained to see through the windshield.

"It will settle down once we get into the lee of the big Island," Max said calmly. "And with the moon you'll be surprised how well you can see."

"I wish I had your confidence, or even his for that matter," he said, staring down at Phil who was comfortably seated at Max's feet.

The seas remained steady but the gusts were getting stronger, and as they rounded the point at Ridley Head a rogue wave hit them with such force it felt as though they had hit ground.

"It's just water hitting the hull," shouted Max as he swung the boat into the wave and then throttled back to fifteen knots and let the boat surf down the back side of it.

Once inside the channel, Max would not only need to trust his advanced navigation equipment, but would also have to rely on past experience to get them through the passage. With the moon now fully overhead, it gave him an eerie feeling that they were cruising into a black and white movie as he took them perilously close to shore.

Ken was staring at the sea as it washed up the beach, and tightened his grip on the arm of his chair as they suddenly sank deep into the trough of a wave a mere ten feet from shore. Then his stomach flipped as the beach appeared to rise above them, "You sure you got this right?" he shouted,

"Don't worry, we have about ten feet of water under us and in another minute we will be out of it," said Max as he made a hard turn to port and aimed the boat directly at a large chunk of coral head that was now fully exposed as the water sank around it.

"It's like threading a goddamn needle," said Ron as the entrance marker to Harbour Island finally came into view.

Just then Phil emerged from below, and Max could see Ken's body relax, and almost feel the relief in his face as the lights of the island came into view.

"I wish I had his constitution," said Ken as Phil stood on the transom with his nose to the air.

"He's made the passage on more than one occasion," said Max as he turned the boat inland.

"Ron, take the helm and aim for the channel marker slightly off your starboard bow," said Max as he unclipped his seatbelt and took his cell phone from inside his vest and stepped out onto the aft deck.

Gino answered with the third ring, and after a brief conversation Max went back inside and took the helm, heading for a private dock to the east of the marina.

Max brought the boat in at an idle. And as the bow neared the dock he pulled back on the port engine, gave throttle to the starboard, swinging the boat around and allowing the winds to bring them alongside the dock.

Ron hopped off and helped secure the lines, and as he scanned the area for activity, Max shut down the engines and then went and checked his gear. Satisfied he had all that he needed, he turned and faced Ken.

"The three Amigos can take it from here if you want to wait this one out," he said in the hopes he would agree.

"Not a chance; I'm with you," said Ken as they climbed up onto the dock.

CHAPTER 38

Max felt the spikes of the bougainvillea tearing at his shirt as they wove their way up the path to the house. As they crested the hill he heard the waves breaking on the beach below. The storm was still intensifying.

"We need to cut through the back yard and get to the east side of the house," Max said as the glow of lights from the living room came into view.

Phil stayed close at his side as they slipped along the edge of the property, and as they got closer Max could see there were two men seated in the living room. But there was no sign of Kate.

"Get as close to the deck as you can, and stay out of sight," said Max as he pulled Ken in close. "We will circle back and try to get in through the maid's room."

And then his face hardened. "If you have to shoot, aim for the centre of the body and put em down."

"Damn fucking straight," replied Ken as he raised his pistol and then waved him off.

They slipped back to the other side of the house managing to keep out of sight. But just as Max got halfway up the steps to the back porch, he saw the hair go up on Phil's back. And then all of a sudden, the door flew open and he found himself staring down the barrel of a 38 special.

A smile spread across the man's face, but before Max had a chance to move Phil uncoiled, launched himself into the air, and was hanging from the man's wrist.

Caught off guard, Phil sunk his teeth deep into his flesh and began ripping his head violently from side to side as the man's face contorted in pain. Max saw the gun drop to the floor and rushed him, bringing his fist down on his neck. But then Phil let go, and as the man's weight shifted he grabbed a hold of Max and they both went crashing to the deck.

Phil came back at him, latching onto his ankle this time as the man kicked wildly at him with his free leg. Max heard Phil yelp as he hit him in the side with a terrifying kick of his heel, and then silence.

"Son-of-a-bitch," cried Max as he rolled onto his back and came up in a half seated position with his gun drawn, putting two bullets straight into his heart.

He scrambled on all fours toward Phil, and as he gently put his arm under his neck he saw his eyes open and then felt his body stiffen as he pushed himself up. He could see the dog was hurt badly, and as he watched him limp toward the shadows of the building he felt his rage boiling to the surface once more.

Hearing the noise, the men inside were now up and on the move. Ken lost sight of the one as he left the living room, but stayed focused on the other as he came to the patio door with his gun drawn. He could see Max was now caught between them, and he needed to do something quickly before they were on him.

Ron heard the explosion, and then saw a mass of red spray across the glass as the patio door shattered and a man fell through it, landing face-first on the deck.

"Behind you," shouted Ron as the third one came running through the open door behind Max and began shooting.

Max rolled toward the wall and came to a stop with his back to Phil, heard the shots, and was pelted with wood splinters as the bullets tore into the deck. Ron dropped to one knee as he steadied his gun and then squeezed off a single shot.

Max spun around just in time to see the back of the man's head splatter against the siding, and then turned his attention back to Phil. He was now sitting up, and Max let out a deep sigh of relief as he crawled closer and began licking his face.

"Did you see anyone else?" Max asked as Ron came up and stood beside him.

"At least one more inside," said Ken as he stood a little shaky, his gun now hanging at his side.

Kate was lying on the sofa by the wall, her hands and feet bound tightly together with extension cords and he could see a bright red mark on the back of her right thigh. His face hardened as he saw the man slip down beside her and take hold of her hair as he placed the muzzle of his gun to her temple.

"You son-of-a-bitches are going to pay for this," seethed the man as he sat glaring at them, a look of pure hatred shooting from his eyes.

"Who else is here with you?" replied Max.

"Go fuck yourself," he said, as an evil grin began to push his cheeks aside.

"She must be quite a piece of tail for you to come running up here while we clean out your bank."

"You still haven't answered my question," said Max as he imperceptibly began to close the distance between them.

As Max stared him down, he again reverted to his readings of Sun Tzu, "He will win who, prepared himself, waits to take the enemy unprepared," he reached behind his back and let fly with a throwing knife.

He heard Kate shriek as it found its mark, and watched as it buried itself deep into the man's left shoulder.

Max could see his look of defiance had turned to one of shock as the gun fell from his hand and he released his grip on Kate's hair.

"I guess we can assume you're the last one," said Max as he walked over and kicked the gun away.

"Doesn't' matter, you won't make it back alive," he said, glaring up at him.

As he got closer, Max recognized a faint but distinctive odor on the man's clothes. It was the same odor he had smelled in the underground parking.

"How's your brother's leg doing?" asked Max. But then stopped when he saw the look of horror on Kate's face as her chin dropped.

"The tattoo on his arm," she said, pointing. "It's what Janet described to me when she told me about her attack."

"Ken, take Janet to the kitchen," said Max, without taking his eyes off the man. "There is a bottle of gravol in the cupboard by the sink. I want you to each take one, they are for motion sickness."

"Did you hurt my friend?" he said when he was sure Kate was out of the room.

"Now that was a piece of ass," he replied mockingly as he

gripped his balls with his right hand. And then he was up, his powerful thighs propelling him forward as he dropped his shoulder and charged. Max sidestepped him, and as he spun around he drove his fist into the side of his head, knocking him to the floor.

But he had resilience, and managed to get to his knees before Max grabbed a hold of him by his head. With his chin cupped in his right hand, and his left hand at the base of the skull, with one swift jerk he snapped his neck and let him drop back to the floor.

CHAPTER 39

The clock on the stove read 3:42 a.m. If they left now, it would just be getting light by the time they got back onto the water.

"You can stay at the Rock House if you want," he said to Kate. "You will be safe there."

But she just shook her head and grabbed onto his arm with both hands. "Not on my life," she replied, as her nails dug deep into his arm.

"It's going to be a rough ride," said Ken. "You sure about this?"

"I'm sure," she replied defiantly.

"Then we're out of here," said Ron as they headed for the door.

The wind whipped the sand up in front of them as they made their way down the path. And as they got near the clearing Max stopped for a second as he considered what they were headed into, but then continued on anyway. He had no way of knowing whether there were more of them still on the island, and either way he didn't feel he had a choice but to head back.

Ron took the bow line and Max the stern, and as they pulled

the boat in to the dock Max helped Kate on board and then hopped on behind her and started the engines. He held the stern line while Ron climbed on to the bow, and then let the wind blow them off the dock as they let the lines loose.

Dawn was just beginning to lighten the skyline when they got to the end of the channel, and Max could see the waves breaking high over the reef as they neared the entrance to the Devil's Backbone. He estimated they were running six to eight feet and, depending on the break, he would have his work cut out.

It would be a rough passage. But with the sun behind them the visibility was reasonably good, and Max was beginning to feel confident as he wove his way in and out of the coral heads at a steady fifteen knots. But his confidence was soon shaken when he heard Ken shouting, and as he turned he saw a boat approaching them from behind.

"Shit, where did they come from?" yelled Ron as he watched the boat gain on them.

"They must have hung behind until we entered the channel." He cursed as he quickly considered his options.

Realizing they were now dangerously close, Max swung the boat hard to port and barely missed a jagged coral head as he tried to shake them. But the pursuit boat, with three, three hundred horsepower outboards had them easily out-powered.

"Looks like three of them on board," shouted Ken as they continued to close the gap.

"Seems to be their magic number," said Max just as a bullet tore past his head and blew a hole in the fiberglass frame in front of him.

Then he heard Kate scream as a spray of bullets blew off the port side glass as shards of fiberglass flew about the cabin.

"Sons-of-bitches," cried Ron as he began firing back.

"Hang on," yelled Max as he hit the throttles and took them in toward the beach.

He knew they were in serious trouble if he didn't shake them, and were at risk of opening up one or both of the pontoons on the coral heads as he wove in between them.

And then he spotted the opening, "Ken, keep your eyes on the shore, port side. We are coming up on a place called preachers cave. You'll know it when you see it. As soon as we pass it you will see an old white fence that runs down to the beach. Shout out as soon as we are directly across from it," he yelled as he turned the boat hard to starboard and took them back into the reef between two coral heads.

"Take this," yelled Max. As he tossed his gun to Ron he noticed Kate had squished herself down onto the floor in front of him and was holding onto Phil for dear life.

The captain of the boat behind either knew the waters or had exceptional reflexes and he managed the turn almost perfectly. Realizing he had no choice, Max gave it more throttle as he tried to put some distance between them. But the boat was soon bearing down on them as the two gunmen began firing.

"Now," shouted Ken and Max spun the wheel hard and pushed the throttles to their limit. He could hear the thunder of his gun as Ron emptied the clip, and then felt Kate press up against his legs as the stern sunk deep into the water on the starboard side.

Max had to brace himself as they made the 180 degree turn out to sea. When he saw the swell crest off to his right he knew they were in the channel.

"You ok?" shouted Max as he looked down at Kate and saw

she had one arm around Phil's neck and the other wrapped around one of his legs.

"Ok, just get me out of here!" she said.

Not realizing what he had been drawn in to, the captain of the boat behind them made the turn but then realized his mistake when he saw the jagged coral sticking out of the water in front of them. He was going too fast now to stop, and before he could pull back the throttles their port engine hit one of the coral heads.

"Holy Christ," shouted Ron as he watched them launch out of the water at a thirty degree angle.

Max heard the scream of propellers as the boat flew into the air beside them, and watched as the boat crashed down on its side on top of the reef just across from them.

The two men who had been firing at them were ejected off the back as the boat came to a grinding halt, and were shredded to pieces as their bodies skidded across the razor sharp coral. The force of the impact sliced a three foot long gash in the hull and ripped off the starboard engine. Max couldn't risk stopping in the oncoming seas, but could see the boat was taking on water as the waves broke over top of it.

Kate had finally emerged from below and stood holding onto the bar on the console. Her face was pale, and her knuckles were white as she gripped onto the handle in front of her and watched as the wall of water came toward them. The channel was acting like a funnel, and Max knew he had no time to waste as he once again hit the throttles, tossing them back against the seats.

"Hang on," he shouted, as he felt the turbos kick in just as the wave began to lift them. And for a terrifying second they felt themselves being thrown backwards as the bow began to rise.

"Come on," shouted Max as he felt them slowly begin to gain

speed, and as he rocked himself forward he felt the boat break over the top of the wave. It felt like an eternity, but a second later they landed on the back side of the wave with a shuddering crash.

"We're out of it," he said as he relaxed his grip on the wheel and eased back on the throttles. He could feel his forearms aching, and his legs felt like lead as he stood drenched with perspiration.

Then he noticed the bright red patch on Ken's shoulder.

"I'm ok," said Ken, seeing the look on Max's face. Then his knees gave out and he hit the floor.

Ron pulled himself inside and reached down and gently pulled Ken to his feet and then sat him in the seat beside Kate. He pulled his shirt back and after a quick inspection could see the bullet had torn through his shoulder but looked like it had missed the bone.

"You'll be ok," he said as he opened a bottle of water and emptied it over Ken's face, and then watched as he blinked away the salt.

"Do you think they survived?" asked Kate as she took a towel from the side locker and handed it to Ron.

"Not the two who went overboard. The captain maybe," he replied as he folded the towel and pressed it onto the wound.

"To hell with them," said Ken. "I hope they did survive so the barracudas come and take what's left of them.

"We can only hope," said Max as he pulled a first aid kit from the side locker and handed it to Kate.

CHAPTER 40

Max was feeling spent and his arms were still aching as he brought the boat alongside the bulkhead.

"Thank God," said Kate as she stepped out onto the transom and helped him set the bumpers.

"I guess it could have been a lot worse," he said as he did a quick survey of the boat and crew. He could see she was clearly exhausted, but Ken seemed surprisingly with it, considering the bullet hole in his arm.

Max turned to get his things as Phil pushed by him, and then watched as he leaped up onto the bulkhead and went and found a tree where he stayed for a solid minute on three legs with his nose pressed into the wind.

"He's one hell of an animal," said Kate as she stood admiring him. "And thank you for bringing him along."

"Yes, he is, and believe it or not he has saved my ass on more than one occasion. Now let's get Ken to the house, I have a pretty good medical kit and Lillis is surprisingly good with it." He helped her off the boat.

"Will do. But what's the plan?" she said as they walked up the back steps to the condo.

"Yeah, what's the plan?" said Ken as he struggled to make it up the stairs.

"The plan is, you are going to go and lie down and let Lillis fix you up while Ron and I plan our next move."

And then Max noticed Kate shivering, and wasn't sure if it was shock or just the effects of the air-conditioning.

"Go and take a hot shower," he said just as Lillis came walking out of the kitchen.

"Good lord girl, you are going to catch the death. You come with me right now," she said as she took her hand and led her into the bedroom.

Max was desperate to get back to the bank, but he knew they needed some time to rest and time to get their land legs back. Then the sweet smell of roast chicken drifting from the kitchen, and the angry growl from his stomach reminded him that they had not eaten in some time.

Ron, clearly of the same mind, followed him into the kitchen, and as the two stood hovering over the stove they could hear Ken calling from the living room.

"Guess I'd better go and take care of him," said Max. "But as soon as Lillis comes back, get her to set the table and let's have some chow."

Thankfully the bullet had hit no major arteries or bone, but Ken had lost a lot of blood and his complexion was pale. Max could see he was in a lot of pain, and likely had suffered some pretty good bruises when he hit the deck.

"Take this," he said handing him a Percocet and a glass of water. "It will do wonders for you."

"Forget it, I'm good as new," replied Ken in a weak and raspy voice.

"No," said Max. And then he gently pushed his palm against Ken's chest as he struggled to get up.

"Going someplace?"

"Damn straight I am," replied Ken as he fell back down.

"I appreciate the thought. But I'm afraid you are going to have to sit this one out," said Max as he saw his eyelids begin to droop.

Kate was just coming out of the bedroom in a pair of shorts and one of Max's T-shirts as Max got up from the sofa, and even after all they had been through he couldn't help but stare at her.

"What?" she said as she stood staring back at him. "I left my clothes on the island."

"Nothing, just gave some meds to Sleeping Beauty," he said as he turned back to Ken who was beginning to snore fitfully.

There was minimal small talk as they sat and ate, and although he was exhausted Max was feeling a lot better, having had some time to rest and to get some fuel into his belly.

"Kate, I want you to stay here with Ken, and Ron and I will take it from here. And I know we have been through it all before, but if you do not hear from me by noon I want you to call Captain Stebbings and get everyone out of here, including Lillis."

Too tired to argue, she just nodded her agreement and got up to help clear the table.

They did a count of their ammunition, loaded what they had into their packs and headed for the door. Aside from the snoring coming from the sofa, the room was empty.

"She cares a lot for you, you know," said Ron as he followed Max out the door.

"We will have to wait a minute," said the driver as Max pulled open the door and motioned for him to slide over into the passenger's seat.

"No time," he replied as he put the car in drive and hit the gas.

Visibility was nearly zero, and the wipers could no longer keep up as they slapped away the torrent of water that cascaded down the windshield. Max kept his speed at around twenty, but then began to accelerate when he saw the road disappear as they entered the low S-curve at Rock Point.

It was an area prone to flooding, and as they began to speed up he could feel the car begin to hydroplane as he steered them into the knee deep water.

"Are you crazy?" yelled the driver as they drifted to within inches of the rock wall surrounding the beach house.

I hope not, thought Max as he felt the water sloshing up against the floor boards, but then there was a sudden jolt as the car found traction and they were back on high ground.

"Never a doubt," said Max with a grin as he reached over and slapped the driver on the back.

The security gates were open when they reached the service entrance, and as they passed through Max could hear the 500 kilowatt standby generator's exhaust resonate over the howling winds. Not only had the storm knocked out the power, but there was no sign of the guards anywhere. Which could only mean one thing: the complex had been compromised.

"Shit, that's all we need," he cursed as he steered the car into the underground parking and came to a stop just in front of the entrance. He scanned the area for signs of movement but saw nothing as he climbed out of the driver's seat.

"Slide over and be ready to go on a moment's notice," he told the driver as he closed the door, and then addressed Ron as he got out of the back.

"Hang here by the entrance and wait for me," he said. "I

doubt we're going to find anyone outside, but I need to check the booth." He gripped his gun and rested his finger lightly on the trigger.

He had to force the door of the security booth open as the wind blew hard against him, and once inside he saw the guard lying motionless on the floor. There was a gaping hole in the side of his neck, and the pool of blood covered half of the floor. He never had a chance.

Whoever these guys were, they meant business. And anyone who got in their way was being eliminated. He was now painfully aware that they were not only on their own, but once again were at a disadvantage. He left the booth and hunched over against the wind as he headed back towards the parking garage.

He needed to find an edge, and as he walked back he thought about his readings of the Art of War, "So in war, the way is to avoid what is strong, and strike at what is weak."

He had no idea how many they were up against, but he had little doubt they were in for a fight. He swiped Ken's keycard and waited for the secure door to open. Once inside they saw dozens of bullet holes in and around the security desk, and as they came around, Max saw the guard lying on the floor.

"Doesn't look like it was much of a fight," said Ron, as he leaned down and grabbed the man's wrist and checked for a pulse.

"My guess is they clearly have control of the building," said Max as Ron looked up and shook his head. They heard the faint sound of footsteps coming down the hall.

Max glimpsed an unmarked door just off to the right of the station, and Ron followed as they quickly stepped inside. "I must have missed this one," said Max as they stood staring at the narrow staircase that led to the basement.

"You still have some of those pig stickers?" asked Ron as he peered through the crack in the door. "There's two of them, and they look like they are carrying M-16s."

"I can do one, but you will need to take out the other," Max replied as he pulled the weapons from his back and handed him one. Wait until they are just past us, we'll take them from behind."

"Ok, but it might wake up the neighbors."

"Not if I can help it," said Max.

They waited until the two had just passed the doorway, and then Max leaped out and in one swift move came in behind the one closest to him and drove the knife deep into his neck. As he lowered him to the floor he saw the other spin around just as Ron drove the knife into his chest.

The corridor lit up with a hail of gunfire, and he could hear the bullets ricochet down the corridor as the second one pulled the trigger. One had a hold of him but as they went down he felt one of the bullets tear through his thigh.

"Son-of-a-bitch he shouted as he pulled out the knife and then brought it across the man's neck leaving a six inch wide gash from ear to ear.

"You're hit bad," said Max when he saw the blood pouring down his leg.

Ron was breathing heavy as he leaned his back against the wall, pushed himself into a seated position and took off his belt. "All I know is you owe me a new pair of dockers," he said, and then grunted in pain as he cinched the belt tight around his leg.

Max kept an eye on the corridor as he picked up the weapons and then waited for Ron to catch his breath.

"I'm good," said Ron as he used one of the rifles as a crutch to push himself up.

"I guess we should have just shot the fuckers," said Max as they took the stairs down to the bottom. There they found a door that led into a hallway just off of the computer room.

"Men from the boys," said Max as he looked up at his friend and winked.

"Easy for you to say," groaned Ron as he limped along beside him, then stopped when they came to the entrance to the janitor's room.

"Come on in, we've been expecting you," he heard a voice say from deep inside.

CHAPTER 41

Max whispered, "There's a chance they haven't seen you: hang back and give me time to suss out the situation." He stepped through the doorway.

Once inside, his eyes immediately fixated on Jim, who was seated in a chair directly in front of the main terminal. There were signs there had been a hell of a fight, and there were dozens of bullet holes covering the walls.

He knew every move would be crucial. He stayed put and continued to take in the room but then stopped short when he saw John leaning up against the side of one of the desks. He could see his eyes were glazed over and his face swollen and bruised, but he was still alive.

And then he felt his heart jump when he spotted Janet just off to his right. She was sitting beside a man who had a look of means that one did not easily forget, and he was sure he'd seen before. Their only backup appeared to be the two burly bank security guards standing in the rear of the room, whom he recognized from a few days earlier.

"Better late than never," said Jim as he motioned for him to enter.

"I see you managed to rally a little inside help," replied Max as he walked toward him.

He needed to buy some time while he got his bearings and formulated a plan. He still needed an edge, and fast.

"If you let her go now, we'll walk out of here and you can carry on with your little plan. But if you don't......"

"Christ, do you believe this guy?" said Jim as he broke into a strange laugh. "How does the saying go? Your ignorance is only exceeded by your arrogance."

"Remember, I gave you fair warning," growled Max as he stepped closer.

"That's far enough," said Amit.

Max could see by the look in his eyes that he wasn't so quick to dismiss him, and then regretted what he'd just said as he watched him grab hold of Janet's hair and yank her toward him.

"We appreciate your offer, but I think I will have to decline. Once the transfers are complete, we are going to walk out of here. And if you behave, maybe I let your pretty little friend here live. So cut the drama and drop the gun."

Max could see his options were running thin, and after a few seconds he dropped his gun to the floor.

"Good boy," said Amit as the gun landed a few feet short of him. "Oh, and if you are wondering about the twin blondes, they're kind of tied up at the moment," said Amit as he turned his head toward the far corner.

Max stepped to his right and as he followed his gaze he felt his stomach tighten. Bjorn and Sven were seated back to back with their wrists bound with electrical zip ties, and appeared to be unconscious.

But as he stared over at them, he saw Bjorn barely open one

eye, and couldn't believe it when he thought he saw him wink. It was the edge he had been looking for, and taking his cue he dove headlong across the floor. Amit was quick to move, but Max had reached his gun, and as he rolled over he fired three rapid shots dropping the guard to his left.

Ripping free with a roar, Bjorn was on his feet and rushing the second one just as Ron stepped into the doorway and carefully aimed the Glock. Max heard the deafening echo of the shot, and watched as a mixture of blood and bone splattered on the wall behind him.

"Fuck you," yelled Amit as he pulled the Katar from his belt and pulled Janet's head back, exposing her throat.

"Move now," Max shouted as Janet drove her heel down on top of Amit's foot, and bolted from her chair. She screamed as her hair was ripped by the roots.

"Bitch," cried Amit as he jumped to his feet with the knife held tightly in his fist.

His face was contorted with hatred as he lunged at Max, but Max was now running on pure adrenalin. He sidestepped and threw up his left arm to protect his face. But as Amit brought his fist around in a sweeping arc Max let out a grunt as the razor sharp blade sliced a deep gash in his forearm.

He could feel the pain but he thrust his arm higher, forcing Amit's head back as he drove his fist deep into his throat. The blow crushed his windpipe, and as Amit dropped to the floor Max brought his foot down and pinned his wrist, yanking the knife free.

There was a stream of blood dripping off of his fingers as he tossed the knife across the room, As he twisted his arm round to survey the damage he caught sight of Bjorn. He was helping Sven to his feet, and although they looked as though they had just gone ten rounds with Muhammad Ali, he was relieved to see they both were alive.

"Let me go and check the janitor's room and see if they have some towels or a first aid kit," said Janet as she trotted toward the door.

"A few stitches and we'll be good as new," said Max as he stared back over at Jim. "Anyone else we need to concern ourselves with, or is this it?" he said.

There was no response. Jim just sat there glaring back at him.

"Found a first aid kit," he heard Janet say as she came rushing back into the room.

"So what was the play here, Jim? Did you think you could just steal a couple of hundred million and sail off into the sunset?" said Max as Janet worked at taping a makeshift bandage onto his arm.

Max saw his jaw flex as he ground his back teeth together and stared defiantly back at him, "You're so goddam smart, you figure it out."

"Help me, and I will help you," said Max as he pulled away from Janet and went and sat down in front of one of the two large computer screens connected to Jim's laptop.

After a few minutes he spun the chair around to face Jim, "Truth is, I don't give a shit about any of the transfers but two, and either you work with me and we get out of here quick, or......"

Jim was in a rage when he cut him off, "Or what? You can't do a goddamn thing without me."

"Fine, like I said before. You had your chance," he said as he motioned for Janet to come and sit beside him.

Her nerves were frayed, and her entire body ached from

exhaustion as she sat down and began to study Jim's computer once again.

"Give me a few minutes," she said as she pushed her hair to the side as she studied the screen.

CHAPTER 42

Max could feel the seconds pulse by as his heart thumped against his chest. After what felt like an eternity he saw her back stiffen as she spun around with a grin on her face, "That was almost too easy," she said. "But we are in."

"Then let's get this party started," said Max as he leaned over. After reading several pages of fine print that covered the screen, he hit the enter button on the keyboard.

He should have known there was a problem. The last time Janet tried to get into his computer it was a total bust. But they were all exhausted, and it wasn't until he saw the slight upturn in Jim's lip that he realized his mistake.

Feeling his body tense, Janet pushed her chair back and stared at him wide-eyed, "What now?" she said.

"It's a set up," shouted Max. "We have to stop it."

But as she turned back, it became painfully clear what had happened.

The system should have been set up so that each individual account would be processed one at a time. The account information would be entered along with a code to the corresponding bank, which would then initiate the transfer. But instead, they had somehow programmed the computer to send the information automatically.

"Too late, you arrogant ass," shouted Jim as he sat glaring back at them.

"He's right," she said wearily as she desperately looked for a way to stop the transfers.

"Calm down," said Max as he rolled his chair up close to her. "There is always a backstop, there has to be. We just have to find it, and fast."

Janet could feel her neck muscles aching as she tapped away at the keyboard with the finesse of a concert pianist, "If I can find a way to cut the connection, I may be able to stop it."

"Not to be too simplistic," croaked John as he came limping over, "but if you shut down the main computer and kill the internet connection it should stop the process."

"Shit, why didn't I think of that?" said Janet as she began looking for the cable connections.

"I'm glad to see you're back with us," said Max as he got up and guided him down into the seat beside Janet.

"This is bullshit," yelled Jim as he made a grab for one of the rifles. But he barely had time to move before Ron hit him with a straight right that almost tore his head off. As he flew backwards Max heard a loud crack, and saw the rifle fall from Jim's hand as his head hit the floor.

"Guess he won't be spending any of that money, after all. Not that I thought he ever would have," said Ron as he limped over and picked up the rifle.

"True, but he's not going to be of any use to us now either," said Max as he leaned over Janet's shoulder and stared anxiously at the screen.

"Don't need him," said John as he reached behind the computer and began disconnecting the cables.

"Holy crap," said Janet as the screen in front of her froze.

"Give it a minute, and once I connect it back up we should be able to overwrite the transfers and get them deposited to their rightful accounts."

Max could see the pain etched across John's face, and his breathing was coming in fits as he leaned into the desk.

"How're the ribs?"

"I've seen better days," he replied as he fell back into his seat.

"I got this," said Bjorn as he came over and in less than a minute had the cables reconnected.

"How will we know if any of the transfers were processed?" asked Janet as she began scrolling down the screen.

"We won't. At least not until we have a chance to check the individual accounts here," said John as he leaned in front of her and punched in a code on the keyboard.

"Whatever we do, it better be fast," said Bjorn as he went and took the chair that Amit had been in. "Just before Max arrived I heard Jim talking to someone on his cell phone, and I'm pretty sure he was expecting others who would be coming to collect them."

"Well, then let's get this over with," said Max. "We only need to deal with three transfers that did not appear to have been processed.

When they were done Max picked up the laptop and smashed it onto the corner of the desk, and then ground his heel down onto the key board until there was nothing left but fragments.

"Bjorn, are you ok to take one of the automatics and lead the way," he asked as he picked up the other rifle.

"Yes sir," he replied.

"I can help as well," said Sven as he came over. But Max could see it was all he could do to keep himself upright.

"How about you give Janet a hand, and the rest of you stay between us? If anything happens I want you to hit the floor," said Max as they headed for the main corridor.

Max was thankful to see the wind had died down to a light breeze and could feel sun overhead as they came out of the security area.

The storm had passed, and it was as though the nightmare of the past few days had been simply washed away.

"Wait here and keep an eye out for company," he said to Ron and Bjorn as he headed toward the limo. When he got up beside the car he saw the driver's head leaning at an awkward angle, and there was no movement when he rapped his knuckles on the window.

Fearing the worst, he began banging harder, and then jumped back when the driver shot upright and sat staring at him through half-closed eyes.

"Christ," said Max as he jumped back and felt his heart begin to pound. He had to laugh at the thought of this guy having slept through their night from hell.

But conscious of their exposure, he quickly waved for the rest to follow as he opened the back door and then instructed the driver to move over. He waited until the rest were all seated in the back and then slid in behind the wheel.

"Keep your window down and your rifle ready, we may be getting company at any time," he said as he stared at Bjorn in the rearview mirror.

They were almost at the exit when he saw a black SUV come

sliding through the gate and then begin heading directly toward them.

"Brace yourselves," shouted Max as he gunned the engine.

"Oh Jesus. Oh Jesus Christ," shouted the driver as he ducked down below the dash. "You are a crazy man."

"Maybe so," Max shot back through gritted teeth. "Wait until I tell you, and then let her loose," he shouted into the back as Bjorn lifted the automatic.

Janet could see they were on a collision course and followed the driver's lead. As she ducked behind the seat Max hit the emergency brake and spun the wheel to the left.

"Give em hell," he shouted as they slid sideways and came to a stop directly in front of the oncoming SUV.

Bjorn took aim, and then held down the trigger and watched as the windshield on the driver's side shattered with a spiderweb of holes.

"Get us the hell out of here," Ron shouted.

But as Max hit the gas they barely moved as the tires fought for traction on the wet pavement.

"Jesus Christ," he shouted. He felt the pain as his arm struck the door as the SUV nailed the back corner of their car. They were hit with such force that they spun a complete 180 degrees and were facing back the way they had come. And as they stared ahead, they heard a thunderous crash and watched as the SUV hit the concrete wall at the entrance to the parking lot.

Max could see smoke coming from under the hood, but saw no movement from the vehicle, so he put the car into gear and hit the gas. They never encountered another single car on the way home, and were back parked in front of his condo less than ten minutes later.

"Hand me my pack," Max said to Ron as he brought the car to a stop and hopped out of the driver's seat.

"This is for you, my friend," he said to the driver as he handed him two freshly banded packs of U.S. one hundred dollar bills. Each band read $10,000.00.

Clearly at a loss for words, and completely overwhelmed at the events of the past twenty-four hours he just stood there staring at the cash in his hands. And when he finally looked up, there were tears starting to form in the corners of his eyes.

"Forget about it," said Max as he slapped him on the back. "You earned it. Take your family to Florida and lay low for a month or so. Maybe go to Disney World. And don't worry about your job, it will still be here when you get back."

He waited until the car was out of sight before mounting the stairs. It had been a long couple of days. Hell, a long couple of weeks. But it was over now, and time to wrap it up and head home.

Lillis, along with Kate and Janet, had managed to close up Max's wound with the help of a dozen Steri-Strips. And after a long hot shower, John seemed to be no worse for wear and in pretty good spirits.

But it took a few calls before a good doctor friend of Max's, who specialized in Mohs surgery came by and took care of Ken and Ron's bullet wounds.

Aside from some cuts and bruises, a fractured cheek bone and two cracked ribs, the Bjorn and Sven team made out ok. They, along with Ken and John, stayed behind to mop up the aftermath with the help of a few of Max's local friends.

CHAPTER 43

Captain Stebbings was standing in the lobby of the FBO, and Max was relieved to see him looking like he'd fully recovered as he walked over to meet them.

"All in all, I'd say we did alright," said Max as they boarded the plane. But then he paused for a moment, and took one last look around before he stepped inside and let the attendant close the door behind him.

Max took a seat across from Kate, and Phil took his place as he curled up at his feet. And for the first time since their encounter, Max felt an awkwardness between them. Kate, sensing his feeling just placed her hand gently on top of his, "we're good," she said. "Now let's get some sleep shall we."

They were all asleep before the plane left the runway, and it wasn't until almost four hours into the flight that Max felt Ron pushing on his good shoulder. As he slowly opened his eyes he saw that big grin on his friend's face, and a large tumbler of what he described as "some golden nectar to help with the pain."

"So tell me, what was the deal with those last transfers?" he said as he pushed the glass toward him.

"All in good time," he said and then emptied a quarter of the glass.

"There are still some loose ends I need to tie up, but trust me when I tell you. You will be pleased with the outcome."

"Have I ever doubted you?" said Ron as he pulled off his boots, sat back, and put his good foot up on the chair across from him. The now-empty tumbler rested comfortably in his lap.

Max was jolted awake when he felt the light impact of the wheels hit the runway as they touched down in Vancouver. He was surprised to see both Janet and Kate sitting facing him, wide awake, mugs of coffee in hand.

"Glad you could finally join us," Janet said with a laugh.

"Complete lightweight," added Kate as she sat staring at him.

"I'm afraid so," replied Max sheepishly as he looked back and saw Ron still sound asleep, with the empty glass still sitting upright between his thighs.

The customs and immigration area was empty, and Max suspected Mike must have made a call because they were processed through without question. As they emerged from the processing area there was a driver already waiting for them.

"Max Duncan, I presume," said the driver, extending his hand.

"If no one has any objection, I suggest we head back to my place and you can all get some rest," said Max once they were all seated in the back of the limo.

Beatrice, having received a call from Lillis already, had a feast prepared and the smell of the assorted Tapas, broiled steak and chicken had the saliva running down the back of their throats and the taste buds popping as they entered Max's foyer.

"And what about you?" asked Kate as they sat staring at each other across the dining room table.

"What about me?" replied Max somewhat bewildered.

"You said we should all lay low here at chez Max, but what about you?"

"Me," he replied as he carefully thought about his response. "I still have some things I need to take care of. And given the circumstance, it would be wise for you all to take my advice and hang out here for a few days, or at least until I get back."

CHAPTER 44

"And so this is where it gets touchy," said Max.

They were sitting in Mike's office, and he was bringing him up to speed on what had happened in the Bahamas over the past few days.

"There are four things I can assure you of: One, is that there is a village on the East side that will be permanently missing their idiot. Two, is that it's amazing what one can accomplish with the right amount of cash, and Three, is that there are a dozen underpaid police officers in Nassau that will never have to work again."

"Correct me if I'm wrong, but that was Three," replied Mike in a subtle but sarcastic tone.

"So it was," said Max, as he got up and headed for the bar. "Too early for a drink?"

"Not today," replied Mike as he watched Max fill two tumblers with Laphroaig single malt scotch.

"And four?" he said as Max handed him the tumbler.

Well, four is the simple fact that sharks are far and away the best means of disposing of,———-"and then his voice trailed as he took a drink and sat savoring the moment.

"And what about the individual accounts?" Mike asked. "What was the final outcome?"

"As it turns out, when John shut the system down, the transfers were either held with the originating or the intermediary banks. But I'm afraid it will take some serious public relations work to repair Morton's reputation."

"Ok, that covers the general matters. Tell me about Global," said Mike.

Max had no illusions that Mike had known his association with Gino from the outset. And not only going as far back as to when they were kids but also his involvement in the public company that had brought them so much wealth.

"Let's just say that the Global accounts are intact and the funds are safely secured," replied Max.

"And the other?" Mike said as he stood up, dug into his pocket and pulled out a ten dollar bill, "As your lawyer, whatever you tell me remains in confidence." He had a mischievous grin.

"Well, as it turns out, our friends the Singh brothers, had just completed a private placement with a Russian Oligarch, probably someone they met through the Czech raider in Nassau. We found the account by accident when we were moving Gino's money."

Although Mike knew Amit was dead, hearing about the money had his attention. And for the first time since they had sat down there was excitement in his voice, "Okay, so where is the money now?"

"You mean the five hundred and fifty million and change," replied Max with a big shit eating grin on his face. He had been dying to give Mike the news ever since they had found the money.

"Did you say five hundred and fifty million?" said Mike as he sat back and began to laugh at the thought.

"And change."

"Well, I'd say it's a blessing that our friend, Amit, is no longer with us. But do tell me, where, pray tell, is the cash?"

"Let's just say our friend, Gino, was very accommodating and the funds are sitting happily in a number of offshore banks that will be virtually impossible to trace."

"For services rendered," said Mike as he got up and headed to the bar.

"Something like that," replied Max, as they both burst out laughing.

EPILOGUE

A security guard at the hotel found Howell lying unconscious beside the path to the parking lot at just after 5:00 a.m. while making his rounds. It took over an hour for the ambulance to arrive, but he was still alive when they finally loaded him into the back and rushed him to the emergency ward at the Island Hospital.

He came to three days later, and had little to no recollection of what happened and after spending an excruciating month in recovery was finally released. He spent the next two months at home before being well enough to go back to work.

Sadly, having still not learned his lesson he took up the cause once more as he tried to nail the people who had stolen the $15 million from them. And so it was, on a beautiful bright sunny morning, he had just gotten out of his car in front of his office when a young man dressed in jeans and a dirty T-shirt came up from behind and put two bullets in the back of his head.

Although there was an investigation of sorts, and much speculation around who was responsible for his death, no one was ever charged and the funds were never recovered.

Morton employed the services of two of the top public relations firms in Canada and the U.S., and, although it took some time, they were able to finalize the consolidation and were back to business as usual.

John, after a one month sabbatical, was back at the helm and in fine spirits.

Ken finally met up with the tourist girls, who in fact were just innocent bystanders. One went back to Canada but the other stayed behind and moved into Ken's place not long after.

The Sven and Bjorn twins received handsome bonuses from FB and T and were offered permanent positions in Nassau. But both declined and moved back home where Sven is now the head of a small private bank and Bjorn became a coach for the National Olympic team.

After coming into unexpected inheritances, tax free of course, Ron and Janet purchased new apartments just a few addresses away from Max, and had signed on full time to join him in running his business. However, they were yet to learn what exactly that business was.

As for Kate, she too had been the recipient of a fabulous inheritance. And although the embers still burned just below the surface, she and Max had not taken their relationship past that of very good friends. And neither had spoken of their lustful encounter on that warm afternoon in Harbour Island since. However, she too had agreed to join the others working with Max.

As for Max. well, he and Phil took what he described as a long needed vacation and flew off in the Pilatus headed for what he described as, "the little latitudes."

BOOK TWO
MAX DUNCAN
THE MECHANIC'S LIEN

THE MONA PASSAGE 1:20AM:

Max had barely fallen asleep when he felt a hand tugging on the canvas that separated the aft birth he had slid himself into less than half an hour earlier.

"All hands on deck," said Colin, and then he turned and climbed the stairway back up to the cockpit.

They were in a JP54 sailboat on their way from the British Virgin Islands to Providenciales in the Turks and Caicos when the weather suddenly turned on them. And although Max was the least experienced sailor on board, he had crossed the Mona Passage twice before and knew it was not a crossing even the most experienced sailor took lightly.

As he woke he could feel his back pressed against the side of the hull, which meant they had heeled over another few degrees in the short time since he had fallen asleep. Not a good sign, since they were only halfway across the passage—a passage which had claimed countless ships and hundreds of lives over the years, allegedly including a fleet of gold laden ships during the time of Christopher Columbus around 1502.

He could hear the wind tearing at the stanchions as he climbed into the cockpit, and as his eyes adjusted to the darkness he saw the tops of the eight-foot-high waves being torn off by the ever-increasing winds. But what was most alarming was the sight of the brightly colored spinnaker still flying high in front of them.

"What's with the spinnaker?" he shouted as he clipped his harness onto the Jackline.

"That's the debate," replied Roger as he put his back to the wind and cupped his hand to his mouth.

"There's nothing to debate," shouted Max as he braced himself on the high side of the cockpit and looked down at the starboard gunwale as it disappeared into the water.

The winds had been a steady force five when he went below, but he could feel they were now gusting to a force seven or higher, and they needed to get the spinnaker down while they still could.

"Take her head to wind, and I'll grab Mike and Jeff and get that sucker down now," he said as he pulled himself up onto the deck.

It took a few intense minutes, but they managed to bring it in. However, before they could bag it they were hit with a twelve-foot wave that washed over the entire deck.

"Get it below and now, don't worry about the water," Max shouted as the three of them forced the sail down the companionway and into the salon.

He had long studied the Southern Islands and their many

passages, and was well aware of the unpredictable currents and fast-forming storm cells that plagued the Mona Passage. It was said to be the deepest point in the Atlantic Ocean, and had been the demise of many sound boats and experienced crews, including Christopher Columbus's, Santa Maria.

"Reef it," yelled Colin as Max came back up into the cockpit.

"Goddamn right," he shouted back as he climbed back up on deck and, with the help of the others, put two reefs in the mainsail as Colin fought to bring them back on course.

They took shifts for the rest of the night as they battled the ever-relentless winds. It wasn't until the first light of dawn that they had a visual perspective of the size of the seas they had been up against. But as they reached the coast of the Dominican Republic, the seas began to lay down and they were back making a steady ten knots right until they reached Samana Bay.

There was barely a breeze inside the harbor, it took little effort to lay the boat alongside the dock as the crew eagerly awaited to jump ashore.

"I don't know about you all, but I need a burger and a beer," said Max as he secured the spring line to the piling.

"Amen to that," replied Colin, as he climbed off the stern and joined him on the dock.

"Forget about it," said Roger as he saw Max staring at the salt build-up on the railings. "I'll hire a few of the locals to come down and give it a good wash, inside and out. It will give us a good excuse to stay an extra day or two while we let her dry out."

"Speaking of dry, can we talk about this at the pub," said Colin as he began making a bee-line for the Rusty Scupper.

They were all exhausted, but there was something invigorating about riding the fine line of control of a sailboat as you battle the elements of a summer storm. His muscles were aching, and he could feel the fatigue of the past two days but there was no way he could have managed sleep.

He emptied the first bottle in two ravenous swigs, and was working on his second Presidente when he heard his cell phone ringing through the pocket of his pack. Thinking the call might complicate his plans, he was going to ignore it. He'd been mildly entertaining the thought of jumping ship and heading back to Miami rather than staying on board. And this could be his ticket out.

It had been almost six months since he had arrived back in Vancouver from his ordeal in the Bahamas, but he had spent much of the time flying in his new toy, or sailing down South. And although he rarely left his dog, Phil, behind, he had not been able to take him on this trip and was beginning to miss him.

So when he finally decided to answer, he could never have imagined the chain of events that would soon unfold as a result of it.

CHAPTER ONE

"Janet, it's great to hear from you. What's up?" said Max as he walked over to the side of the bar and took a stool looking out over the marina.

"Sorry to bother you, Max. I can't imagine that you've read any of the Vancouver news online recently?"

"Can't say that I have, I've been Island-hopping the past few weeks."

"Well, I know you think I live in a constant state of paranoia. But I was reading the Sunday paper and I came across a story on page six about an old mechanic who was being forced to sell his small shop on the East side."

"Ok, and so what is so interesting about the old guy?"

"At first nothing. His property is at the end of the block near the tunnel for the new transit line. The block was recently assembled by a local realtor, and is to be rezoned for high-rise condos."

"And the old guy doesn't want to sell," said Max as he got up and headed to the bar to get another beer.

"Correct. And from what I can see, his property is not a make or break part of the deal. In fact, I did a little research and it turns out he offered to sell his density back to the developer and keep the property."

"Thanks," said Max as he put the phone to his shoulder and took the beer from the bartender. "So what's the big deal? The market has been on fire for a long time; developers are all over it. What makes you so interested in this one?"

"Like I said, at first nothing. But when I passed by the site on my way home I was stopped at the light and read the re-zoning sign and the name of the company that owns the adjacent properties…" she said as an air of excitement crept into her voice.

"Look Janet, I just made the crossing from hell on the Mona Passage, and just want to sit and appreciate my beer. And not that I don't enjoy talking to you, but can you get to the point, if there is one?"

"777000777 B.C. LTD. It's one of the companies I came across when we were doing the FB and T thing," she almost shouted. "It's a numbered company owned by a Bahamian Trust."

"And this is relevant why?" he asked, as he sat watching three young women cleaning the deck of a large Sport Fish.

"Because that same trust is the one FB and T bought when the whole mess started. And listen to this--I traced the beneficiary of the trust back to a holding company based in Ireland."

There was a long pause, and Max thought maybe the line had been dropped and was about to end the call when she came back on "You'd better hold on to your deck shoes, sailor; it's owned by the Whitmore Group of Companies."

"Janet, please, Whitmore is a billionaire with countless businesses. Including real estate development, so what?" he said impatiently. There was a long pause. Then it hit him, "How did you find out who the beneficiary of the holding company is? That's an almost impossible task in and of itself."

"When we were dealing with Global Enterprises I met one of their executives in Dublin who I became friendly with, and he proved to be very helpful. Anyways, what we didn't know at the time, is that not only does Whitmore indirectly own 777000777, but the company was one of the major shareholders of several of the Singh Brother deals. Including the last one that they made all the money on."

Max went silent. And after a moment he stood up and felt a slight sensation of imbalance, which was common for sailors to experience after being at sea. The French call it, "mal de debarquement," or disembarkation sickness. But he knew it wasn't the time at sea that was rocking his world. He grabbed the bar and then sat back down.

"I need you to call a friend of mine at the FBO in Vancouver where I keep my plane. Ask him to run the tail numbers on all the Citation Xs they have at the hangers, but keep it quiet," he said and then emptied his beer.

"Ok, will do. But when are you coming back? It's been almost six months since we wrapped up in the Bahamas and everyone is going a little stir crazy."

"I'll be back in two days. Meanwhile, you and Kate get me everything you can on the mechanic, the properties, and whatever you can dig up on the triple seven company."

"Anything else, like maybe pick the winning trifecta numbers for you to play on Friday?" she said with a playful hint of sarcasm.

"Yes, tell everyone to get some rest; it looks like we are going back to work." He ended the call before she could respond.

Max sat for a moment and picked at the label on his beer as he thought about the implications of what he had just heard. Why in the world would someone like Whitmore be involved with the likes of the Singh brothers? And given he did not believe in coincidence, what were the chances that the jet on which his father had flown the Singh group to the Bahamas would be registered to one of Whitmore's companies?

It had been six months since he had put the Bahamas behind him, but now he felt the uneasiness creeping back in as he thought about the call. All of a sudden he felt a hand on his shoulder, and as he gripped a hold of it and spun around he found himself face to face with Colin.

"Whoa, cowboy," he said as he stared back at him with a startled look on his face.

"A little jumpy, are we? I got just the fix for that," said Colin as he handed him a tumbler of dark rum and ice.

"Come on, forget business or pussy or whatever you were yapping about. It's time to relax, we deserve it after that trip," he said with a grin.

"Sounds good," said Max as he followed him back to join the rest of the crew.

"I don't know about you, but I think we've got some serious drinking to catch up on," said Max as he tried to force the conversation he just had with Janet somewhere deep into the back of his mind. There would be plenty of time to think about it on the trip home, but tonight he needed to blow the carbon out.

And for the rest of the night, they pretty much took over the bar and Max took care of the tab for those who hung back after closing. They played pool, and had the staff dancing in the kitchen while they made batches of chicken wings. He wasn't sure exactly what time he shut it down, but he knew daybreak came far too early.

The sun was high overhead when Colin finally emerged from his bunk and headed into the galley to start a pot of coffee. There he found a note sitting beside the old fashioned aluminum percolator:

My dear friend, thanks for last night. And sorry to abandon ship on you, but you have an able crew that will get you the rest of the way to Provo. And the good news is, you won't have my cantankerous ass to deal with for the rest of the journey.

I've been away long enough and it seems my presence is now required back home. Stay well, and I will look forward to our Alaska trip this summer.

Max

CHAPTER TWO

The drive from Samana to the airport in Punta Cana took four and a half hours, and doing it when slightly hung over and with no air-conditioning was almost as bad as the crossing. So by the time Max arrived, he was relieved to see the text message that a plane would be waiting for him at 9:00 a.m. the next morning.

The driver took him directly to the Melia, where he checked into a suite and went and took a long cool shower. He was feeling tired after the long night of festivities, and after checking his emails he lay down for a short siesta. When he finally woke, he was surprised to see it was almost dusk. He had slept for over eight hours and could feel his stomach rumble as he slipped on his sandals and headed to the buffet.

He was sitting in the lounge waiting for his plane when he felt his phone vibrate, and when he saw it was Janet he checked his watch and saw it was only 5:30 Vancouver time.

"A little early for you, isn't it?" he said.

"Good morning to you too," she replied with far too much energy in her voice.

"Dare I ask why the call so early?"

"Well, if you would have answered your phone last night I would not only have gotten a good night's sleep, I wouldn't be up at this hour, now would I?"

"Oops, sorry about that. I had the ringer off so I could get a good night's sleep. Guess I owe you one," he said a little sheepishly.

"Guess you do. Anyway, you asked and we are delivering!"

"The mechanic, by all accounts is just a nice old man who spent the majority of his life working in his shop. However, the property is larger than I originally thought and would make an excellent location for one of Whitmore's new boutique grocery chains. But he's not selling, or at least he's fighting it."

"They can't force him to sell if he doesn't want to," said Max.

"Well, not so fast. It turns out he had to have some work done to the property a while back. It was fairly extensive and although he claims he paid for the works in full, the improvement company filed a mechanic's lien against the property and managed to get judgment against him. He has thirty days to pay or they liquidate."

"The assembled properties will be a windfall for the developer. They are across the street from a recent redevelopment which is anchored by a local credit union and one of the new Fried Green Tomato restaurants."

"And let me guess," said Max cutting her off, "all part of the Whitmore Group of Companies."

"Correct, you are," she replied.

"And the numbered company?"

"Still working on it."

Call it intuition, but there was something about the story that just wasn't sitting right. And he just couldn't shake the feeling that he needed to help the old guy.

"Ok, go to the courthouse and get a copy of the liens and then go to the bank and get a draft payable to the treasury for the total amount and have the lien released today. Use the Philco account," he said as he saw a rather attractive woman in a captain's uniform coming toward him.

"Mister Duncan?"

"One and the same," he said as he got up and extended his hand.

"I'm Captain Jones," she replied with a smile. "Hope you don't mind having a woman behind your controls."

Anytime, he thought to himself. And then, realizing he was still holding her hand, "Not at all, lead the way," he said.

Once they were in the air Max went online, and not knowing what he was looking for he started with some research on a few of the Whitmore Companies. But after an hour of surfing he felt himself going in circles and decided to put the computer away and have breakfast.

It was 11:30 when he felt the wheels touch down at the Miami Executive Airport, and after a quick exchange of contacts with the pilot, Max headed into the lounge area to meet Captain Stebbings. They had met almost a year ago when Max was doing some consulting for the law firm he used to work for. They had hit it off right away, and Stebbings had proved himself to be one of the most solid pilots Max had met.

"Good to see you, Max," he said as he came walking out of the pilots' room with a large Starbuck's coffee in one hand and his pilot's case in the other.

"Good to see you too, Robert. How's our time?"

"We are good to go as soon as you are."

"Well then, if it's ok with you, let's get the beast into the air."

"Sounds good. I notice you requested a co-pilot so I take it you are not flying today?"

"Nope, I have work to do, but I will check in on you as we go," said Max as he picked up his bag and followed him out to his G IV.

"Janet, how did you make out?" said Max when he heard the connection.

"Sorry, she is still at the courthouse," replied Kate. "Where are you?"

"Looks like we are just over Orlando," he said as he felt a smile creeping across his face. He had not seen Kate in a while, and just the sound of her voice gave him a much needed boost.

"I thought she would have been back by now; it's a simple process to make the payment and file for the release of the lien, is it not?" he replied.

"One would have thought, but it seems there is a judge's note on the file that an application for release must be heard, either in court or before a judge, before it can be released."

"That's strange," said Max as he opened up a new web page and began searching the public announcements for filed liens.

But after a half an hour of searching he couldn't find any listing so he pulled out a note pad and began making physical notes:
1. Land assembly of East 6th entire Block from 801 to 899.
2. Development Company owned by 777000777 B.C. Ltd. a Whitmore
3. Company owned by the FB&T subsidiary Trust owned by a holding company in Jersey.
4. Anchor property owned by mechanic; Ben Weinstein. Owned the property for over fifty years.
5. Retail across the street owned by Whitmore Group.
6. Jet father was flying to Bahamas - Whitmore fleet?

Was there a connection to Whitmore, the Singhs and his father? And what about the mechanic? What possible relevance did he have in all of this? And what had both him and Janet so concerned about him? After all, there was certainly nothing on the surface to indicate anything was amiss.

But then that was soon about to change.

CPSIA information can be obtained
at www.ICGtesting.com
Printed in the USA
BVHW032020070220
571783BV00001B/3/J